TALES FROM
BRACKISH
HARBOR

AN ANTHOLOGY OF ELDRITCH HORROR

EDITED BY
CASSANDRA L. THOMPSON
DAMON BARRET ROE

TALES FROM
BRACKISH
HARBOR

AN ANTHOLOGY OF ELDRTICH HORROR

EDITED BY
CASSANDRA L. THOMPSON
DAMON BARRET ROE

QUILL & CROW PUBLISHING HOUSE

TALES FROM BRACKISH HARBOR:
AN ANTHOLOGY OF ELDRITCH HORROR
EDITED BY CASSANDRA L. THOMPSON, DAMON BARRET ROE
PUBLISHED BY QUILL & CROW PUBLISHING HOUSE

Copyright © 2022 by Cassandra L. Thompson. Stories by William Bartlett, Nick Bennett, Amanda M. Blake, Amanda Casile, Fox Claret Hill, Lucas Mann, Matthew Siadak, Teagan Olivia Sturmer, Mary Tait, R.B. Thorne, R. Thursday and Wendy Vogel

Cover Design & Interior by William Bartlett
Printed in the United States of America

ISBN: 978-1-958228-02-9
ISBN (ebook): 978-1-958228-01-2

Publisher's Website: www.quillandcrowpublishinghouse.com

Table of Contents

FOREWORD, WILLIAM BARTLETT...9

I. LURE, AMANDA CASILE...11

II. SALT & FOG, R. THURSDAY...29

III. TASTES OF DESPERATION, AMANDA M. BLAKE....................47

IV. A BED OF EELS, FOX CLARET HILL.................................67

V. REAPING FOR MOTHER, LUCAS MANN.............................87

VI. LOW TIDE, NICK BENNETT..101

VII. THE GIFT OF RAKOSKA, WENDY VOGEL.........................117

VIII. FROM BELOW, R.B. THORNE...131

IX. BLOOD UPON BLOOD, MARY TAIT..................................147

X. THE SILENT SONATA, MATTHEW SIADAK..........................169

XI. THE ORIGINS OF CORA DEERING,

TEAGAN OLIVIA STURMER..187

XII. UNFETTERED GREATNESS, WILLIAM BARTLETT.............207

ACKNOWLEDGMENTS...227

AUTHOR BIOGRAPHIES...229

TRIGGER INDEX...233

FOREWORD
William Bartlett

Of all the subgenres of horror, nothing encapsulates the existential insignificance of humanity like cosmic horror. Horace Walpole kindled an ember by applying the word "Gothic" in the subtitle of his novel, "The Castle of Otranto," and inadvertently created the flame that would give life to Gothic fiction. This inspired other writers to focus more on the horror shade of the genre, like Mary Shelley, giving birth to Gothic horror. Many authors helped the genre take form, and others helped it evolve by pushing boundaries and taking risks, like Edgar Allan Poe. Howard Phillips Lovecraft worshiped Gothic horror, and desperately wanted to make his mark on the genre's evolutionary process. He studied the origins of human fear and discovered it embedded in the unknown.

Ancient humanity took shelter in caves and depended heavily on fire. The darkness of the night outside our fire-lit caves led our imaginations to wild possibilities. Those imaginings were horrifying, and kept us inside until the morning's light could illuminate what was previously unknown.

H.P. Lovecraft dove into those wild imaginings. He imagined the most terrifying possibilities of what could be slithering around in the most unknown aspect of our existence, outer space. He decided that something as simple as the tentacle, a limb so far from humanity that it seemed almost alien in nature, was the best way to portray the dark slithering of darkness.

Being a devoted fanatic of the genre myself, I have always felt what truly defines cosmic horror is the philosophy behind it and the deep thought that its stories provoke. Nothing, in my opinion, is more terrifying than the frailty of our mental health, and more importantly, the worthlessness of our existence in the grand scheme of the universe. The possibility that our reality is truly nihilistic.

To put it more simply, horror, in its purest form, lies within the truth that religion and spirituality is all fictional and that life is truly meaningless.

What makes cosmic horror so frightening is the mystery and ambiguity of the creatures that exist outside our realm of understanding, that are never fully revealed. It is the fact that our finite minds cannot comprehend the reality of it that makes it so terrifying.

With humanity's limited vocabulary, I cannot properly express my honor and gratitude writing alongside these talented storytellers as Quill & Crow Publishing House attempts to push the boundaries of cosmic horror and encourage the genre's evolution. This anthology will blend the traditional elements of Gothic fiction and the newer elements of Eldritch Horror, and focus on the psychologically terrifying fact that there is more out there than our limiting five senses allow us to perceive. We hope you enjoy this thought-provoking, mind-opening, existential-crisis-inducing collection of short stories that all take place in the enigmatic town of Brackish Harbor.

CHAPTER ONE

LURE
Amanda Casile

The air was thickest near the water. A humid soup of anticipation hung around us as I led my family to the dilapidated dock tucked behind an old crab shack. We were at the start of something new. Electricity buzzed just below the surface, a promise. I wiped a bead of sweat that had dribbled down my brow. They didn't know it yet, but this would be my redemption.

I bought the island for a song, which was fortunate, since a song was all I had. Harriet may never forgive me, but at least she decided to stay. For Fiona. For us. Staying because she had nothing left to run away with.

A fishing boat bobbed at the edge of the dock, squat and black, arms jutting out like crab legs. I stepped gingerly towards our ride, unsure of my footing on the uneven boards. Gray wisps of clouds grew, billowing ever upwards like smoke from a fire that had yet to be lit. I hoped a storm wasn't on its way. Quiet laps of waves and rhythmic clangs of rope against mast swallowed all other sounds.

11

Fiona's shriek sliced through the hushed silence like a knife through canvas. An audible tear in the fabric of the moment.

Harriet swooped in first, arms spread wide like crows' wings. "Button! What's the matter?" She wrapped her arms around our daughter and handed her the overpriced trinket—a water-filled magnet with plastic fish sloshing around—we had to buy her when we passed through the tourist town.

I'd tried to tell Fiona, "Those tourist traps are just out to get your money. We're the ones who set the lures, not the ones who take the bait." But she and Harriet both insisted, so I was forced to capitulate.

I tried to coax Fiona onto the dock, but she shook her head, staring at the boards below through her tears. It was a practical fear—I had to give her that.

"It's quite safe," I said, stomping a foot. "The wood might look old, but people out here know how to maintain their docks."

She looked up at me with fire in her dark eyes, a flare of anger and disbelief beyond her young age.

Harriet took Fiona's small hands in her own. "This is a big move, isn't it, Button? I know how far away California feels from here. But I'm sure you'll make friends in Brackish Harbor. I moved when I was nine, too—remember how I told you?—and it went all right. You'll see. I know how hard this is for you. For all of us." The last line, I was sure, was directed at me.

"I'm doing this for us, you know," I said through gritted teeth.

Harriet slid her hands over Fiona's hair as though to smooth it, but let them linger over Fiona's ears as she hissed, "You should have thought of that before you blew all our savings on nothing—*my* savings. And now we're stuck chasing your last gamble to God knows where."

"Not 'God knows where.' This island made the former owner billions. It's only a matter of time for us."

She opened her mouth to respond, but I was already walking away towards the boat. They'd see, I thought. They'd see soon enough.

The island emerged from the gloom in snippets, a black and white photo torn to pieces and scattered on the wind. The intermittent glare of an unseen lighthouse. A dock extending from the fog like a charcoal tongue, before being swallowed once more. The twisting edge of a widow's walk, rusted and coated in algae. A chimney, bricks faded to gray in the gloom. The gnarled fingers of a tree branch reaching out, as though offering us its handful of lichen.

And then we were upon it. The boat lurched and groaned before settling into its berth. Quiet descended upon us as the motor sputtered and silenced. Even Fiona had reduced her tantrum to the occasional hiccup and sniffle.

Tentacles of fog slithered away from each other like a stage curtain parting, allowing us a full view of the main street leading up the small hill into town. The shops all appeared shuttered tight. It seemed a storm was indeed on its way. I pulled my phone from my pocket to check the weather, but the words *No Signal* glared back at me. Harriet held her lips in a flat, pressed line.

"It will look better in the sunshine," I responded.

I threw Fiona's duffel bag over my shoulder along with my own and helped Harriet haul her overstuffed travel trunk up onto the dock. The boat captain fired up the engine again and spun back out to sea before I had both feet upon the dock.

"First thing I'll change," I said, huffing as the trunk dragged behind me, its small castors bumping and cracking across the dock boards. "Marketing. We need to get the people here to see how wonderful a place it is."

Harriet snorted. We reached the edge of the dock and found ourselves on a narrow, cobbled sidewalk, with not another soul in sight. Fiona took in our surroundings with a doubtful look, her hands stretching out the bottom hem of her shirt.

I rifled through my duffel bag for the deed paperwork and the old metal key the baron's estate had shipped to me after I completed the purchase.

Fiona walked a circle around where Harriet and I stood. "I'm hungry," she said, eyeing the shops shut tight.

Harriet pulled a granola bar from her purse. "Just to tide you over."

Two crows landed a few feet in front of Fiona.

"Oh! Look at you!" she said, and took a step closer. Their feathers were matted and thinned in patches, eyes milky. One fluffed its wings and hopped towards us.

"Um…Button? Let's keep moving." I shook the wrought iron keys. "The house is at the top of the hill. The estate manager told me it has a great view."

Harriet followed, but Fiona didn't budge. Her sneakers were the only bright objects, glowing against the damp sidewalk. Rooted to the spot. I glanced over my shoulder at Fiona, at the birds, at the gray sea beyond. Exhaustion began to weigh on me as much as the black duffel bags I held. My skin tightened, itching to move. To get on with this and get settled into our new home.

"It appears there won't be a car," I said with what I'd hoped was a hint of levity. Enough to get her moving, rather than inciting her to dig her heels in even more. I waited, the double duffel bags chafing my shoulder raw, travel trunk bruising my thigh. Another two crows joined the first two. "And Fi, I think you should move away from those mangy birds."

Fiona stared into the distance just beyond the hill. Her lips moved, but no sound came.

Harriet reached out a hand to her shoulder. "Come on, Button. Let's see our new place. Dad says there's a lovely view. We're almost there."

Her lips continued to move.

I leaned in, the blasted bag threatening to slide off my shoulder again. "What? What are you saying?"

The faintest of whispers, brushing my cheek like sea spray. "Rotten."

"What?" Harriet shot me a look, her eyebrows pressed together.

"They're rotten. It's all rotten."

I glanced around at the boarded shops through the fog that had thickened around us once more, sealing us onto the island. One was a butcher, another a bakery. A hat shop, a cobbler. A fishmonger. Some with signs too weathered and moss-covered to read. Not just boarded up for a storm, abandoned.

It didn't matter. I would raise these businesses from the dead, give them new life. I took Fiona's hand and we marched past the crows and up the hill. Each clack of my shoes against the stones rang like a cash register bell in my ears.

"I wonder where all the people are," I said to Harriet as we huffed up the hill. My breath came in bursts, as Fiona resumed her quiet whimpering at my side. She pulled her jacket hood up.

"You own this island now. Do you not *know?*" Harriet asked.

"There's still much to explore," I responded around the tightening of my jaw. From the top of the hill, our view extended down to the opposite side, where I could just make out a few chimneys through the fog. And beyond that, the ever-present pulse of the lighthouse lamp. "That looks like a town down there," I said to Harriet. "We can explore later, after we get settled in." I came to a stop. "Home, sweet home!"

Harriet's dismay radiated outward and crashed over me like a wave.

"It has character," I tried, as we gazed up at the old Victorian. The wood had been weathered down to a muted driftwood-gray, and a velvety coating grew across the roof from the gutters up to the widow's walk. "At least it has all its windows. And look, it even has a wraparound porch. Maybe we can hang a swing! What do you think, Fiona? A porch swing?"

She stared at the house. "Rotten," she whispered, digging a sneakered toe into the damp, mildewy ground.

"Right. Well, let's get our bags in, then."

The porch steps creaked and buckled as I hauled Harriet's trunk over each one. Piles of leaves banked up against the edges, rustling in the light sea breeze. I tried the key, and the front door opened with its imitation of a whale song, a long, melancholy whine. We stepped over the threshold and into the darkness of our new lives. The opposite of being born; it felt as though we were swallowed by some unearthly beast.

Into the belly of the whale.

Dust swirled in eddies around us, so thick my lungs threatened to seize. Fiona coughed into her elbow, and Harriet blinked rapidly. I reached for a lightswitch, which sent up a dim, flickering glow from two sconces bookending an old, stone fireplace. A few items, furniture I hoped, gathered under white sheets in the center of the room. "It's fine. We can definitely make this cozy. A fresh coat of paint, some new light fixtures, and—"

Fiona began pacing circles around the clustered furniture.

"Fiona, honey, could you stop?"

"With what *money*, Todd?" Harriet cried.

"How can you sound so defeated when we've only just begun?" I eyed Fiona's ever-tightening circles. "*Button!* Could you please *stop?*"

"'Only just begun?' Really? This is the *end*, Todd. Your last chance."

Fiona's feet hammered against the floor in staccato. *Thud thud thud thud.*

15

"Once we get the town up and running again, and the tourists—"

Thud thud thud.

Harriet lifted her arms—whether it was to emphasize her protest or to bodily attack me, I'd never know—because a door slammed on the far side of the house, stealing the breath from the room.

Fiona came to an abrupt stop. She raised her eyes, blank, to the far wall. "Rotten!" she cried, her voice bordering on frenzy. "All rotten!"

"Jesus." I gestured to Harriet. "Take her to pick a room. Maybe she'll get some rest. I'll see what the noise is."

I was impressed with the nonchalant confidence in my own voice. If I were honest, I'd have to admit the cold fear snaking up my spine as I eyed the dark hallway to the back of the house. I gave Harriet a moment to refuse, to tell me not to go, but she didn't. So, I forced myself down the blackened hall and burst into the kitchen beyond, where the back door stood open, swinging on its hinges. "Must have been the wind," I muttered. The deep scent of old, moldy air hung in the kitchen, enough to make me hesitate closing the door. But I knew Harriet wouldn't feel safe with it open, and we couldn't have it banging all night.

Reaching through the threshold to close it, I noticed a dark pile in the corner of the back porch. Upon first glance, I thought it to be another slope of leaves, as in the front of the house, but the darkness drew my eyes for an extra moment. Long enough for me to notice the matted black feathers, twisted wings, stiff talons. A pile of crows, at least ten, in various stages of rot. Some were so fresh, it was as if they'd leap into flight any moment. Others were gutted, green growth in patches across their sparsely feathered bodies.

My greasy, tourist-town lunch roiled uncomfortably in my stomach. I brought a handkerchief to my nose and backed into the house, my vision swimming. Dead crows. What could this mean? I wasn't a superstitious man. Must be something with the house, I thought. Perhaps a raccoon or...or...something on the porch that attracted them, and...

It didn't make sense. I had to get this cleaned up before Fiona or Harriet saw. For now, I slammed the door shut, turned the deadbolt, and leaned against it, my breath shallow. It was fine. It was going to be fine.

I returned to the sitting room to find Harriet and Fiona perched on the edge of a threadbare sofa the color of mold. The sheet that had covered it lay crumpled at their feet.

Harriet stroked our daughter's hair. "She wasn't ready to go upstairs yet," she explained.

"All right. Well, how about we wash up and see if we can find anyone in town." I hoped I could find someone to clear off the porch before we returned. "There's a bathroom right here." I gestured to a door I had passed in my rush down the hall.

Harriet gave a numb-looking nod, and she and Fiona shuffled off. A moment later, I heard a startled screech.

"What is it?" I rushed in, expecting a large insect. Harriet and Fiona stared at the faucet, which sputtered and sprayed water intermittently.

"I thought it was blood!" Fiona cried, gesturing to the brownish-red liquid that splashed across the sink.

Harriet ran her hands across her forehead and through her hair. "Rust. The pipes are just rusted because this house is older than your grandmother."

The water flowed more steadily, shedding some but not all of its bloody tinge. However, rather than running clear, it came with bits of debris like grasses and curling strands of roots. Neither Fiona nor Harriet complained, but I found that more disconcerting than the rust.

Harriet quickly plaited Fiona's hair into braids and I changed out of my travel clothes before we headed out. The day had dimmed, and though we couldn't see through the fog, I knew the sun was lowering in the sky. The soft boards of the front porch were slick beneath the evening's dampness. "Nothing a pressure washer won't fix," I muttered as Fiona squatted down to poke at a clump of moss growing along the edge of the top stair.

"Did you know moss can live for years without any water? Whenever it gets watered again, it comes back, like from the dead," Fiona said.

I inhaled the moist air. "I bet the humidity here alone would keep it going. Besides, there's water all around."

Fiona stood, her fingers stroking the air. "No." She shook her head. "Moss can't live in salt water. An island surrounded by sea would be a prison for it."

Harriet strode on ahead towards the village we'd seen earlier. She must have been hungry to ignore the promise of a scientific conversation. Harriet enjoyed every opportunity to display her knowledge. But my own stomach growled at me, so I took Fiona's hand and we caught up to her mother.

"I hope the food here is good," Harriet said, her words as crisp as her slacks. "Is there a restaurant?"

"I-I'm not sure," I faltered. "The island looks different than in the advertisement. So…I don't know."

"A grocery store?"

"I certainly hope so," I said.

She stopped so abruptly I nearly ran into her. Her arms flapped to her sides. Crows' wings again. "Jesus, Todd, do you not *think* before you do anything? Research? Plan? You didn't check if there was a *grocery store* on this island? We could have at least brought provisions. This, after you bought that goddamned Badlands property without even—"

"It wasn't the Badlands. It was just outside San Diego. Still in San Diego county, actually."

"I don't give a damn! It was in a wildfire zone and *everyone* knew that. Except you. You, who emptied our whole life savings to purchase it."

"It would have been prime real estate, if—"

"If it weren't about to burn up, Todd. No one in hell would give you permits to even break ground on it. You bought a wildlife preserve for the gophers and coyotes." She broke into a walk again, brisk, huffing breaths in time with each step.

"Gophers and coyotes deserve a place to live, too," Fiona chimed in. "Maybe you can find a way to protect them, Dad."

"Forget it. I'm going to sell that land, first chance I get," I said. "Gophers and coyotes don't pay rent."

Harriet let out an exasperated huff. "The land won't sell, Todd. That is the whole problem!"

Fiona took my hand, meeting my stride. "It doesn't matter. We'll stay here forever anyway."

Harriet glanced over her shoulder, a look of horror painted across her face. "Not forever," she said quietly to herself, like a prayer.

I stared at the sight in front of me. I'd hoped for signs of life on the island. A larger village, if not a vibrant commercial scene. I swallowed back the bitter taste that grew in my mouth as I gazed over the hill. It would be fine, I told myself as a bead of sweat traversed my temple. We could make something of this.

The road curved, and the land to the right of us dropped sharply. Below, a smattering of chimneys reached up like hackles on a dog's back, bordered by a beach the color of ash and strewn with seaweed. Beyond the beach, a rocky spit of land jutted into the sea, the lighthouse standing sentinel atop it. Here, though, the grays of the island had been replaced by greens. The chimneys were shrouded in plant-cover, and an emerald layer of flora grew around the lighthouse like a jacket.

Our steps grew quiet as we descended. I looked down to see a thick, leafy layer stretching across the cobblestones beneath our feet. Fiona's hand tightened in mine, and I thought I heard a whisper of her word on the wind again. *Rotten.*

Our feet slid and slithered across the slick cobblestones as we descended towards the beach below. My head throbbed from the full day of travel and lack of proper food. There was no relief from the blinking glare of the lighthouse, exposed as we were on the treeless stretch of hill. Not even the fog remained to buffer the ever-pulsing rhythm of its light. It had retreated upwards but remained a constant cover of overcast gloom.

The groundcover thickened at the bottom of the hill, where we found a cluster of several squat stone structures, all faded and wilting around the edges. They surrounded a field, in the center of which stood a well. The plant life that covered the ground appeared to be emanating from the well, spreading up and over the stone ring and the little wooden roof that covered the pulley. The moss swallowed sound and humidity the way a fresh covering of snow did, lending an intimate air to the tiny village.

"Is this all there is?" Harriet whispered, apparently feeling the same claustrophobia.

I shrugged and looked around, circling the green. I became aware it was actually a cobbled square, not a field, smothered by layers and layers of overgrown blankets. A single crow alighted on the top of the well, slid a bit on the moldy shingles before regaining its footing. I eyed it in my periphery. Did its feathers have a greenish tinge?

A cough sounded from one of the houses, then echoing coughs in a few others. There was a scent of herbs in the air, and the strong smell of cooking vegetables. My stomach rumbled, and Fiona turned to me with a half-grin, though it didn't obliterate the awe and fear in her eyes.

A door opened from the home nearest us, and a short, waif-thin woman emerged. Her red hair hung bedraggled on her shoulders, and her clothing—a stained apron over a peasant dress—seemed a remnant of a bygone era.

She blinked at us and rubbed her eyes. "Who're you then?"

"Hello, Miss….ah…" I swallowed. "Well, hello. I'm Todd Packett, and this is my family: Harriet, my wife, and Fiona, my little girl. We've… ah…purchased this island and have just moved in. Just today, in fact. And we were just looking for something to eat. Is there a…um…restaurant around here anywhere?"

She stared a moment longer. "We don't get a lotta visitors here, you know."

"Yes, so it would seem." I could hear Harriet's teeth grinding to my left. "But we aren't visitors, see, we've moved here. For good."

That earned a small exclamation of horror from Harriet, but an approving twitch of the lips from the woman in front of me.

"We're up in the baron's old estate."

"No restaurant," the woman said with a shrug. "But the island takes care of its own. You all can join me and mine at our table." She blew her nose into a tissue and tucked it back into her apron pocket.

"Yes, thank you," I said.

At the same moment, Harriet whipped out her phone and announced, "No need. I'm calling a water taxi and getting us the hell out of this infernal place." She stifled a cough as she stared at her phone a moment too long.

"I'm afraid there's no service out here," the woman told her. "We get the barge with supplies once a month. Should be here in a few weeks, as we just had a load dropped off not a week ago."

At this, Harriet seemed to freeze, as though she was made of salt and the slightest breeze would blow her away.

"I told you, Mama," Fiona whispered. "We're here to stay."

Harriet sputtered back to life like a windup doll. She shook herself. "No. No, that can't be. We can—call the woman who brought us here, Todd. Call that fisherwoman. What was her name? Sonya? Your phone must work, right? Someone here must have a phone!" She poked at her phone's screen with increasing frenzy.

Harriet's hysterics drew more people from their squat houses, faded just like the first woman. They sniffed and squinted in the island's gray substitute for sunset. Chatter ran around the square in hushed whispers.

"Well, this is awkward," I said, with the same half-smile I used when I charmed Harriet into marrying me. "I didn't intend for the introductions to go this way, but, hello!" I raised my voice to make clear I addressed the entirety of the growing crowd. "Some of you may have known the baron. He owned this island and used to live up the hill…a long time ago, I would guess, by the state of things. Apologies for delivering the news this way, but the baron has passed on, sadly, and I have purchased this land from his estate. So…I don't know if that makes me mayor or just owner or…no, none of that sounds right. In any case. I aim to turn this town around, bring in some more tourist traffic, and get things bumping again. Back like it was in the Brackish Harbor heyday." I spread my arms wide to emphasize my point. "Eh, are we excited about that?"

A man stepped up behind the first woman who'd approached us. He resembled the fog, with his gray hair and moth-eaten sweater. "Appears this might call for a celebration," he said, sucking his teeth.

"A celebration," the rest of the crowd chorused in unison, not with the jubilance one would expect, but with the monotone toll of a bell.

They all moved at once. Cauldrons were hauled from stone huts, bags of ingredients tossed over shoulders, buckets of water raised from the well. One man leaped onto the edge of the well and, to my horror, grabbed a perched crow by its neck and shoved it into a sack. Fortunately, neither Harriet nor Fiona seemed to have noticed.

Barely anyone spoke. The red-haired woman emerged from her house with a tray of chipped mugs. "Some tea while you wait?" she offered.

Harriet coughed again.

"Might do you some good, especially."

"No, thank you." Harriet turned and wandered the square, holding her phone out in front of her like a guide.

Fiona and I greedily grabbed the cups of murky liquid and brought them to our lips. Anything to satisfy the emptiness inside. The tea tasted of grass and earth, and faintly of salt water and low tide, but I drank it up anyway, letting it settle my stomach as well as my jangling nerves.

The fog returned as we sipped our tea by the well. I rubbed my itchy nose with the back of my handkerchief as I searched for signs of Harriet and her damn phone. But she was nowhere to be found. She would settle in here; I was sure of it. These villagers were even throwing a party in our honor, not something she would have passed up lightly. Perhaps she'd gone back to the house to change her clothes.

Fiona squatted down beside the well, fingering the clumps of moss again. "There are no bugs here, Dad," she said. "Not even ants."

"Maybe you haven't seen any because they haven't come out yet. It's probably just the start of the warmer season," I said, leaning back against one of the well's boards.

She looked at me for a moment. "No. You always see ants. Maybe the island doesn't have any. But I haven't seen any flies either." She raised her eyes to the air around her.

"Perhaps flies don't like fog," I said with a chuckle.

The red-haired woman returned to take our mugs. "You can follow me to the beach," she said. "My name's Margot, Mr. Packett. But names don't always matter here."

She led the way down a path worn in the moss, which stood tall here with capsule-heavy sporophytes reaching skyward. I realized the seaweed I thought I'd seen from above was actually more of the same plant, long streaks of it growing through the sand and reaching out to sea where it browned at the edges.

A group of men hauled driftwood across the sand and built three bonfires on the beach. A group of women set up tripods over each fire and hung the cauldrons. They laid out blankets on the soft ground and unloaded sacks of plant matter. Stalks and leaves and clumps of moss, which they threw into the cauldrons. I spotted Harriet with the women, running her hands over the stalks, long thin fingers stroking absently. I knew she would settle in, find some friends.

Margot placed a blanket in the center of the beach and instructed us to sit. We complied, and I watched as the man who'd grabbed the crow from the well hunched over his bag some paces away. Black feathers drifted around him, landing on his graying hair and faded jacket. He approached the cauldrons, dropping a pale, pimpled object into each. A wave of sick horror shuddered through me, and for the first time, I wondered what I had gotten myself into. I eyed Fiona to see if she noticed, but she stared at the lighthouse through the darkening evening, her eyes blinking in time with its rhythm.

Margot and a few others gathered near the fires. The two men banged on crudely made drums while Margot crooned a song I hadn't heard before. Though the song's tone was melancholy, like the dark depths of the well put to music, some of the villagers took up dancing. Their bare feet pounded the ground, kicking up sand and bits of plant matter. The lighthouse kept time with the beat of the drum.

I scanned the crowds for Harriet once again, and spotted her on the edge of the beach, phone raised and screen glowing against her face. Still searching for a connection, I thought.

By the fires, bowls were unloaded from another sack and a man used a large ladle to fill each one while the women passed them around. A small girl, not much older than Fiona, bowed low and handed us each a bowl.

"Thank you," I said. "What's your name?"

"You can call me Briar," she said, not meeting our gaze.

"Hi Briar, this is Fiona. You must be about the same age. Maybe you'll see each other in school."

Briar looked up, an eyebrow raised. "School?"

Something cold snaked its way inside me. "Yes, of course. You're in school still, right?" I had researched the schools. The realtor who sold me this property made a point of mentioning the wonderful schoolhouse on the island. I gazed around, looking for a building like the one I saw in the photo. But there was none.

Briar ran off to get more bowls of soup to pass out. I turned to Fiona. "It'll be okay," I said. "She's probably just confused."

"No," Fiona said, lifting her bowl to her lips. "She isn't. She knows."

My stomach rumbled as the soup's steam wafted up, but I thought of the mangy crows and swallowed back bile instead.

Fiona slurped her soup. Tentatively at first, but then with larger sips. "It's good, Dad. Try it. I think it's…chicken?"

My stomach lurched again. All I could see were black feathers, matted black feathers, piles and piles of them. But I brought the soup to my hungry lips anyway, and tried not to vomit as it slithered down my throat.

The music intensified as the sun set, though there were no stars visible through the cloud cover. Fiona watched the townspeople dancing circles around the fires, but made no move to join in. She leaned against my shoulder, her breath slow and even.

"We should probably get back," I said, patting her shoulder. "Where the hell is your mother?" I slithered out from beneath Fiona and stood, casting my gaze around the beach. There she was, in the center of the dancing crowd, arms flailing and leaves strewn in her hair. Her hands were empty and moved around her like birds in flight, no cell phone to be seen. "What the hell?"

"Leave her." Margot's husband was there, suddenly, his heavy hand on my shoulder, his breath cold as the fog. "We'll take good care of her.

The island takes care of its own, and you're one of us now. Go ahead, get your child to bed. We'll look after your wife."

I searched his words for a hint of irony, or something more sinister, but maybe he was right. Harriet was enjoying herself—finally—and I didn't want to ruin that. So I gathered Fiona by the hand and led her away.

"Are we leaving Mama?" Fiona asked, her words slowed by drowsiness.

"She'll come later," I said.

Fiona nodded. "The island will take her."

"Take *care of* her, yes," I clarified.

Fiona nodded again and we climbed the hill home.

I barely slept at all that night. I lay awake as Fiona snored beside me in the small, lumpy bed. I listened for the sound of the front door, of Harriet's footsteps in the front room. Had I made a mistake leaving her at the party? The lighthouse beamed through the bedroom window like a slow-motion strobe light, in time with my heartbeat, in time with my breath, as though it were a part of me.

When I finally did drift off to sleep, my dreams were muddled. Waves crashed on moss-covered rocks in the swirling fog. Featherless crows circled overhead, their caws fit to shatter eardrums. Harriet's voice called from somewhere deep, rippling with echoes. Mildew crept across walls, children screamed, a grotesque angler fish blinked its lure, bright and insistent with need.

I awoke caked in sweat in the wee hours of the morning as light blazed through the bare window. Briefly, I entertained the thought that the sun had made an appearance. Surely Fiona would be happier here if she could see the beach in all its summer glory. But the moment I had the thought, the light blinked away again. Through the muted air, my nemesis winked. I scowled as the light spun on to the waves beyond and then circled back. A beacon. Or a warning.

Curtains. Today we would get curtains.

I reached beside me for Fiona, but the other side of the bed was empty, cold. I descended the stairs on tip-toe to allow Harriet to sleep in. I found Fiona in the sitting room. She stood at the picture window, wearing a new dress of white linen. Her hair was tied back with a red bow, the burst of color shocking after seeing only varying shades of fog.

"Well, aren't we up bright and early today! Excited about exploring our new town, Button?"

Fiona didn't turn, continuing to stare out the window. The lighthouse's glare silhouetted her at regular intervals. She grazed her fingers along the rotted window-sill, across the patch of fuzzy emerald growth that sprouted there, as though petting a cat.

"Fiona, darling?"

My footsteps felt thunderous on the old, creaking floors. I placed a hand on her shoulder and she startled, turning to me. Her eyes were wide, her pupils nearly obliterating her chestnut irises. "We can't stay here," she whispered. "But now we can't go."

I forced a light chuckle. "Now, now. I know this…doesn't quite feel like home yet," I said with a gesture around the dusty room. "But you'll see. We'll make it a home. We can stay here."

She nodded her agreement, whispering. "Now we have to."

I swallowed. "Is your mother awake, yet?"

"She's not here," Fiona responded, turning her gaze to the window once more.

"Nonsense. She must have come home last night. Let's go check her room."

Fiona shook her head and resumed fiddling with the blasted moss. So I headed back upstairs to find Harriet and settle this nonsense.

But Fiona was right, I realized with ever increasing panic. I opened every door and found nothing but empty rooms in various states of disarray. Only one held a bed, and it was empty, the mattress bare and moth-eaten. My pulse quickened. Would she have stayed down by the beach? Harriet?

I thought of the strange people, the squat huts, the boarded town center. The well. The island seemed to spin around me in disconnected images. What had I done? *What had I done?* I ran down the stairs again. "Let's go back down the hill," I said to Fiona. "We need to find your mother."

"I told you. She's not here. The island took her."

"The island took her—what are you talking about? Come on. She probably just drank too much and passed out on the beach." Yes, I thought. Now that makes more sense. An anger flared inside me, more comfortable than the fear. She probably met some rustic islander, went off behind some beach rocks. Just to spite me. That must be what happened. Well, I wouldn't allow her to make me a cuckold in our new home. "Come on," I said to Fiona again, and she jumped to follow me.

The growth that spread itself across the ground and houses seemed to glow in the morning light. The weather-worn stones of the well shone especially bright. Margot was there, drawing up a bucket, her red locks circling her head like an octopus's tentacles.

"Mornin'."

"We're looking for Harriet. My wife," I said. My eyes traveled to the beach, expecting to find her there, hair mussed and clothing askew.

Margot unhooked the bucket from the well and walked towards her house, letting the bucket slosh against her leg. "She's not with us," she called over her shoulder.

"Not with you." I scoffed. "What do you mean, 'not with you.' Where is she, then?"

Margot shrugged. "You're welcome to look around. It's your island, Mr. Packett."

"It is my island. Yes, yes it is! And I will look around if I please!"

She disappeared into the shadows of her home.

"What do you think of that, Button? Happy to feed us last night, then turn their backs on us today. Hmm?"

Fiona shook her head. "The lady was right, though. Mom isn't here."

"Well, where is she, then?" I stamped a foot, dissatisfied with the damp slosh it made against the soft ground. "Damnit."

Fiona pointed at the lighthouse. "Look."

My jaw slackened. The structure stood dark against the morning sky. Absent was the light that taunted, swirled and blinked. I could finally see it clearly; the upper levels crumbled, the iron structure that held the lantern long rusted and knocked askew. "Maybe the light stops in the daytime," I said, though I'd started to tremble.

"It was on yesterday." A roll of thunder rattled my eardrums.

I eyed the dilapidated tower. "Come on." Lightning flashed over the ocean. The burgeoning storm had finally arrived.

We ran across the beach, past the blackened fire pits and beaten earth where the dancing took place. We scrambled over the slick boulders leading to the base of the lighthouse. A crow landed nearby, on only one foot. The other was a gnarled stump. Its beak was broken at the tip, ending instead in a jagged hole. I shivered and turned away.

Further up we climbed, barnacles scraping our knees and the palms of our hands. Another roll of thunder, and the rain was upon us. My brow dripped with sweat and rainwater, and my knees ran with blood as we reached the bottom of the lighthouse. I reached out to grab the wet foliage that covered its curved, rocky surface. The leaves and fronds slithered between my fingers like snakes trying to escape. Like the pieces of my life slipping away. Unexpected tears pricked my eyes. I gazed upon my daughter who stood next to me, eyes wide. "This island was meant to be my redemption, Button. We were gonna make it big here."

Fiona shook her head. "The island takes care of its own."

"I am its own! I am!" Thunder echoed as my rage crescendoed. "I belong to the island. We belong here, Button. Tell me how to belong!"

"You said you owned the island. Not the other way around." She gazed up at where the light used to blink not so long ago. She gave a nod and returned her eyes to the base of the lighthouse.

Soft ridges piled with flora made the ground uneven. Rocks, I thought. But upon closer inspection I noticed the jutting of a bone from one, a damp blue sweater peeking from another, a flap of black nylon, a glint of pink polish. "Jesus." I bent down. It was her jacket, her nail, her hair poking through the surface. "Harriet? Harriet!"

Fiona and I squatted down, peeling moss off her in clumps until I noticed her skin, grayish and pocked, stuck to the plant as we peeled.

Fiona whispered, "Rotten," and blinked away tears. "I told you it was all rotten."

"I…I. Oh God." She had no pulse. "I didn't know! I'm so sorry I didn't listen!"

Fiona ran her hands into the moss around her mother, and curled up beside Harriet's stiff corpse. "It's all rotten," she whispered again, and closed her eyes. "All rotten."

CHAPTER TWO

SALT & FOG
R. Thursday

Simon shuffled between creaking rows of swollen shelves and found himself yet again cursing salt. It was impossible to keep out—to fortify the tiny library that was his whole world—against the perpetual onslaught of the sea and its co-conspirators: wind, rain, and mist. He regarded it as nothing less than a mortal enemy and, he had to confess, it was winning. The wooden boards of the stacks expanded and contracted, as if birthing the books weighing them down. Books with faded, blistered covers, brittle and stained papers, and words running down the page as if to escape. The card catalog was constantly beset by mold, requiring him to write multiple new cards a day just to replace them again a week later.

Most of the town buildings were warmed with stoves or fireplaces. This was obviously impractical in a building filled with tinder, but the heaters offered by the council were always breaking down, choking on the corrosive air and exhausted by the futile fight against the chill. The salt seemed to get beneath Simon's skin, grind itself to silica between his joints.

Brackish Harbor ages everything rapidly, all peeled paint and pickled people.

Now, he glared at a new hole in one of the sea-facing windows, as if he could scold it back to wholeness. The possible culprits were many: he occasionally found evidence of vandalism or efforts to break into the library. It was closer to the outskirts of town and looked unoccupied, making it an attractive shelter for the bedraggled strangers who sometimes made their way through town towards more charitable locales. Simon gently, but assertively—or as assertively as he could fake when required—sent them on their way: they could read or they could leave. He didn't look down on the indigent travelers, he just preferred not to look at them at all…too often they looked like his neighbors.

Or perhaps a bird had flown into the window, salt-blinded and turned around. He didn't notice any blood or trace of a broken body, but it had happened before. Silvered cracks threaded their way across the glass like choking ivy. Well. Sometimes things just broke. This meant he would have to go out—during the day, no less—walk several blocks to what passed for the hardware store, and passing the secondary harbor where—

Simon stopped pacing.

To be totally clear, Simon stopped breathing.

Just for a bit, just to let his thoughts slam into a cliff-face of realization before tumbling into a sea of awful possibility. He checked his watch. It was still early enough. Maybe the dark figure wouldn't be there yet. Maybe Simon wouldn't see him. But he wanted to. In the sunken cavern of his chest, he knew he wanted to. He shook his head. Whether or not the harbor was empty, the window would still be broken and the salt would claim more bibliographic victims. He pulled a heavy coat over his cardigan to spite the bracing sea air. Checking the door—twice—to make sure he'd locked it, Simon made his way down the short hill towards Main Street.

He didn't have friends. Brackish Harbor, in general, wasn't a friendly place. Even when the tourists visited, the town itself tolerated them, indulged them with welcoming smiles and empty eyes, and quickly sent them on their way.

But that was before Simon's time; all he had ever known the Harbor to host was the sullen, festering resentment of abandoned isolation hanging in the air, like it hitchhiked in on the fog. The families of Brackish Harbor were spread out and apparently infertile: his graduating class had boasted a mere thirty-five scholars; of those, maybe eight still lived in the area. Maybe less, Simon had no idea.

A frail, bookish boy, he had grown into a thin, bookish man with little interest in the masculine pastimes of his town: sailing, fishing, and, increasingly, drinking and muttering. A sensitivity to light—a leftover, he'd been told as a child, from some 'odd genes' somewhere down the family roots—complicated social activities even further. The Harbor wasn't often sunny, not this close to the ocean and its cold fronts, embracing the town in gray clouds as if to promise that, if nothing else, *it* would never leave. Still. Simon kept to the library during daylight as much as was (mostly) humanly possible.

His footsteps echoed dully off the pavement that constituted the main thoroughfare. In a few more yards, he would clear the cannery complex, its concrete walls crumbling like an old castle. Simon gritted his teeth, told himself not to look, that he was on an errand—a quest, even— that every moment the wound in the side of the library remained, his beloved texts would be at the mercy of the cursed salt-air. But his traitor eyes slid sideways the instant the view wasn't blocked by ruined chimneys and rusted silos. There was the secondary harbor, the one they'd closed up once the cannery was more trouble than it was worth; there was the short dock in a losing territorial dispute with algae and barnacles; there were the anchor posts with their painfully unnecessary riggings, hanging limp and rotting in the silty water; and there was Thomas, and his easel.

Thomas wasn't a local, one of the interchangeable faces of Simon's childhood, and so wasn't as easily cataloged and dismissed. He had shown up a year ago with everything he owned: a single change of clothes and a hardy A-frame easel. He claimed he wanted to paint a few portraits and just…never left. As far as anyone knew (this, Simon was aware of because it was intensely discussed at a council meeting he'd only attended to beg for funds to repair the sagging library roof), the artist came to the same spot and painted the same thing: the fog. Every day.

Simon found his feet turning, his legs in a secret treasonous alliance with his eyes, moving him towards the dock, the sharp stones that made up the beach, and the tall man in the heavy black coat and gray scarf. Simon told himself he was just being friendly, but even he wasn't sure what that meant. The stones crunching beneath his shoes sounded suspiciously like snickering. He stopped, off to the side, and considered the tapestry. On the ground sat a small crate with dozens of colors, most unopened. The already-off-white background was blossoming in smoked and soft grays, tans like long-ignored coffee stains, and brief bursts of white. The easel was partially buried, grooves in the compact sand below the shale well-worn and solidified. One of its legs was chained to a heavy stone, reminding Simon of old ball-and-chain manacles from less enlightened times.

Thomas, too, seemed anchored to the spot, unshifting as he stared at the horizon, long fingers holding the brush lightly, like he was afraid he might bruise it. His face was partially obscured by curling black hair that surfed over his scarf on the morning breeze, and his eyes were bright and pale, shifting between gray and blue and green, like he had spent so long staring at these frigid waters, they had colonized his irises. Sometimes, his hand moved without him looking at the canvas. Sometimes, he leaned forward to add a line so fine, Simon wondered if it was in a spectrum of light he couldn't perceive.

When the possibility that he was being a voyeur slipped into certainty, Simon cleared his throat. Thomas turned his head without moving his shoulders. There was no hint of recognition in his steady gaze, but Simon expected that. They'd only spoken two or three times, the first a memory that still burned Simon's cheeks. After that encounter, he was sure Thomas considered him another one of these backwards fish-folk, demanding to know why he wasted his time painting the same meaningless swirls, as if *they* had room to judge. Thomas's eyes had gone flat and hooded, withdrawing into himself so quickly, Simon felt a riptide pull at his heart in the wake. Months passed before he approached the painter again. Simon didn't remember what jumbled mess had dribbled out of his mouth, but he doubted he'd created any meaningful impression.

"Good morning," Thomas said, summoning Simon back to the potentially-disastrous present.

"Good morning," Simon echoed. The pause after was a chasm whose bottom no stone would reach.

Thomas turned back to his easel.

Simon scrambled for anything to say that wouldn't inspire the sand to open its silica maw and swallow him whole. "Anything...new in the fog today?"

Thomas's eyes darted towards him in surprise, his brush frozen midway to the canvas. He considered Simon again, properly registering him. "There was a deer washed up this morning. Chunks missing. But in the time it took me to set up, it had vanished."

It was Simon's turn to be surprised. Deer weren't common in the area. Wrong climate, wrong topography. The specimens Simon had come across were only heads—stuffed, still, and staring from bar walls and trophy cases. So how could one have washed up on shore so far from its usual habitat? And how could it have disappeared again? Simon had no answers, but, emboldened by what he was fairly certain was human conversation, he continued it. "I have to go into town. Could I bring you back something? A...a coffee? Or, um, if you don't coffee—a tea? I think they still make hot chocolate?"

This time, Thomas didn't turn his head to respond, but he smiled, and Simon's wretched brain wondered if salt would seem so terrible if tasted on—

"A coffee would be appreciated. Thank you."

If Thomas noticed Simon's exit bore a striking resemblance to 'fleeing,' he had the good grace not to comment.

The hardware store occupied a building that mocked traditional concepts of spatial perception. From the outside, the store didn't appear impressive: a steepled façade backed up by a flat, squat roof. The insides were mostly lit by a series of skylights that turned the already gray sky the color of weak tea, and stretched every shadow like taffy, giving the impression of a deeper structure of murky borders. It never didn't smell of rotting roses and greasy popcorn. Simon considered how much of his life was spent staggering among stacks, piled and uneven shelves, how liminal his universe was: these rows of nails and the velvet shadows, the shore and the sea, the printed pages and the heavy breeze. Being alone and being lonely. He thought again of Thomas and his fog, the liminal made visible. Maybe every border was so porous.

It took a bit to find all he needed, partially because he refused to step around the outer edges of the shelves near the shadow-obscured walls, to be any closer to the outer limits than strictly necessary, which required backtracking to the center before moving onto the next aisle. And, as far as he could tell, he was the only person in the building and, therefore, unable to ask for directions. When he returned to the lone register, Silas Devers was behind it.

Silas was old in the way that most folks of the Harbor were old: thin white hair, a face wrinkled by surf and salt and a lifetime of scowling, a wispy beard that looked desperate to jump ship, and heavily-lidded eyes that had already sized you up and dismissed you.

Simon wrangled a hefty roll of silver tape, a tube of heavy paper, three flattened cardboard boxes, and a painter's sheet onto the counter.

Silas eyed them and snorted out a number Simon knew was just shy of extravagant, but he pulled out his wallet without argument. While Silas packed everything but the boxes into a large paper bag, he paused on the sheet. "This for the fog boy?" Silas rumbled.

Simon bristled, though he wasn't sure why the dismissiveness should bother *him*, it was just how people talked there. Maybe it was more the surprise that Silas would make a connection between them. "No," Simon replied, keeping his voice even and crisp, "there's a hole in one of the library windows. I want to cover it until the city replaces it, and I don't want to scratch the surrounding glass."

Silas snorted, though whether that was in acknowledgement or judgment of Simon, the library, the city, or the existence of holes, was unclear. "Shouldn't be so close to the water," Silas continued, dropping the sheet into the bag. Simon knew Silas wasn't referring to him.

"He's not hurting anything," Simon reminded himself he didn't need to be defensive, but the retort escaped regardless, "and no one uses that harbor anymore anyway."

Silas fixed him with a stare and Simon felt like a schoolboy who made an embarrassingly obvious mistake in front of the class. "That's right. They don't. Shouldn't be so close." And with that, Silas grabbed a broom and made his way into the depths of the store, vanishing into the gloom.

It took more doing than Simon cared to admit, juggling the paper bag, boxes and two ludicrously hot coffees back from town, but he managed. The cafe seemed to be exclusively staffed by rotating sets of teenagers from out of town, which made for a brief but friendly change. Thomas was exactly as left, shifting his gaze from the harbor mist to the canvas, pausing only to refresh the paint on his brush, and when he noticed Simon awkwardly holding out a sleeved cup.

"That was quick," Thomas said.

Simon felt this was objectively false, but didn't debate. Instead, he scanned what Thomas had added to the canvas. While there were certainly more swirls and streaks, particularly near the edges, his eyes kept sliding towards the bottom center. It wasn't a busy section—in fact, there seemed to be a definite *lack*, a kind of softly pulsing *waiting*.

Simon was about to ask what would fill the pale void when Thomas said, "I'm sorry for not recognizing you. You look after the library no one uses."

Simon opened his mouth to protest, to rally in defense of his beleaguered career, but something in Thomas's heather-gray eyes made him pause. It wasn't pity, Simon couldn't have stomached that, but a kind of cool, clear understanding, like a very deep, glacier-fed lake. Simon clenched his jaw, not trusting himself to speak, and simply nodded. He looked out over the water and tried to identify where the gap in the painting came from, but the fog was a monotone wall of faded bruise.

Simon shivered. What Silas had said—patronizing as it was—stuck with him, and he couldn't think of anything to say that wouldn't lead to blurting out, 'Are you sure you're safe here?' so, after accepting Thomas's thanks and making apologies, he staggered his way back up the hill to the library.

The morning rumbled in, ornery, a spouse demanding attention, a hunger growling in the skies before dawn had even shrugged on the first pale shafts of light. Thomas stared out a window that had likely never known a gentle hand: spiky growths of brown encroached from edges, every inch filthy save the parts that were just cracked. Relatable.

Thomas had slept badly. Thomas always slept badly. Spiky growths of certainty encroaching from the edges of his mind insisted that if he didn't keep an eye on himself—a vigilant, muscle-locked control at all times—his flesh would fly apart, soft and brittle as old ashes. Even through the closed window, the heady mix of petrichor and brine promised heavy, wind-punched rain, and a day that would never brighten past crepuscular. Thomas smiled. The fog would be beautiful.

Three hours later, he was drenched, shoulders sagging under the weight of his water-logged greatcoat and the knowledge that whatever *it* was—the effervescent something always *right there*—would elude his paintbrush once again. But still, he added lines, layers, if he could just capture a shadow of it…Sometimes he put down what he snatched from the corner of his eye; a wisp, a flicker. Other times, he stared at the obscured horizon line, as if daring answers from the waves. They crashed against the harbor, mockingly as relentless and ineffectual as he, each break hissing dully as a slurred blasphemy. His nostrils stung with a scent like chemical fire, all burnt hair and devastation. His hands were beginning to shake from the chill, the tension, the frustration. He looked between the canvas and the water. It wasn't *right*, he knew he was close, he had to be, he just couldn't quite *get* it.

Thomas carefully packed away his brushes, and pulled the tarp over the easel. He didn't sigh, ever, always afraid that such a spontaneous expulsion of air would be impossible to cease once released, until it pulled the breath, the throat, the lungs, the blood of him, past his lips, leaving him little more than an emptied, wet shredded skin smeared across the sand.

He would try again tomorrow.

"Does it smell odd to you?" Simon asked, his face caressed by a frame of steam coming off the top of his tea and mingling with the spectral condensation of his breath.

Thomas took another sip of his coffee, feeling it scald his throat and finding himself unbothered. It was a pang that kept him here, now. "Define odd."

Simon smiled, small and brief. *Fair enough.* "Like…sharp."

The fog was a slate wall punctured with iridescent blues, a smoke-swirled opal. Simon avoided looking at the water. Recently, it seemed massive and belligerent, like he was beneath its notice but not its wrath. Not unlike most people in Brackish Harbor. In any case, if he pretended not to notice how *immediate* the endlessness was, how dark the water got only a few meters from the shifting ground he stood on, he could almost hold what passed for human conversation. He preferred to look at Thomas's canvas, the seamless blend of sky and sea, less overwhelming through the Claude glass of the paint strokes.

Thomas nodded, though Simon didn't know if it was in response to his observation or to some thought drifting through his mind while he concentrated. The water closest to the shore seemed unusually viscous, the waves always returning a little more sluggish than they came in. From his peripheral vision, Simon thought he saw speckles like pox scars or tiny eyes. He refocused on the dark figure in front of him.

Thomas's face was very close to the easel, strokes staccato jabs. The picture looked darker to Simon than the actual harbor, but he didn't comment. If asked, he would have immediately disintegrated into a swarm of bats, but to himself, he could admit he enjoyed sitting and watching Thomas work. He didn't require a great deal of conversation, so he sat on the sand, feeling the damp chill slowly colonize his spine.

Thomas stooped as he focused on a lower section of canvas. The goopy deposits were beginning to build up in the wet sand as the tide receded. Sometimes, one area seemed to swell, an oleaginous lung inflating.

Simon strained to see if the void was still there in the painting, perhaps even more apparent with the tenebrous hues Thomas was using. Sure enough, not in the same place and far bigger—closer?—the barest suggestion of a similar outline, but maybe only because he was looking for it. He was about to ask when Thomas made a low groan in the depths of his jaw, straightened his back, and glared out into the water. "What's wrong?" Simon asked, tentatively.

For a long time, it seemed like Thomas couldn't hear him, perhaps had forgotten he was there. Then he turned and there was the same wild brightness to his labradorite eyes. "I thought I had it this time, but it's gone."

Simon bit the inside of his cheek, but forged ahead. "What's gone?"

Thomas's eyes clouded over again, that sinking inward that immediately made Simon regret having said anything, having ever spoken in his life. "There's something. In the fog. I don't know. You'll think I'm mad. I am…" he paused, gathering up his brushes, wrapping them in paper towels and returning them to his bag, "…quite certain I am."

Simon became aware one side of his own face was copper, was leaking, no, was bleeding, he had bitten too hard inside, and he forced himself to relax his face. He didn't feel he was equipped to comment on the sanity of others. "What will you do when you've got it?"

Thomas heaved his bag onto his back and began to walk towards town. He glanced once over his shoulder, and Simon could have thrown himself off the pier and felt less a sense of drowning than what Thomas's eyes threatened to pull him into. "Be less alone."

Simon watched Thomas trudge towards town. He finally allowed his eyes to drift to the slate-gray shore. Hundreds of tiny jellyfish were stranded along the sand, their mass protean pulsating as they failed to return to the water. Simon could see why: what he had mistaken for spots were the ends of what he would expect to be long, trailing tendrils. Instead, every single jelly sported nubs jutting a short way out beneath their hooded heads, ends dark and livid. All their tentacles had been sheared off, leaving them unable to propel themselves to safety. Soon, they would dry out, nothing more than a sticky web across cool sand. Simon didn't stay to watch.

The next morning boasted acclaim as one of the rare sunny days, and Simon knew he couldn't go outside. There was plenty to do: the library seemed to be constantly—even actively—disintegrating around him.

By mid-afternoon, his hands ached from sweeping, scrubbing, sorting, and shuffling; and his mind demanded more stimulation. He felt vaguely guilty as he perused the folklore section for any titles about…well, he wasn't sure. Fog, perhaps, sea monsters, local tales. He was surprised to realize he'd never really looked into local myths, but concluded he'd dismissed the possibility of anything about his hometown being remotely interesting. The citizens of Brackish Harbor were pragmatic people who kept their thoughts to themselves and their beliefs to whispers shared in corners.

The section housing folk and fairy tales wasn't extensive: children's books were shelved in a separate section—which, he reminded himself, he needed to brush the cobwebs from, and soon—and the more…unsavory-yet-valuable titles were kept on a totally different floor under multiple locks even he didn't have the keys for. Every few months, the District Manager—a gaunt woman with severe bangs who never aged, as far as Simon could tell—would pass by, check the Restricted Titles cabinet hadn't been disturbed, and pat Simon's shoulder in an unparsable mélange of irritation and sympathy, telling him he was doing his best given the circumstances, before vanishing to some other, probably less sodium-enriched location. He had never asked about the Restricted Titles, and no one had ever inquired after them.

All this meant that the pile he carried to his favorite reading table—close enough to the windows to let light in, but at an angle where it didn't fall directly on him; wood so old, it had almost petrified and was smooth against his skin, not too far from the kettle—was not particularly impressive.

The first book he flipped through was an anthology of coastal hauntings, and while Simon appreciated the author's poetic flourishes, it wasn't what he was looking for.

The second title boasted truly terrible cover art that the book itself seemed ashamed of: the cheap glue had disintegrated and it slid out from the spine upon pick up. His suspicions were confirmed by the publication page: self-published author who provided the cover art. In large hand-drawn letters, the title, *The divine radiance of the lady of Gillcrest Cove*, encircled a glowing figure in white, and indicated an utter lack of interest in capitalization expectations. The rest of the cover was dark gray with silhouettes presumably representing the iconography of Gillcrest Cove. The text was both overwrought and somehow prosaic, describing an encounter with an ethereal being appearing in a town not unlike Brackish Harbor. Details were contradictory or vague, but the back of the book contained a surprisingly thorough bibliography the author claimed had been helpful for determining context.

Carrying the decayed codex with him—and leaving the offensive cover behind on the table—Simon searched Earth Sciences, Paleontology, Biology, Animals, Memoirs, and Music. The last had only seven books in total, and yet, by some dark miracle, one of them was a tome he'd sought: *The Drowned Man's Shanties: an anthology.* He had less luck with the sciences, though both *On the Anatomy of Piscian Majoris* and *Agarthan Topography* sounded promising, if absolutely ludicrous.

The real gem though, was the Journals. Simon loved journals, loved their oiled leather covers, the tangled thong clasps, the way the stiff, aged paper demanded delicacy. After only a few years as librarian, Simon had defied conventional library set up by moving the Biographies, Memoirs, and Journals section to the side of the library with the least exposure to the windows, and put the older copies in glass cabinets. They weren't kept locked—*why bother?*—but protecting the historical treasures from the elements had always been deeply important to him.

Simon carried the thick tome with both hands and laid it reverently on the table. Beneath the brown hide cover, someone had attached an index card in a way that made him both grateful and infuriated. *The Collected Journals of Antwerp Johannson: Keeper of the Harleson Point Lighthouse, 1756-1858.* He breathed in the peppery scent of the past, then set the book aside. *Later.*

The collection of shanties was thin and dripped barnacles, murder, and a great deal of attraction to monsters. One even mentioned Brackish Harbor by name: a cautionary tale about the hubris of man, the implacability of nature, and paying attention to your surroundings. Though he'd never heard anyone mention the events recorded in the lyrics of this particularly morose number—with, he felt, an overfondness for the word 'indescribable,' a bold choice considering how difficult it was to rhyme—Simon made a note to dig deeper into *The Raising of the Greenworm Ford.*

At some point, he realized the sun had buckled under the weight of warming such a dismal patch of shore and was sinking below the water, staining it in shades of flame. The dimming light washed the exposed pages under his fingers incarnadine, and the invading shadows invited the illustrations before his tired eyes to dance. Creatures with fins and fangs and too many eyes and too many bones, too big and too clever to be anything but myth and nightmare, swam along the borders of maps, the marginalia of diaries, the sketches of credulous interviewers. Despite not knowing quite what he was looking for, Simon was certain he was close to capturing it, and, as his head drooped down and his eyes closed, he wondered if this was how Thomas felt every day.

Simon stood next to Thomas. The sea was angry and mourning, using the wind to scream and to warn, and the rain was sharp and cold. Simon opened his mouth to say…something, but the roar of the waves stole his voice, pulled it under the surface, and drowned it.

Simon stood next to Thomas. The sea was angry and mourning, using the wind to scream and to warn, and the rain was sharp and cold. Simon asked Thomas what was happening, but when the artist turned, his eyes were gone and seaweed streamed from the empty sockets, then crabs, tuna, jellyfish, a speckled octopus, an aquarium's worth piling up at his feet.

Thomas opened his mouth and a net full of garbage fell out, plastic and aluminum, shards of steel, sea glass, tangled fishing wire, so many bones. They kept coming, until Thomas's skin could no longer keep itself up and he collapsed into a wet pile of flesh, slowly pulled apart by pincers and tentacles and sharp edges.

Simon stood next to Thomas. The sea was angry and mourning, using the wind to scream and to warn, and the rain was sharp and cold. Simon told Thomas he cared for him, wanted to invite him to the library, show him all his favorite books, discuss Antwerp Johannsen and his uncannily long life, make tea together.

Thomas blinked, turned back towards the canvas. His voice sounded distant and echoed as if underground. *Thank you, but no. I'm here for the fog.*

The sky laughed. The sand laughed.

They pressed Simon above and below, compressing his spine—sliding off, disintegrating cheap glue, poorly made cover—heavy, heavy. The sea didn't laugh, the sea sighed in an un-parsable mélange of irritation and sympathy; the sea *understood.* Simon walked forward, into the embrace of the water, pulled below the surface, and drowned.

Thomas never looked away from the easel.

Simon stood. Thomas seemed very far away. The fog was everywhere. It rolled off the water like logs, like avalanches of smoke. Simon walked forward, he had something to tell Thomas, he was *right there*, so close. It was very important.

The sky laughed. The sand laughed.

The fog rose, expanded, solidified.

Thomas never looked away from the easel.

The fog—or something camouflaged within—reared or roared, Simon wasn't sure, just everything was heavy and loud and he had to get to Thomas before—

The fog smashed down, painting the sand in incarnadine shades of Thomas.

Simon stopped.

The monster oozed forward, away from the harbor, towards the town. Soon, Simon's whole world would be smeared with Thomas's bloody absence. He began to run towards the malignant fog, that hateful void. No point staying, no one would miss him, he didn't even wonder if they'd notice. The monster would just be the latest and last thing to crush him with indifference.

He stepped into the path.

The fog came down.

Everything was quiet.

Simon stood, knocking his chair over, startling himself to complete wakefulness.

Multiple books were open before him, though in the early morning twilight, they seemed much more mundane, the illustrations simple photocopies of drunken legends, the scientific descriptions only a reference to creatures long-extinct, songs to keep sailors focused on long, dull swathes of night.

He stretched, the tendrils of stiff sleep still sunk into his muscles. *Well.* The information—generous though the term might be—he'd come across was little more than suggestive, a faint sketch or outline...not unlike, he mused, one of Thomas's paintings. Like if he just found the precise text, all the pieces would merge—or, he shook his head, running a trembling hand through disheveled mahogany hair, he was grasping at nothing more real or corporeal than the fog, none of it meant anything, and he should choose better places to sleep. Maybe there was something out there in the harbor. Maybe there was something out in every harbor, the border of matter thin and amorphous, making other veils—spiritual, astral, perceptional—more porous. Whatever the case, metaphysics or madness, Simon knew he wasn't equipped to deal with any of it. Certainly not without a nap first.

The next day brought with it a storm as if punishing the folks of Brackish Harbor for daring to glance at the sun. The clouds were low and full of fury, the lightning flashing often enough, each mass of mist and vapor was almost chrome. Rain came down, sharp and cold. Those who could, stayed inside. A few of the elders looked towards the coast and muttered about foreigners, but the youngsters misunderstood them. Whole sections of town lost power, adding to the overall gloom.

Nobody should have been outside. Simon knew it, knew any reasonable person would be bunkered down to wait out the gales, would never tempt fate by going out knowing the mean, insular former fisher-folk wouldn't bother rescuing anyone fool enough to defy the salt and storm of it all.

Simon knew this, just as deeply as he knew Thomas was *not* a reasonable person.

Whatever survival instincts the painter may have been born with had bled away into the sand, drowned out by pandemonium mists. He would be out there, every streak of color immediately vandalized by rain, but still, brush in frigid hand, Thomas would be painting, each stroke like that of an oar before river rapids, desperate for release. He wasn't of the Harbor. No one would come for him nor mourn his vanishing.

Simon grabbed his coat and pulled open the door. The force of the wind was great enough that several index cards and more than a few books tumbled from their perches. He felt, more than heard, the wooden door slam behind him. He didn't bother locking it.

The salt burned his eyes, embedded in his clothes, weighing them down as he stumble-ran towards the secondary harbor. Something was happening in the cannery, the sounds of twisting, shearing metal rising even over the wind and waves. Not a dozen feet away, lightning came down on one of the chimneys, and he wondered why it smelled like charring meat and turpentine. He was vaguely aware of falling, that the wet trailing down his leg was more copper than brine—though, being from there, he wouldn't have been surprised if he'd bled tidepools—but he refused to register the pain.

There were creatures of shadow and scales, native to the between-places of the world, harbor hauntings, and a storm married sea and sky in a way that could only make the zone between dimensions thinner; or, there were krakens and leviathans from deep caverns leading to a world below the crust of the earth, where crushing darkness bred life bellicose and twisted; or, he was going to go tell this soft and strange man that he cared for him and the resulting silence might swallow them both whole.

But no matter what, *he was* not *leaving Thomas out there alone.*

The cannery was swallowed by the mist almost as soon as Simon passed it, and there was the secondary harbor and there was Thomas, without a scarf or coat, hair lank around his face and neck as he furiously dipped brush to paint to canvas.

Simon stood next to Thomas. The sea was angry and mourning, using the wind to scream and to warn, and the rain was sharp and cold.

"You shouldn't be out here!" Simon shouted. "It's not safe!"

"It's here, I'm sure of it!" Thomas's eyes were wide and wild, moon-like and locked onto the easel. "I just need to...need..."

Simon put one hand on Thomas's shoulder and wrapped the other around the fingers holding the brush. Conjuring more courage than he'd ever required in his quiet existence, he stepped forward and pressed the side of his face to Thomas's drenched cheek. "*I'm* here. With you. You're not alone."

The paintbrush clattered to the stones.

Simon held his breath in the eye of all the spiraling panics about rejection and apathy.

Thomas put his arm down without letting go of Simon's hand and turned to face him. His eyes were still almost too bright to look into, especially now that they were focused entirely on him, but the azure and viridian swirls within were warmer, so present—*right here*—and in them, he saw surprise, trepidation, and a brittle joy, wavering like a ship's lantern.

There were many reasons why, later, they wouldn't be able to describe the thing that heaved itself from water, oozing into corporeality long enough to leave a trail of destruction along the waterfront before returning to whatever place or plane of existence it usually occupied. The fog was heavy and moved with a cruel sentience, the sky was dark, the rains were heavy. Much was obscured.

The most obvious reason they couldn't describe its likeness was that it crushed them both and left no trace.

However, the truest reason was, in that instant of recognition, the shared understanding of connection, they were as utterly oblivious and indifferent to the horror as it was to them.

When they reach us—and they will—from beyond the borders of coastal shores, may we all be so blessed. When they breach whatever subtle forces have spared us so far, may we all, each of us, find such a beautiful distraction.

And when facing the certainty that all that will be left of us is salt, may we be given the choice between solitude and connection.

CHAPTER THREE

TASTES OF DESPERATION
Amanda M. Blake

They live together like ghosts, same as everyone and everything left on the island. Fishing nets are cobwebs, residents merely spirits fading to gray like wharf wood. Each day much like the previous and the next, changes small rather than sweeping, and breaking down more quickly than what has endured. The steady rise and fall of an indifferent lapping tide. Their little upthrust of rock holds life like a tide pool; wholly insignificant from a distance, yet, up close, churning with throat stones and stomach acid, because the island doesn't care but the islanders do.

They pause for the ferry horn, as though one day, a different ferry will escort them, but also because the sound is its own kind of electricity, briefly jolting life at seven-thirty and eight-thirty in the morning, and again at seven-thirty and eight-thirty in the evening, arrive and depart, arrive and depart. Whenever the ferry leaves again, everyone left returns to their work, their meal, their chores, their tea, their cards, their binoculars, but even the industriousness is listless, restless, wandering—drifting in the churning foam of the northside current.

Sarah's bob bounces on the water's surface to let boats and the ferry know that she's diving the shallows, although she needs it less these days—all the more reason to use it, really, because the boats that still go out aren't as careful as they used to be. There are worse ways to go, but around here, not many. For most, it's a hard life meeting premature old age. Or they disappear into thin air—most escaping to the mainland without a word, to find a life while they still have a chance.

The shipwrecks have been picked clean by scavengers of both the marine and island variety, but people still toss trash over the sides of their boats and the ferry, and sometimes that trash is aluminum. She gathers beer and soda cans—mostly beer—into her bag, surfaces like a dolphin to take a breath through her snorkel, and dives again.

Should have, should have, should have rocks with the water that rocks her and knocks the bob like a bell. She could have, could have, could have, too. She could have waited tables longer, maybe long enough to become manager, or taken night classes at the community college. She could have figured out something else to do except fall for a mainland fisherman and bring him to the island, like a stolen selkie skin, to take over where her weary parents left off in the house that they left to her, which leaks more and more every time a storm blows through, and she has to find more and more buckets to bail the water out the back door to keep them from sinking.

Once she has a trash bin's worth of crushed cans in the garage, she'll take it to the mainland for fifty bucks—if she's lucky—a chunk of which goes to the ferry round trip.

As a child searching for pocket money, she'd shared the shiny with scale-flashes of fish schools and the toothy yawn of eels, but these days, among the thinning kelp of the sound, she is mostly alone.

Leo sits in *Ocypode*, surrounded by the accoutrements of a trade gone to molder. Owning a boat is worse than owning a home. Entropy accelerates; everything requires constant maintenance—repair rather than replace—for as long as possible, and longer. Whenever anyone asks what boat they should buy, as though what he does is the same beast they're looking for, he always tells them the same thing—buy the fish, rent the boat.

Even so, he was proud as paint when he left his father's boat to run his own after marrying Sarah and moving south to the island, which was already deep into its slow, fetid rot in the hazy sun. But he eked out a living off his nets and traps and even got the Witts' two boys to help out. Until the Witts moved to the mainland, leaving Sarah's parents' home standing in confused fugue, two houses empty on either side, and pushing his prematurely-deteriorating body to take on the work of three for the yield of less than one.

Every morning before sunrise—if there is sun—he leaves before Sarah wakes, same as he did when there was a point. Perhaps this is limbo. Perhaps they are already dead and death is simply familiar repeating patterns, even when it accomplishes nothing, like brushing their hair in front of a mirror that doesn't show their reflection.

Leo is not a man of particular imagination. When he stares at water, he sees water, and when he guts the fish on the cutting board arranged on his knees, he sees food. But he is not without his moments of association, like the old navigators who saw shapes in stars no longer seen.

He eats the perch raw, because it's better that way and because it's not worth the effort to cook when he has the stretch of day before him, simmering under the sun. Underneath his coarse beard, his skin scales and peels like chapped lips.

When he's finished, he wipes his hands, and grabs the net as he stands. He mended the holes in it that morning, and would mend the holes in it tomorrow. At this rate, the net would soon be more repair-nylon than rope.

He wears his father's clothes, bought his uncle's boat and all of its gear—his uncle had to retire from the sea after a bad back turned paraplegia—and lives in his wife's parents' house. Everything his is somehow secondhand, such that it feels like he only paid for the opportunity to borrow what would be repossessed, but really, it possessed him, didn't it? Jute-calloused hands, pickled cheeks, scarred-over splinters, mercury aching in his veins, and everything smells, so much that he doesn't even smell it anymore. Nose-blind and nearly deaf. Just another reason the mainland turns up its nose at him when he doesn't have catch to sell—and these days, even a good catch isn't good enough for lean markets, where only commercial boats gather the numbers needed to barely break even.

His boat is a shipwreck floating like a corpse, sinking under debt, but at least it sometimes catches a decent dinner so that, even if he can't come back on the ferry with money in his pocket, he can put something on the table. Something to sink their teeth into. But was that enough anymore, or was it all as much memory echo as everything else?

Even so, the motions: cast the net, gather the catch, throw what's found on ice. If he has enough by evening, he will exchange fish for bread from Mary Shelton, eggs from the Barretts, root vegetables from the Larabies. And Sarah maintains her own garden, providing vegetables and herbs that somehow taste the way the island looks, as though already overcooked. He swallows the bland without complaint, because it's supposed to be better than nothing.

Perhaps it isn't just his hearing that's nearly gone. He thinks he sees clearly, but all he sees is gray; he thinks his poisoned blood still runs warm, but all he feels is cold. No matter how many sweaters Sarah knits, he is always so cold, and no matter how many quilts she layers on their bed, it is always so empty. Just like his nets.

There's not enough to go around. Algae blooms lap the shores of the sound and snag in the inlets, the kelp browns and beaches in dead clumps, and the fish move further into waters surrounded by only horizon. Too many desperate fishermen, too many commercial boats with bigger nets, bigger crew, and a belly full of ice. All he has are instincts instilled in him from another time. He is a shark searching barren feeding grounds until his insides shrivel.

He circles around to the inlets. He's not supposed to use the net or traps this close, but the old-timers are already off the water and the lighthouse keeper just likes the ambience. Leo readies the rod but casts the net once more.

He has to come home with something, or he might as well not come home at all, because God knows he offers her nothing else. She's the reason they have a home. She's the reason they have a space heater in the winter and a window unit in the summer, freezers in the cellar, but he's the reason they light candles in the dark. He's the reason Sarah cans, pickles, preserves, cures, and smokes mornings and nights between trash collecting and scavenging the rooted shipwrecks of the island's abandoned homes for the fourteenth, fifteenth, five-hundredth time—although they're usually picked clean by the Nero brothers before Sarah gathers her courage to creep like the thief she's become.

Eden Inlet at dusk floats in a haze—not quite fog—pierced by glaring light in a slow, steady rhythm from the lighthouse, like the island's heartbeat. Leo switches on a lantern to see between rotations, keeping it dim enough that he will not be so easily seen. Feeling his way, he closes the submerged net and swings it up over the deck.

It writhes as though full of eels during spawning season. His twisting, unsettled stomach loosens from its fist, because it's something, something to share, to trade, not enough to sell so late but at least *something* to bring home.

The lighthouse lamp shines on something huge amid the haddock, eyes gleaming like great silver dollars, slime plastered like black spider silk over a slick, fleshly body, more eel than fish, but ending in a horizontal fin that fans out the width of the net.

Leo recoils, stumbling against the edge of his boat, a grunt escaping like blunt nails in his throat.

When the light swings back around, Leo approaches the net, expecting that his limited imagination nevertheless elaborated upon a sturgeon or shark.

Those silver-dollar eyes blink, inner eyelids like a crocodile, but this is nothing from that family. Instead, the creature's skin is smooth, interrupted by slashes above the barrel of its human-like ribs, and humans only need ribs like that, to cradle lungs.

Leo reaches for one of several knives in his jacket, tries to cut loose the desperate soul, but it lashes out, floundering its marine-mammalian, eel-slick tail that extends from a long torso which leads up to a black mouth ringed in sporadic, uneven conical teeth, like a moray. The slashes above its ribs ripple like a sea snake, useless over the dripping surface. But its throat works, too, and Leo thinks it screams, that hissing sound through the muffled drum-pounding of waves against unforgiving cliffs below the lighthouse.

Leo lowers his knife as the thing grabs at the haddock around it. Skeletal fingers grasp the slippery flesh, dig rusty-nail claws in to bring the fish to where it stifles its scream with ripping, staining its face as black as its mouth in the dark but glaring red when the lighthouse lamp illuminates it.

Until he has to believe what he sees. He just doesn't know what to do.

Sarah sits in front of the fire, knees tucked up near her chest, toes pressed to the edge of the metal tub. She stares at the firelight flicker in the glass window, ink-blot nothing on the other side.

The back porch isn't usually where Leo enters, but she's relieved when she recognizes the weight and carelessness of his step, not that she's feared thieves in years. The only thieves on the island don't trespass on occupied land. The only *convicted* thieves. She supposes many who remain would be considered thieves by some reckoning or other if anyone officially cared about the desecration of a corpse.

He enters without boots. His socks have holes in the heels and toes, but he won't let her darn them, and although she knits new, he always disintegrates the old before he considers replacement.

He brings with him a cooler of fish, but she indicates the stove, where she's done what she could to temper the brine of canned mackerel in the stew's gravy.

Leo sets the cooler on the kitchen counter as though he carries a greater burden than feeding his family. He hasn't brought home anything else, which tells her that he didn't exchange what limited catch he manages these days, so there's nothing to supplement the stew but what she picked from the greenhouse, which is held together by silver tape and prayers to the cardinal winds to hold until they can replace the windows, which might be never.

He hovers in her kitchen with an indeterminate uncertainty but doesn't complain when he ladles the stew from the simmering pot into a bowl, only wrinkles his face against the initial ache of salt, as though his tongue is an ill-used slug.

She suffered the same while she ate alone as night blanketed the island, had to temper it with someone else's wine—which edges on vinegar, but she'll take fermentation where she finds it.

Sarah steps from the cooling water, then opens the drain that connects to a hose leading out of the house—more convenient than in the time of pioneers, but she still needs to heat water in the fireplace kettle to take a hot bath. Leo will have to heat up his own. She dries off and wraps herself in the thick robe that holds hearth heat much better than the bathwater.

She leaves him to his cold bath and salty stew. He knows better than to let the food crust on dirty bowls or in the pot, and he knows better than to slip between sheets with her without soap cutting through the saltwater, like dry-scale film, on his skin.

She heads into what was once her childhood bedroom—turned sewing room after she left. It could have been a nursery after she returned, but she eventually painted the walls from pink to white for a catch-all. An office where red-stamped envelopes, opened but restuffed, go to die. A reading room that mingles the insinuating ocean air with decaying paper and ink. A sewing room once again, with her mother's sewing machine, which was vintage when her mother used it and is now antique, and her grandmother's knitting needles and crochet hooks and boxes and boxes of collected yarn. A craft room for mermaid's tears and bits of shell, shipwreck, and driftwood that she can sell to the nautical-obsessed along with the discarded possessions of the disappeared.

It was somewhere to go that wasn't the kitchen, where she pickled her fingertips, bloodied her rubber apron, and bathed her face in steam so that they'd have something to eat in increasingly leaner times. Somewhere to go that wasn't the bedroom, with its window facing an endless ocean that was the same rippled gray every day and would be the same rippled gray in the days to come, as though time didn't move forward or backward, but in an endless loop for sins she wished someone would tell her she'd committed—sins greater than marrying a fisherman like her father, like her grandfather, when she should have known better, but it really was all she knew.

And she must have loved him once. She remembers it like dreams of the past, dreams of a future in brighter colors than this. Quite different from the way she loved her father, because Leo's silence was borne from hearing loss, not from a father who taught bootstrap stoicism, as her father passed down not to his sons, but to his daughter.

Her brothers left the island, never to return. For all she knows, they're dead, because they didn't come to the funerals, never invited her to any wedding or christening, as though she'd already taken the place next to their parents on the island cemetery plot. Perhaps her disappearance from the mainland was like the disappearances from the island—inexplicable, unspoken, obituary in and of itself.

Beloved sister, lost at sea.

She makes jewelry by candlelight long into the night. The hall outside creaks under her husband's footsteps on his way to the bedroom. He hesitates outside her door, rocking over a particularly warped floorboard that he probably doesn't know he disturbs, but his ghost doesn't disturb her.

By the time they moved into her parents' house, they didn't need words, but their shorthand turned into haunting, crossing paths instead of crossing over. He goes out during the day to fail because he's given up. She sees it in the seventy-year-old wear on an almost fifty-year-old man. She goes out during the day to try. And when their parallel lives shift into the perpendicular, they neither speak nor shorthand. He doesn't look her in the face even if she wants him to read her lips, and her wedding band tarnishes from sea spray.

If she asks for help, who would hear her?

She wakes to singing.

Not her own half-hearted hums to stave off silence—when seagulls won't screech and the ocean forgets to roar, air so still she isn't sure she can breathe—nor Leo's tuneless memory of radio songs from his youth. He sleeps next to her, behind her, his body heat collected beneath the quilt with hers, but only their feet touch. She emerges from the quilts too hot from fading tendril dreams to reach for her robe in the cold room, but he doesn't stir.

Although he wakes before the sun, he's slept through gale-force winds while she reinforced boarded windows and replaced buckets as needed through the night before he woke to the aftermath. He sleeps like the dead.

Sarah walks through the house on the pads of her feet without lighting a candle. The swing of the lighthouse lamp pierces through the windows in slow intervals, enough to confirm that she's following the worn-smooth wood and threadbare patches of carpet to the living room.

The damp air chills and tightens her bare skin, but there's no one to see her, and she still holds the bed's warmth within, so she steps out onto the porch. The singing is stronger, weaving in and out of the wind and breakers on the beach. It hovers without structure around her, wraps like summer's humidity over her surface cold, and makes her forget she ever left the quilts behind.

Sand grits under her bare feet as she follows the music, otherworldly and yet familiar—like the dream she can't remember, except it smells like the wet green of Eden Inlet. Her parents took her there as a kid, but when she was old enough, she rode her bike to the lighthouse on her own, swung from the tree rope her parents had swung from in their youth, what seemed like a thousand summers from forever ago.

Slimy tangle around her ankles and finger grip on her thighs. Seaweed on the surface, two eely eyes above the spread. She tries to find purchase in the memory, but she's not even sure it's real any more than the give of sand and sea spray against her nakedness.

Ocypode is tied off at the rocks at the end of the street, a dock for row boats, kayaks, and canoes, the kind of boats that the retirees take out for pleasure. It's not really built for professional vessels, but this isn't the first time Leo has used it after returning too late to the marina. As long as he doesn't make a habit of it, the sheriff doesn't cite him.

The dock is rougher on her feet than the porch, but her soles, like her hands, are scarred and calloused from a lifetime on and around water, barefoot most of her young and working life. She climbs onto Leo's boat, which is even rougher.

She's used to everything smelling like fish, until she can barely smell it, but here the scent is thick in the mist—a fresh catch in the early stages of decay. It's not like Leo to leave a catch to decompose on his deck, especially these days.

When the lighthouse lamp hits the deck, she searches for the lantern, stumbling on less familiar terrain, and swearing from the scrapes on her knees and shins when she walks into the traps. But on the next pass, she finds it where he keeps the coolers for personal catch rather than commercial, not that he uses the hatch much anymore. She switches the lantern on brighter than Leo prefers, coloring the deck and her skin orange-gold like a dying campfire.

Black hair tangled in rough net, fish guts splashed on the deck in black blood from the massacre. Other than the ripple of its throat and shift of tongue behind gleaming teeth, it is as still as the dead fish—whole and in parts—around it. Its song moves more than the thing itself, wreathing her mind like good wool, tightening her skin further than cold, until she feels fifteen again: a head full of desire, and a young creature circling her in the inlet pool when she thought she was alone.

Different melody, same voice. But she doesn't remember it being so thin, an abacus of ribs and concavity beneath, eel-long body a narrower, loose coil in the net, cheekbones prominent against the stretched rubbery press of its aquatic flesh.

It reaches winter-twig fingers through the holes in the net as it sings. Gray shoots through the black of its hair, much as it has her own. Scars mark its flesh like the old bull sharks they drag out of the ocean when someone spots a dorsal from the mainland, or they infiltrate inland on brackish currents. From sharks, seals, shallows, boat propellers; distinctive patterns that might fade but nevertheless tell the same story, like the scars on her own body. She remembers tracing its raised scars—fewer then— remembers the bite mark on its shoulder, remembers blood crusting her sides in the mirror after she took off her shirt. The stains washed out, and the impressions gradually smoothed and pearled to glint against her suntanned skin.

Sarah crouches on the deck, head stuffed with fog but the rest of her amazingly alive, as though from too many cups of coffee, heart racing, cheeks flushed against cold she can't feel, a frantic cellular vibration.

It rises on the bed of dead fish to bring its eyes level with hers. The years have been unkind to both of them, skeletons too prominent, but they're still here, aren't they? Still hungry but here, consuming what they can to fill the emptiness growing hollower by the day.

She brings her hand to its beckoning fingers. They interlock between the rope.

Fever burns hotter in her face, pulses between her thighs, and she remembers how the black secretions coated her neck and shoulders where it tasted without breaking through. She'd furiously scrubbed that off before emerging from the water, legs trembling as though afraid they would merge and their tails would knot around each other, like rat snakes in their season. By the time she climbed back up the cliffs, it was a mere shadow in the lagoon glow as it swam out of the inlet, and with the fading of the song, she forgot, or thinks she forgot. Blood and bruises were from slipping on the rocks, and so were the blank, empty hours lost.

Hard to tell in the darkness, hard to tell in its sea-cave eyes, but she thinks it remembers her, too.

"Sarah."

Not the thing. Not in its song. Not in her head.

Leo on his boat. The thing in his net. And her on the deck, hair damp and heavy against her scalp and sticking to her bare skin.

He catches them stark in a flash of brilliance from the lighthouse lamp, and although perhaps she should feel guilt, it furrows his forehead instead.

Leo doesn't talk much anymore, although it's her that really lost her voice. Neither she nor Leo know much sign language, either; some of it they might have just made up as part of their shorthand since taking classes so many years ago. The only reason he agreed to learn then was to teach his deckhands enough that they could work together. Sometimes she goes weeks without signing or saying a word, not until she ferries to the mainland to sell.

The thing's grip on her hands becomes almost painful, and it clicks its teeth through the shifting of the song. It doesn't speak, like her, but like her, it makes itself understood.

Free. Hungry. Dead.

A bed of fish beneath it, but the fish were going bad. Under other circumstances, its dexterity might have loosed it from the net and it could maneuver out on its own, like a raccoon unlocking itself from a trap, but its seaweed hair was hopelessly tangled, and the thing was heavier out of water, harder to move the way it wanted to.

It must have thrashed all night to try to free itself from the net before singing to snare something in its own.

Leo kneels next to her, as awkward as a stranger, but he hasn't yanked her back, nor has anger twisted his features into something unrecognizable. They are only ever this close in bed, but it has been so long since true intimacy, and he'd pulled on a pair of pants and an undershirt before following her out to the beach, perhaps in her footprints. "What are you doing out here—like this? Do you know what it is?"

He can't hear it. Or if he can, the song doesn't reach as deep. She knows his hearing is worse, but she didn't realize the loss carved so much away that his flesh marbles from cold rather than the music seeping in, creeping deeper, insidious, centering in a low, long thrum like those thin fingers entering her to pluck at the bass strings of her spinal cord.

When she speaks, it's not so much to be heard as to remind herself that her voice is still there—cracked as summer dirt and rusty as everything, but there. She speaks for him to watch her lips, because she doesn't know the sign. "Siren."

She reads his skepticism, even though the creature is right there, but she understands, because she's not positive this isn't a vivid dream, the kind that spills into her bedroom like heavy smoke, rising into baleful shapes that she can't trust.

With her attention elsewhere, the siren intensifies its song. The sound hits her like feather pillows, but she still reels and would stagger if she were standing.

"Sarah?" Leo understands more than he sees, although their world has always been small; everything's been seen before, until they can barely see at all in the wash of watercolor gray, nothing but an anonymous lamp to guide them in circles like moths.

But the thing in front of them is new, a different kind of gray from a different kind of water, except it isn't new to her, is it? Is *he*?

Want.

When last it sang, the long flexible tail wrapped around her, then around itself, her mouth filled with the briny taste of its tongue, and a rare, tender, sour song. Blood stained her shirt, but also her shorts, and she stumbled to her bike, rode home like her period started before she was ready, convinced herself that's what happened for a while. But her grandmother sat on the porch, her cane planted between unsteady legs with swollen ankles. That was just a few months before she died, another gravestone in a ghost town, although she was a fisherman's wife back when the getting was good and more than the dead and dangerous sang on a breeze.

Nana took one look at Sarah and sucked on her cigarette, on her sunken lips, then tapped the ashes on the cinder cone of her ashtray. Although her eyesight suffered, she squinted at the blood and Sarah's dazed, dizzy walk in the sand.

"Never, never." Nana's voice groaned like the porch wood under her rocking chair. "Never trust a man when he's hard. Never trust a serpent when he's scared. And never trust a siren when he sings. They'll all of them eat you alive."

Now, the siren tangles its fingers in her loose hair, as though to bind itself as fast to her as it was to the net. Its tongue slithers between its teeth, undulating with the shiver in its song, and she can imagine it heavy over her, the sound of its body on hers and the wooden deck that of a fighting swordfish, its song mingling with her moans. She can imagine how it scores new marks, how it fills her, and how even if its teeth never pierce beneath the surface, it leaves her hollower than before.

"Sarah." Her husband's hand weighs heavy and warm on her shoulder, reminding her that she's cold under the song's cocoon and would shiver if it let her.

She loved him once. It isn't the slow death and decay of the island that took him from her or left her gasping on the beach within reach of the rolling tide. And it isn't the siren who gives her the breath she keeps forgetting to take on her own.

She closes her eyes and leans her forehead against the siren's, grimacing from the ache beneath her lungs.

Hungry.

Sarah extricates a hand from the siren's hold, fumbles to the side for one of the weights on an unused net. Then she swings with all her might at the face in the black tangle, the shine of its twice-blinking eyes. She hits it once—a glancing blow—then swings the other way to catch its temple.

It slumps, silent, among the rotting.

Leo doesn't say anything, but his eyes gleam like glass from the lantern and the glancing lighthouse lamplight, as though seeing a stranger.

There they are, three strangers on a boat, and one of them dead.

She stands, finally shivering now that she feels the damp cold, and opens the net to let the fish spill forth. She finds a pair of gloves, when what she needs is a heated blanket and hot water bottle at her feet. The gloves will do for now as she takes the bad fish and throws them overboard for seagulls and other scavengers to pick through.

At first, Leo remains on his knees below her. Then he awkwardly stands to find his own gloves, joins her in eliminating the useless before the stench intensifies. He'll have to scrub the deck either way, but it could be worse.

Then there's only the siren, bigger sprawled out on the deck.

Where she can't undo the knots of its hair from the jute, she rips the strands individually or in small sections, until Leo can push the net aside. Leo tucks his hands under the siren's shoulders, dragging it to toss overboard like the rest, but Sarah covers one of his hands and shakes her head. Indicates the direction of the house, although there is no light to distinguish theirs from the abandoned. Home has always been the north of her heart, the destination of her limited migration, and Leo followed her, to the family nest that might as well be the end of the earth. They always find their way home, even without the lighthouse.

Sarah lifts it by its tail, draping the narrower end over her arm but holding it more tightly where it's thicker. The siren separates them more than they might have expected, the tail alone twice her length, frilled and dense in her arms.

She can't tell if she really killed the siren or just rendered it unconscious, but the cave-in of its skull suggests it won't awaken midway.

When they reach the porch, Leo lowers it, but she tilts her head toward the door. He appears confused, hesitant, but raises the body again and carries it—blood, black saliva, fish tail, and all—into the house. He follows her lead to the dining room, where he rests his part of the siren at the head of the table, as though to prepare it for a funeral. She carefully drapes the tail over the other side. It flaps wet and final, a sodden train on the smooth floor.

She removes the fishy gloves, throws them onto the kitchen linoleum, then goes out to the porch to feel around for tarps, the ones she nails over the holes in the roof when it's going to rain and plastic wrap and duct tape aren't enough. She drags them in and hands one to Leo to put beneath the siren while she arranges the rest around and under the table, scraping the chairs back and covering nearby rugs and furniture—ragged though they are, fraying and crumbling to pieces, like the island into the sea.

"What am I supposed to do with this?" He holds the tarp as though to cover his nakedness, although he's the only one in the room who's clothed, watching his mad wife scramble about at three in the morning— no, four-thirty, according to the kitchen clock, although it hadn't felt that long under the siren's thrall.

She doesn't answer. Instead, she digs the matches out of the junk drawer and lights the fire in the hearth, lights the candles on the mantel and on the sideboard behind him, and fills the room with candlelight in darkness, like a solitary ship in the middle of the ocean—brighter than the lantern to bear witness, and steadier than the lighthouse lamp.

Awash in gold, the siren shines, and so does she, fantastic made real. She returns to the kitchen, where she retrieves the cleaning kit and hunting knives that her father and his father used, and that she keeps sharp all these decades later to clean what her husband kills. But she's her father's daughter and her husband's wife. She's always known how to catch what they need, if it came to that. The hollow within tells her it's time.

She takes out the fillet and butcher knives and holds them in the light, waiting for Leo to follow her, as he always has, for better or for worse.

Leo takes a breath, then another, then shakes out the tarp and works it underneath the body.

He jerks back. "It's still alive."

Sarah feels the siren's chest. It remains unmoving, but there's a mouse-quick, unsteady rhythm within—furiously struggling, although the rest of it seems so serene.

She hands Leo the fillet knife, then stabs the butcher knife into the belly above the subtle transition from eel-fish to human. She doesn't stab too deep, and as she pulls the torso to part, she takes care not to poison the meat.

He's never seen her like this.

Well, that's not true. He sees her like this all the time. But she's never taken on something this big, with a face that looks like hers and gills spread above the closed wings of human ribs, and she's certainly never done so without clothing.

She is calm, methodical, careful, efficient. She usually wears gloves and an apron, but blood from the freshly dead body spills over her hands and arms, splashes onto the plastic. She continues until the flow thins.

And once the first cut is made, there's no point in leaving her to do it on her own.

Leo carves a Y around the cloaca, then makes his own practiced cut down the length of the tail to the fin. Blood spatters from waning pressure and stains his shirt, turns it tacky against his chest, cold in spite of the fire Sarah started, but she's stopped shivering, although the blood must be drying cool on her skin, too.

She turns on the hose, pouring cold water into the bathtub before the hearth, then opens the drain, an improvised cleaning station. She starts with organs, empties the torso into a cavity, wraps each piece in butcher paper and places it in one of the vintage coolers that litter the house, detritus from all the fishermen who lived and live under its roof. When one is filled, she packs it with ice—temporary storage. Most will be repacked in the root cellar's freezers, amid the shelves of bottled preserves.

Leo has never gutted a fish so strange and rare, but this half of the siren is still relatively familiar and mostly consists of the creature's intestinal tract and reproductive organs. He's efficient but distracted, because Sarah seems just as familiar with the body she's steadily dismantling. She stabs, cuts, trims with certainty, without hesitation. Sometimes he twitches, as though the tip of the blade enters his skin instead.

He runs the back of his hand under his lip, barely registering the smear left behind.

When she's done with the organs, she skins the creature, then carves muscle from the bone in cuts both familiar and strange, like everything else about this fever dream of a night—as though at any moment, the sun will rise behind the fog and they will wake in a sweat under too many quilts, only to freeze when they emerge, separate and alone, the way it has been, until the end of time, sleepwalking through the mist. But here they are, in darkness and fire, covered in the blood of something impossible that will satisfy them all through winter and into spring. A nightmare from which he does not wish to wake, a red-stained dream that never bled into his wildest fantasies, because he was never wild enough to hold sirens as she did, with such firm conviction as she portions the abdomen, then the chest.

At the tub, she lovingly washes the blood from her hands and the meat, licks her lips, bites. Leo stops cutting through the tail and almost drops the knife as she slices a sliver away and brings it to her mouth.

She hums around her fingers, chews, swallows, closes her eyes to savor. Then she cuts another sliver, thicker this time, and kneels next to him in offering. A risk, but all of this work is for nothing if the catch is inedible. A new delicacy must start somewhere, and on both land and sea, raw has its place, with some trial and error. He takes what might be sashimi, might be tartare, on his tongue like some oceanic communion, tastes blood from where he smeared it on his lip, but also the meat.

It isn't how he imagined human might taste, nor is it quite fish. Closer to eel, though, a dark-meat-and-mushroom taste with denser fishy texture, and he thinks that, like eel, it would cook well.

If this is even more like eel, if the creature's lower half is an indication of its danger, they really should have cooked it first.

He's a fisherman by birth and blood. He knows how to handle almost everything that swims, whether straight from the sea with salt still under its scales, or cooking it off on his burner, a sear or all the way through, breaking through protein and parasite alike. But this is new—the stuff of legends, but new to them, nothing in any scroll to tell them how to consume mythology.

They watch each other, frozen in spite of the fire, knives in hand and blood on their bodies, relishing and waiting, but nothing happens.

Of the creature's protective adaptations, toxicity is not one—at least not immediately. But this night is never-ending, and the tomorrow they're in might never come. There is nothing else that matters to him now but the gold fire in her blue eyes and bloody arms down to clean hands that she bloodies once again, continuing her work.

He carves from the tail to taste it, the risk already well within his bloodstream, which rushes with forgotten intensity. After all those days and nights of open-eyed slumber, has he ever been so awake, with siren singing on his tongue? Is this what it was like for her? Perhaps it is all the same song, a different kind of toxicity, but if it doesn't kill him, he accepts this dark red clarity.

The tail tastes like the human, and he cuts more to offer it to his wife, a whole handful this time. She paints her lips with the meat, closes her eyes again, her moan a thrum through the table, through his hand with the knife resting there.

He drops the knife to taste the meat in her mouth, catching the last of it and chasing it with his tongue. If they die from delayed poison, then they will never escape this damned island even in death, but at least they will go out in fire instead of ice, a moment alive before the end, with something to fill their endless, aching hunger.

He kisses her hard, knocking her back against the table and sending both knives clattering, muffled, on the plastic-covered floor. She braces herself on the body, her hand sinking into flesh, but then she wraps her arms around him. Heat and friction make the blood of the dead on their skin seem just as alive, slicker with every second.

He loved her from the first moment he saw her on the mainland and trailed her home, remembers a wedding bed of a certain kind of urgency, but it has been such a long time since it has been anything other than biological imperative, and he's not sure how much of her side was merely marital obligation, even that infrequently, especially these last five years— or is it ten?

But on this endless night, they bleed together, desires merging with their bodies.

They slip on the plastic and stumble, fall. Coagulating blood squelches under her, but she tugs at his shirt, almost rips it away, tears her nails through his back as he rises to discard the shirt, doesn't matter where. Pain follows behind her fingers, up to his shoulders as she pulls him down over her again, over his rear as she pushes down his pants. He's not sure how he removes them, only that he doesn't want to leave her to do it, groans as her teeth catch the meat of his tongue, his fist in her hair tearing strands away. He sheds the last of his clothes, crawls between her legs, enters her like she's held him off all twenty-seven years, although it was never her denial that stopped him at the threshold of their bed.

Sarah shudders beneath him, but he feels her heat, which means she burns more brightly than him, even more so when she rolls them over to take him in at her own quicker, more desperate pace. She grips at him, slipping on the blood but finding purchase by drawing blood of her own. She kisses and bites him, her moans a hum all over his skin, creeping through him, prickling and tight, because he can hear her, as he hears so little.

Love. Need. Hungry.

And over and over, *More.*

She makes him want to keep up, makes him want to give her everything, his slippery siren whose song he feels in his flesh. She's the most real thing in the world, the most alive, her touch a brand, and her teeth and nails like knives. He gives her every last bit of him, even knowing that he could die for her, because he knows that he would, that he does not have to decay with every footstep, that there is something left out there to wake up for if she wakes up with him.

He doesn't know how long they feed upon each other, supplementing their feast with cruder slices of meat when exhaustion threatens to end the meal before they are satisfied. But he comes more times than his weary body should, aches everywhere, seeps from rent veins to mingle with the creature's and hers—impossible to know whose—and she still shivers with the after-effects of her last climax when they emerge in the blood to finish with the body, down to the bone.

Sarah wakes with the candles burned down, morning shining gray through rain-pattered windows, casting an old reality on the bloody scene of their living room. She can't call it a crime, though, so much as a revelation.

She's tucked against him on the couch. Neither of them are young enough to sleep like this, but they were too exhausted to make it to the bathtub, much less the bed. Parts of her stick to him as she reluctantly extricates herself from his embrace. She passes the tub, the plastic, to step onto the porch, then the beach. There's no one to see her, no early-morning fishermen in this rainstorm, no tourists, no neighbors. She spreads her arms to let the rain bleed her clear into the ocean lapping foam at her feet.

Leo presses a kiss to the back of her neck, and they stand there until they are clean, scrub themselves with salt and sand, taste purer skin, but they are otherwise satisfied for now.

She makes coffee while he gathers the tarps to take to his boat, where he'll clean them when he goes out. Blood isn't out of place on his deck. The bones, he wraps in one of the unstained tarps and carries down to the cellar. She'll clean them, perhaps to sell as a false oddity—no one will ever believe they're real, but they'll clamor for such a good fake—or perhaps to keep them down there, preserved with everything else. She stops him before he can take a washcloth to where the mess dripped or smeared beyond the plastic. She'll address that herself.

Her grandmother had hung a map of the island on the living room wall—some differences today, expansion followed by diminishment, money and property changing hands, eroded shorelines, but still largely the same.

Her husband beside her, Sarah follows the sound shore with her fingertip to the lighthouse and Eden Inlet.

She speaks as she signs, her eyes wide and shining in the dark room. "*More.*"

CHAPTER FOUR

A BED OF EELS

Fox Claret Hill

A porcelain boy squats on a barnacle-covered dock, hidden beneath a coat that belonged to a much larger man. He shivers as he tries to warm his thorn-pricked, nettle-stung legs against his bony chest. His fingers, exposed by open-ended mitts, are swollen with the bluish beginnings of frostbite. Hoping to revive them, he removes the sodden gloves and wraps his hands around his waist. The comfort the hug offers slows his hummingbird heart, and he unfurls reluctantly once defrosted. He wipes the wet residue on the satin lining of his makeshift shelter, and uses his now-capable digits to pluck a cigarette from a silver tin, lighting it with a matching Zippo.

Inside his woolen cocoon, the smoke languishes in a suffocating pool. Smoked out after mere moments, he is forced to stand, and on numb feet, he paces as he continues to puff. The wind whips the smog away, and the mist wets the paper, but the cigarette keeps burning. He doesn't look old enough to smoke, despite his twenty-third birthday's close proximity, but he hopes to prune his face into maturity with enough nicotine.

He takes another puff and blows smoke rings towards the horizon, and when he spots the approaching ferry, he encircles it in gray. He frowns as it nears. The tourist-bait poster promised something resembling luxury—handsome seamen aboard an ample-sized craft, gilded by a fresh lick of paint—but what sits at the end of the dock is anything but. This boat, a rusty dinghy with no dry patch to sit on, is more mollusk than metal, and belches black exhaust as it putters towards the dock. Victor, who has never seen the ocean in person, thinks of turning back, but by the time the Ferryman dismounts his stead, it is already too late.

Clomping boots shake the rot-worn wood, and the stranger's features are shrouded by fog at the end of the dock, but his massive height of seven-foot-three is evident through the milky veil. Victor straightens the slouch in his spine into a hard line, trying to seem as tall as possible in the face of a giant, but only reaching an unimpressive height of five-foot-six. At least, from a distance, his narrowness provides three phantom inches stacked above his crop of black hair.

Thud, thud, thud, the boots amble down the walkway, and the man accompanies them. Victor's heart rate spikes, and he braces for impact as the skeletal man emerges from the haze. The graying 90-year-old, whose skin hangs loosely and stretches taught over prominent bones, glares down at the young man. His tufted nostrils—which seem small only in contrast with his elongated beak of a nose—flare at the scent of the cigarette, and his eyes light up hungrily. As the gap between them shrinks, liver spots and acne scars appear in rapid succession, and by the time Victor smells the old man's aquatic scent, there isn't an unmarred patch of skin left. The Ferryman reaches an enormous, spindly hand, and his uneven, yellowing nails—that must require bolt cutters to clip—graze Victor's flawless hand.

"Could I trouble you for a smoke, lad?" the old man asks in an accent torn between countries and periods, much of which Victor cannot identify aside from the notes of old sailor amongst the amalgamation.

"Yes, of course," Victor says, his own accent sounding very posh in comparison, thanks to his English mother. He offers the tin to the man, who nods in gratitude.

"Are you wanting to go to the island?"

"I am," Victor says, picking up his suitcase in his enthusiasm.

The Ferryman paws at his hairy chest, the tufts visible due to the sagging fabric of the filthy long johns beneath his waterproof jacket. Fleas spring from the fluff, using the strands as trapezes in their private circus, and Victor takes a step back to keep some distance from the jumping flecks.

The Ferryman mercifully doesn't seem to notice Victor's rudeness. "What the hell are you wanting to go to Brackish Harbor for?" he asks, bemused, moving his scratching paw to his balding head.

"I found this on the corkboard by the payphone in that pub," Victor replies, removing a folded flier from his pocket and gesturing to the red brick building behind him. "It says 'room and board available in Brackish Harbor.'"

"Oh, yeah, that." The Ferryman exposes his rotten teeth in a broad smile, each fang a gnarled brown twig that sits millimeters apart from their siblings. "Old Harold does need a hand at the shop now his boy's left, but the pay ain't much," he says, eyeing Victor's high-quality garb.

"That's not important," Victor says curtly. "I just need off the mainland."

The Ferryman squints at him. "You're not in some sort of trouble, are you, lad?" Victor shakes his head fervently, though perhaps not convincingly. The Ferryman laughs and shrugs. "Frankly, lad, I don't care if you're the latest Jack the Ripper so long as you can lend a helping hand. The village is in desperate need of someone like yourself."

Victor looks down at the flyer. "Should I call ahead and make sure the spot hasn't been filled before we depart?"

The Ferryman laughs a gnarled, wet thing that sticks in his throat and comes out of his sinuses. "No phones where you're going. No electricity either." Victor frowns, and the Ferryman continues his phlegm-filled chortles before falling into a bout of seriousness. "Now, I must warn you. I only come back once a week for supplies and mail."

The Ferryman nods toward the beach, and Victor turns. He flinches when he spies a man who wasn't there before. Wild red hair frames his face like a lion's mane, though he's certainly not as impressive as the animals Victor has seen at the circus. Dressed in scraps and rags and surrounded by hessian sacks, the man is a filthy enigma, and Victor smiles awkwardly at him. The man grins wolfishly back, and Victor finds his attempt at conviviality wither as he realizes the man's eyes are trained on his soft, exposed throat. Whether he desires to bite it or kiss it, Victor is unsure, but he frowns, and the Ferryman grumbles with displeasure, as a dollop of saliva slips from the slathering gob of the wild-eyed stranger.

Victor turns away, and the Ferryman nods approvingly. "You stay here. Don't get too close. Once I load the last sack, you're welcome to come with me if that's what you want."

Victor nods, staring out at the sea as he waits for the Ferryman's surprising feat of strength and back-breaking labor to end. When it does, he picks up his suitcase and boards without looking back, anxious to put as much distance between him, his old life, and the off-putting man as possible.

The Ferryman tries to pass the two-hour trip with polite conversation, but between the roar of the ocean and his own retching over the railing, Victor can barely hear a word the old man says. His seasick tongue covered in excess saliva, his severely-parted hair coming loose from the velocity of the gags, Victor looks at his companion with bloodshot eyes and offers him nothing more than nods in response. The Ferryman overlooks his muteness of mouth and continues to regale him with stories of a mundane life.

Victor gags again, and this time, when the splatter hits the inky water, it's not the ocean that eats the creamy contents. An eel breaks the surface, its sharp teeth snapping at the scraps with vicious fervor.

And then he sees them. Hundreds of skinny, black worms writhing beneath the rocky surface. They're small at first, the creatures that make up the writhing mass, but as the boat continues its journey, the eels grow broader than a strong man's thigh.

By the time they are within thirty minutes of Brackish Harbor, the slick ocean monsters are too thick to wrap your arms around and longer than the boat. When a particularly large one swims close enough for Victor to see his reflection in its beady eyes, he reels. He looks to the Ferryman as he collapses onto bony buttocks, and plants his dainty hands into murky puddles collected from the salty splashback.

The Ferryman, who is quick to laugh in a way that grates on Victor worse than a fine-toothed comb on feverish skin, shakes his head. "You alright, lad?" he asks for the dozenth time, though his tone features no progression of concern.

"I'm fine," Victor snaps, staggering to his feet, his knobbly knees knocking together in the struggle. "I didn't know eels could get so big."

"Ah yes, the Brackish Harbor eels are famous. Tasty, too. People would come from all over just to try a slice of battered eel."

Victor's stomach churns again. "I'll take your word for it."

"It's true! This boat used to be full to the brim, coming and going, but eels that size are hard to catch, and we all got too old to try. Now you're lucky if you get to eat one of the little ones," he says wistfully, and Victor imagines, despite himself, peeling back a breaded layer to reveal slimy black skin. He gags at the idea of sinking his teeth into the rubbery flesh, and returns to the railings to continue his unrelenting bout of sickness, but, this time, he keeps his eyes closed lest he see any larger monstrosities.

"We're here," the Ferryman says, and Victor straightens up and opens his eyes, which stream at the sudden intake of cold, gray light. The island, much like the boat, is weather-worn and smaller than it appeared on the flattering retro posters he'd seen. The Brackish Harbor advertised was a quaint yet thriving fishing town full of smiling adults and chubby-cheeked children. The sun shone upon the bustling shops and overpopulated houses—of which there were at least fifty—and the sandy beach housed numerous suntanned tourists in large hats.

Today, the town is squashed under a heavy layer of fog, and though it's still a distance away, the only inhabitant that Victor can spot is a mangy dog. The houses have halved in number, and a sharp cliff-face has replaced the sloping beach on the far-left side.

"What happened?" Victor asks, staring at the rubble.

"Poseidon was hungry," the Ferryman answers gravely, his bloodhound eyes hollow.

They arrive at an even more weather-worn dock than the one they left behind, and as they unload the cargo, a repetitive thumping alerts them to a rocking chair at the end of the pier.

At first, Victor thinks it's only occupied by a phantom born of the breeze, but on closer inspection, the pile of rags and cloth in the wooden seat contains a woman so shrunken from age, she's no bigger than a child. Her unseeing eyes stare at nothing, and her hands furiously knit something made of murky blue wool.

"The town soothsayer," the Ferryman informs Victor with a whisper before raising his voice above the elements. "What are you doing out here? You'll catch your death!"

The Soothsayer reveals empty sockets and gray gums as she welcomes Victor with cackling glee. "I'm just making something for our guest," she says in the loudest whisper she can muster and lifts her offering to the sky with shaking, sinewy arms. The gift is a cable-knit sweater the color of the ocean, though the oils in the wool mean it'll never become one with the water.

"Thank you," Victor mumbles as he takes the jumper and drops his coat and case. He slips the offering over his head, and the last of his bone chill fizzles out with its warmth. The fit is glove-like, and he realizes it must've taken weeks to make, especially with the Soothsayer's stiff hands.

"Did you know I was coming?" he asks, staring into thick cataracts.

The Ferryman leers over Victor, the scent of fish and salt thicker than when Victor directly faced the ocean's spray. "She knows everything. She's had the sight ever since she was a little girl."

Victor addresses him. "So, did you know I was coming, too?" His tone is accusatory. He can't help himself. He doesn't like not being in on the joke.

The Ferryman shakes his head, grumbling, "Nobody tells me nothing 'round here."

Mumbling to himself and ignoring Victor's protests, the Ferryman picks up the suitcase and lumbers toward the village. He takes the rudimentary wooden steps three at a time, and as Victor attempts to follow—on much shorter legs—the Soothsayer reaches for him. Her fingers squeeze at the slightly soggy wad of cash in his pocket before pulling away. He'd thought the sweater was a gift, but he draws a twenty free of its rubber band belt, not wanting to offend such an important local.

She gasps and puts a hand to her chest. "Not for me," she says, aghast. "A tip for the boys."

"The boys?" He answers his own question before she gets the chance. Two burly men with faded black tattoos on bulging biceps have materialized at the bottom of the steps. They're dressed in black pants, white undershirts, and knee-high galoshes. Their beards are thick and coarse, with flat caps atop dark stringy strands. Identical twins. Victor is in awe; he's only ever read about them in his father's medical books.

The men puff from their pipes in sync, and their feet stay rooted in the sand. "They're here to unload the supplies," the Soothsayer says, hand still awaiting the money.

Victor doubles his offer and hands the forty dollars over without thinking anything of it.

The old crone pats him affectionately. "Good boy." As he reattempts to follow the Ferryman, she grabs his wrist with a vice-like grip. "To know you were coming, I've seen where you've been. Does that money feel like a stone in your pocket?" Her voice sounds strange, doubling over itself and moving out of time with her rapidly moving, lipless maw.

"I don't know what you mean," he hisses and yanks himself free.

The Soothsayer falls still. After a moment, as if nothing happened, she whistles like one would for a border collie amongst the sheep, and the twins begin to walk over.

Victor freezes as they stride toward him, seemingly oblivious to his presence. At the last second, they part and pass by on either side, close enough to exchange body heat. As they continue towards the boat, he scurries away to the stairs, the Soothsayer's cackles and crows following him like a shadow.

At the top of the steps—which seem to be designed to break ankles—the Ferryman is nowhere to be seen, and Victor spins wildly, desperate for guidance. A signpost with directional indicators offers no assistance as the wet has wiped the wood clean. The surrounding buildings are also of little help. Most of them are boarded up, the letters in their signs rendering their previous purposes unintelligible, and those that aren't abandoned are no more approachable. Sour-faced people drinking from paper bags sit in doorways, and snarling dogs tied up with rope guard them. Victor doesn't smile, and neither do they.

Only one building in the immediate vicinity looks promising: the fishmongers'.

Victor approaches the warped glass window, peers inside, and watches a tremendous boar of a man with a swollen, red nose like a tomato, gut a huge gilt-head bream. He slices with an ease that must come from decades of practice. His thick, hairy arms move surprisingly daintily as he continues his work, and Victor watches with intrigue as the chum bucket in the corner fills up with pink slop. The Fishmonger doesn't notice the patches of heat adhering to the glass from the pointy-faced boy, and continues to snort and snuffle from the cold as he works by lamplight. Victor uses his gift of invisibility to gawk at the bountiful display that appears in great contrast to the sad state of the rest of the island. Though he's glad he cannot smell the array of fish, cephalopods, and crustaceans, his bile-filled stomach gurgles with hunger.

Despite his encyclopedic knowledge, he only recognizes half the offerings lying on beds of ice. Marling, salmon, mackerel, trout, mullet, hake, sprat, pollock, cuttlefish, squid, octopus, and various crabs are things that he knows. The rest of the slimy creatures, he's never seen. Miniature sharks that look hard like bone, jellyfish constantly changing colors even in death, pufferfish with five eyes, and starfish with more than a dozen legs only begin to cover the bizarre array. He makes eye contact with a pile of iridescent eels, their flat humanoid faces arranged in an array of cadaverous expressions, blubbery lips hanging open to reveal hungry mouths, almond eyes lazy and cruel.

The Fishmonger whips around, knife in hand and unibrow knitted together, as a scream sounds.

It takes a moment for Victor to realize the yelp is his own. Pain courses through his bare leg. He looks down and finds a dog, snapped rope around its neck, has sunk its teeth into his calf. He shakes weakly to try to free himself of it, but the dog only latches deeper, and blood runs rivers into knee-high socks. The shock of the gore renders him still.

A door slams open and a deep voice yells unintelligibly at the mutt before throwing a fillet knife in its direction. It misses by several inches—a warning shot—and sticks in the wet dirt. The bloody-mouthed dog runs away with its tail between its legs.

Victor watches it go with relief and turns to thank his savior, only to come face to face with another blade. He raises his hands to his face, protecting his finest asset.

"Who the hell are you?" the Fishmonger growls.

"I'm Victor. I'm looking for someone named Harold. I'm responding to his advert," he whimpers.

The knife is sheathed, and the Fishmonger examines the sweater hidden beneath the coat. "Oh, yeah, the Soothsayer said you were coming. Harold lives just up there, on the edge of the cliff. Biggest house on the island. You can't miss it."

Relief floods Victor as he realizes the Fishmonger is not Harold, and he won't have to live above stinking fish guts during his stay. He thanks the man, who inhales a trickle of snot back into his nose before squeezing his bulky frame through the narrow door of his shop.

Keeping his eyes peeled for the vicious dog, Victor staggers along the muddy, beaten path, past bearded men and frail women dressed in dark and dusty colors. Everyone looks at least forty, and there's not a single child in sight. The village seems designed for death, a pre-dug burial plot or a coffin with an open lid, waiting for the occupants to fall into its dark clutches. With no children, Victor wonders what will become of the village once the youngest person dies. He supposes that, eventually, the gods of the sea will eat the rest of it, too.

At the end of the dirt path, surrounded by dead grass, is a house unlike any Victor has ever seen. It sways in the wind with ground-rumbling creaks, the sunken windows sliding in their sockets, the base threatening to part from its concrete foundation. It's painted white, but like the rest of the village, the peeling paint reveals the natural color of the wooden slats beneath.

So preoccupied with tilting his head in time with the house, the man standing before it goes unnoticed until he calls out. Unlike the other islanders, his smile is gleaming white, and his skin is golden as if he's been holidaying in the tropics. He looks thirty-five at the oldest, and Victor finds his heart racing at his handsomeness. He puffs on a pipe, dressed in expensive cream slacks and a matching cashmere sweater.

The man waves before he notices the blood, and his face turns serious as he jogs over, unconcerned about his muddying dress shoes. His arm is quickly around Victor, who inhales the scent of cinnamon, tobacco, and leather. He unconsciously leans into the man's embrace.

"I see you've met the resident dogs," he says breathlessly. "You must be Victor."

Victor nods. "Are you Harold?"

"I am."

"You weren't what I was expecting. I thought you'd be old." Victor laughs, and Harold mirrors him.

"Why on Earth did you think that?"

"The Ferryman called you Old Harold. He said you had a son."

Harold pauses at that, his even pace missing a beat, but he shrugs it off. "That's just my nickname," he says, but he doesn't mention his son.

They reach the door and Harold opens it revealing a world of knowledge and warmth. Every available space is covered in stacks of books, to the point that the wallpaper is hardly visible past the walls of paperbacks and hardcovers. Two worn armchairs and a drinks cabinet sit by the fire, which casts a golden light on the otherwise dark living room and kitchen combo.

Harold invites Victor to sit with him and pours him a scotch, without even asking, before retrieving a first aid kit from behind a slack cabinet door. Victor gulps his drink greedily and tries not to gag from the burning heat in his throat. His glass is refilled before he can even put it down, and only once the second drink is drunk does Harold go to work on Victor's wound.

"When I asked for new blood, I didn't mean this," Harold says with a wink, looking up at Victor, whose Adam's apple bobs as he sucks spittle down his gullet.

"S-sorry."

"Don't be. You'll be of great use to us humble folk."

"What will I be doing here, exactly?"

"This and that. But don't worry about that today. Let me show you to your room and let you get some rest." Harold jumps to his feet with great athleticism.

Victor looks down at his perfectly bandaged leg and stands with all the grace of a newborn foal.

As they climb the stairs, the alcohol settles, and Victor asks, "What happened to the rest of the island?"

"Ah, so you've noticed we're missing a piece. Nothing dramatic. A crumbling cliff and a dozen or so houses."

Victor's eyes widen. "Was anyone killed?"

"Just one. A hermit who lived in the furthest house. He was afflicted by a bad hip and old knees and couldn't get out in time."

"That's awful."

"It was fifteen years ago," Harold says, as if that softens the occurrence of drowning in your own bed. "He always said the ocean was his only love, and now they get to lie together forever."

The way Harold says it reminds Victor of the things people say at funerals to make themselves feel better. *He's in a better place. It was her time to go. It's God's plan.* Victor hides his distaste behind the dregs of drink in his gut.

Victor is woken by a weight at the foot of the bed. He startles, sits up, springs creaking in the lumpy mattress, and opens his eyes.

Black.

Not the black of night and dark rooms, but the black of a blindfold, and when he tries to move his hands to his face, he finds them bound behind his back in satin strips. He yelps and thrashes, a wild animal caught in a trap.

"Who's there?" he whimpers when he realizes escape is futile; his ankles, too, are bound with a fortitude only a sailor's hands can muster

The weight at the end of the bed shifts, and a large hand presses on Victor's chest, pinning him against the headboard. Victor can smell who it is as the other man's face nears, and he opens his mouth expectantly despite himself.

Harold exhales through his nose, bemused by the boy in the bed. Silently, a mountain lion stalking its prey, he straddles Victor and places a hand on his glass jaw.

Shivering from cold and anticipation, Victor holds still, waiting for Harold to pounce. They stay frozen, teasing, expectant, before Harold finally strikes. Jumping to his feet, he picks Victor up and flings him over his shoulder in a fluid movement, and as if Victor weighs nothing, he jogs down the stairs and out the front door into the cold.

Victor has whiplash in his neck and his crotch, and it's only once they're bobbing down the street, his ribs bending against Harold's muscular shoulder, that he doesn't remember going to sleep.

The sound of a door creaking open and slamming behind him makes his heart race. He'd heard tell of human trafficking and black-market organs from his anxious mother but never thought he could fall victim to such a scheme. Harold sits him down hard on a rickety chair that wobbles as he struggles.

"What are you going to do to me? I have money! I can give you whatever you want! Please don't kill me, I can be useful!" Victor begs. His lip wobbles and wet patches appear on the blindfold.

A room full of people bursts into roaring laughter, and his sight returns with the untying of a knot.

"Surprise!" yells the room full of villagers, and Victor's tears dry at the sight of smiling faces. He's cut free by the identical twins, and Harold approaches him with a fond look. As Victor stands, he's embraced in a bear hug. The moment his feet return to the floor, beer is thrust into his hands, and an accordion sounds as the band in the far corner of the tiny pub starts to play.

He looks down at his clothes; a set like Harold's but vivid vermillion. *New blood*, he thinks, but he doesn't linger on the thought. As he stares around the tavern at the seated, dancing, and drunk occupants gathered to celebrate his arrival, he spots a few more young, beautiful people amongst the withered hags and filthy trolls. They, like Harold, have perfect teeth and smooth skin, and stare at Victor coquettishly. He feels like a prince, all the years spent ignored—resigned to a corner, seen but not heard—wash away as he's bathed in all the luxury the rustic islanders can afford.

Even amongst the younger islanders, Victor is a pearl birthed from an old oyster's mouth. He's shiny, pure, and pale compared to the salt-licked and briny. Victor's sense of belonging gives way to something he thinks is love. The shriveled organ that had once resembled a heart grows like a parasite and sits heavy and happy in his chest, pounding against his ribcage. He'd heard tell of family through the fiction he consumed in his father's study on dark nights, and this group—so newborn to him, it stinks of placenta—ticks the identifiable boxes.

Finally at home, he drinks, eats, and talks more than he ever has in a single sitting.

As the music swells, a burst of energy finds him dancing in circles, arms linked with smelly strangers. It doesn't take him long, especially when he becomes partner to Harold's drunken spins, to collapse on the chaise longue by the fire. Sweat beads roll down the bridge of an aquiline nose, and drip like a leaky faucet from its tip to his lap. He doesn't remember the last time he worked up a sweat, and an elderly woman sits beside him, offering a glass filled with water. Dust floats on the surface, but he laps it up thankfully and shoots her a panting grin.

"What a blessing you are," she croaks as she watches him gulp. She makes him think of the grandmothers he never met, and he leans his skinny frame towards her stout figure.

Victor shakes his head. "I'm so pleased to be here. I've never met such nice people," he says. What he's feeling is more than pleasure. He identifies the feeling, from slumped shoulders and slack limbs, as relief. Running from his past has worn his soles thin, though his sins are recent. Until tonight, his crimes have pecked at his exposed flesh like a murder of crows, and he's had to sleep with the soreness and patches of ooze.

Harold pulls up a chair, one that rocks on uneven legs with repetitive thumps as he leans into Victor with drunken enthusiasm. "You're our saving grace," he whispers, his breath bristling fuzz on Victor's jawline. When they part, Harold thrusts a whiskey into Victor's palm and stands. Victor downs the drink, eager to re-join the festivities with him, but two-thirds into the beverage, his hand goes limp, and the glass hits the floor with a *thunk*.

Once again, Victor wakes in the dark without having remembered falling asleep. This time he feels no anxiety. He'd been drunk, warm, and exhausted. Drifting off makes sense under the circumstances, and as he opens his eyes, the eager grin remains on his face.

Until his eyes adjust.

In the dark, lurking at low levels, some squatting, some on all fours, some lying on their bellies on the table, are the town's occupants, wearing papier-mâché masks. The masks are poorly made, rough at the edges, and the paint hasn't seeped into all of the cracks, but the resemblance is unmistakable. Eels. Their fangs of sewing needles and glass shards are bared, waiting to strike. As he leans to the right, they move to their left, honed in and vicious.

He laughs at first, ignorant of any genuine malice, waiting for the band to break into song once more and the prank to be over. He looks for Harold and finds him behind one of the nearest masks, recognizing his cream ensemble and veiny, bronzed forearms. As he gazes into the blue eyes, sunken behind cut-out holes, Harold's eel mask darts forwards, as if to bite him.

Victor flinches and laughs again, though it's reflexive and uncertain. Victor hisses back in jest, and having sobered up from his nap, he moves to stand and poke the waning embers in the hearth. None of this comes to fruition as he realizes he is bound again. This time, he's tied by rough rope rather than fabric strips, and the cuffs are tight to prevent slippage or circulation.

The remaining whisper of laughter dies in his throat, and another figure joins Harold at the head of the pack. The person, small and thick, intertwines their hand with Harold's. Removing the mask reveals the ancient woman who had cooed and comforted him before his deep sleep. Harold removes his mask and they come together in a sticky, open-mouthed embrace.

Victor recoils, making his disgust known through audible retches.

Harold flashes a piercing glare at him and speaks in a tone that makes the other eels retract. "This is my wife, Agnes." He coils protectively around the much older woman. "We founded this village together back in the 1920s."

Victor is confused. Very confused. His head aches with the white-hot whistling of a kettle left on the stove, and he barely hears a word from Harold's pretty mouth over the panicked shrieking. The year is 1988. "But that would make you—" Victor cuts himself off, unable to perform the equation through the pain.

"Ninety-five years old. Agnes is ninety," comes the matter-of-fact answer. It doesn't help. It doesn't answer the million questions breeding on a hungover tongue.

"How do you—"

"Look so young? Well, after the old Hermit's house fell into the sea, something odd happened: he didn't die. He became something else. We'd watch him from the shore as he sat in his sunken living room and enjoyed a book. It was as if he didn't notice he was underwater. But over the course of that first year, he changed. He grew barnacles, and his fingers softened into tentacles, and he became too frightening to look at anymore. So, we pretended he wasn't there. Until, one day, the eels came to us all in dreams and told us that the Hermit was hungry and that if we fed him, we'd be rewarded. Can you guess what he wanted to eat?"

"A human." The answer is obvious, but it sickens Victor all the same.

"Exactly right. A sinner, to be exact. Supposedly, they taste the best. Lo and behold, the next day, our local psychic had a vision of a fifty-year-old man fresh out of prison and unsuccessfully looking for a job on the mainland. So, we put an advert in the pub, and soon enough, he came to us." Harold is haughty and proud, and panic rises in Victor as he recalls his own trespasses.

"We let Harold go first," Agnes says. "He was eighty-one at the time. A fifty-year-old undid plenty." She looks back and forth between Harold and Victor and sighs. Her husband comforts her with a skin-whitening grip. "You'll only make me sixty-eight, but it beats dying in my sleep."

"We'll find more. There's plenty of other scum out there."

"Was *your son* one of the scum?" Victor asks, his hackles raised.

"Mercy me, no!" Agnes yelps. "We never had our own children. Our 'son' is just part of the story. Makes you young'uns feel like a missing puzzle piece. Though I suspect you had little interest in being Harold's son."

The pair laugh cruelly, and Victor feels shame for his desperation at Harold's house. The guilt only sinks deeper as Agnes chides him, his memories growing serrated roots. "Your poor parents. You awful boy." The semi-healed scars on Victor's buttocks and back sting as much as the memories of a study, a glass paperweight, a sickening crack, a pool of blood.

Harold interrupts the self-flagellation as he checks his pocket watch. "Five, four, three, two, one, and midnight!"

The room explodes into applause.

"It's time," Agnes croaks, though it needn't have been announced as a great, underwater bellowing shakes the pub.

Harold carries Victor to a chair, where he begins to violently shake as he's tied down by more ropes. Once secured, the twins pick him up on his throne and carry him from the pub to the dirt road, where the procession of eels pours out and follows the leader dutifully.

It's a somber parade, lit by torches and accompanied by booming rumbles. Both Victor and the ensuing horde balk at the roars. Victor screams until ragged, hoping his shrieks will alert nearby boats, but the slow-rotting death of Brackish Harbor's economy and population means there is nothing but monsters and water for miles. Both of which he knows will be consuming him soon.

On the edge of eternal nothing, the screams run ragged and culminate in a whimpering cough. Victor doesn't beg; what would be the point with a man whose love is pointed like a dagger in a different direction? Instead, he asks a question, his thirst for knowledge not quenched yet by saltwater and briny lungs. "Are you scared of death?"

Harold looks at him with a cocked head and replies with a question of his own, "Aren't you?"

Victor ruminates on his life in a series of flashing memories. At least *that* part of impending death has turned out to be true. A series of identical images present themselves: a skinny boy with no friends, a mother with quick hands, and a father who lived in shadow. "No," he answers decisively.

Harold looks out at the water as another bellowing growl reverberates in everyone's bones, and a rock tumbles from the cliff. It takes a long time to hit the water, and Victor counts each second that it falls. Harold sighs once the grumbles cease. "You're too young to be scared. You're much too young to know how short life is." Harold looks down on Victor. He seems much too familiar. He looks like he could fit in Victor's wool coat.

"I think I've gotten a pretty good idea," Victor says, the cold making his jaw quiver, turning his words into a bitter laugh.

The eels swarm, making the black sea even darker.

Harold pauses, looking up at the moon, the white light masking the perfect face with sagging skin and deep lines. He offers faux humor of his own, but his contorted pictures paint a clown, not a man. "You're lucky you'll never get old. The eels have nothing on inhabiting a corpse."

"Why is your life worth more than mine?" Victor asks.

"It's not." The answer is not what he expected. "But hers is."

"Then sacrifice yourself. You've sinned enough," Victor spits as the twins cut him free.

Harold hums thoughtfully. "I think I understand you now. How can you fear death if you've never felt love?"

As Victor thinks of a response, he's picked up from the chair by his armpits and dangled over the cliff's edge. Refusing to look down, he stares out at the horizon and ignores the clacking of teeth beneath his feet. When an espadrille slips from his foot, he shuns the sound of wet leather being minced by a hundred hungry jaws.

He only turns when he hears a dry, chap-lipped kiss from behind him and sees Agnes saunter away, escorted by two women. He watches her as she undresses without shame and changes into a white smock—momentarily exposing her sagging nudity to the cold light—before climbing down a rope ladder on her own. He can hear Harold hold his breath as she makes the descent, and feels the warm exhale on his nape as she disembarks onto the beach. Everyone watches as she wades into the freezing ocean, walking as far as to dowse her hips and legs in the salt.

The cold barrel of a 19th-century gun, the kind that spits spheres made of lead, distracts Victor from his spying. He realizes he's not going to drown. He'll be dead before he ever hits the barrier between above and below. The monster will eat him once he's already gone. It reminds him of his childhood pet, a mighty boa constrictor diminished to eating frozen mice in a glass box. *How disappointing to be the God of this island,* he thinks.

The gun cocks, and muscle memory guides a dainty hand to a sharp knife tucked into a hidden pocket in his underwear. The blade cuts the hand that grips Victor's armpit before the bullet can be freed. It misses bone but severs enough nerve and muscle that Harold yelps and drops Victor down, down, down into the black.

The impact of the sea from such a mighty fall hurts, but not as bad as a bullet might, and after a second of shock spent underwater, Victor decides that he lied. He *is* scared of death. He tucks his body and floats to the surface, riding a bubble to the top before surfacing and swimming with the spare sprinkling of athleticism he'd been given. The gun fires, a sparkler of celebration in the night, but it misses again and again. Victor swims towards Agnes, a pale piranha stalking his prey.

Too busy basking, too busy freezing, she doesn't notice until it's too late. As soon as Victor's swimming limbs hit pebbles, he stands, and his slender frame cuts through the water at tremendous speed. The gun stops firing when he reaches her, and the screams start as he presses a knife to her wrinkled throat. Beads of blood line the blade as he drags her back into the ocean. Harold, panicked, his neat demeanor collapsing into something ugly, descends the ladder, but by the time his shoes hit the beach, the two are already submerged.

She turns to deadweight quickly as he holds her close, her bones become lead weight, and her panicked swallows tell him she won't survive the trip. He places a hand over her mouth and nose after her last exhale and kicks with all his might. He keeps his eyes open despite the burn, and though he can't see anything, he keeps them moving towards the reverberating hum in his eardrums.

Through the water, a greenish glow draws him like a moth to a flame, and he puts all his brutal swimming lessons to good use. He soon realizes the light is further than he thinks, and as his breath inflates his chest to the point of bursting, he comes to an almost imperceptible film. He touches it with his free hand, then penetrates it, and as he drags himself and the near-dead woman through the veil, they're both coated in a thin membrane.

Once on the other side of the bubble, the hole repairs itself, and he feels warm and dry. These sensations urge him to open his mouth. Oxygen floods his system, though he still swims and moves hindered by the water.

Agnes, semi-unconscious, hasn't realized what her captor has, and her cheeks are speckled with burst veins. Victor tries to gesture that they can breathe—not out of kindness but out of necessity—but though she tries to inhale, the water already in her prevents the rewards brought by the dome. Victor pumps at her ribcage, not caring if he breaks bone, and when she spits up rising bubbles, he sighs in relief; he needs an offering worth eating.

As they continue, she doesn't bother struggling anymore, and they're soon blocked by a bed of enormous eels, much larger than those that gobble at the surface. Agnes screams silently, but Victor pursues them, fear diluted by the adrenaline in his system. The eels part, forming a slippery, ropey tunnel for the pair. At the other end, the green glow brightens, and Victor realizes it's coming from the windows of the Hermit's house.

He approaches the porch, no longer carrying Agnes but dragging her, like a weightless balloon, by her scrawny wrist. As they land on the porch, he realizes the house is in better condition than most on the shore, and he peers through the windows at the time-capsule rooms. When none of them contain the Hermit, he creates a lure by carving further into a fleshy part of Agnes. Crimson blooms around them.

The sand at the bottom of the ocean stirs, and a behemoth beast—many times larger than the house—rises from its resting place.

Victor inhales, and the dry liquid around him burns his throat. As many people would, he urinates, and Agnes faints in his arms.

The creature's maw gapes, bone-lined like the maw of a whale shark, toothless but vast, and Victor feels its suction even from a distance. Attached to the top of the massive mouth like a parasitical fish are the Hermit's head and torso. From his body—once human-sized but now an enormous bloated balloon of tangled purple veins and waterlogged hide—four giant tentacles have sprouted where his legs and arms used to be, and he uses the appendages to navigate the ground as his senses draw him towards the blood.

Victor holds Agnes towards the creature so that he might smell her meat and see her sin.

The beast begins to suck ferociously, a whirlpool appearing by its hungry mouth. She wakes, and her limp body is sucked away with a soundless scream. He doesn't know where the body goes, into the hermit or into the whale, all he knows is that he doesn't want to find out.

For a ridiculous moment, Victor thinks he might be thanked, but the suction doesn't let up, and he's forced to grip the beams of the porch as the creature sups at the sacrificial lamb. He opens his mouth to plead his case to the once-sentient beast, but no words escape his dry throat, so, instead, he opens the front door and swims through the perfectly preserved house, the dinner table still set with soup for one, and moves through the backdoor and up to the surface.

When a kraken-sized pink tentacle wraps around him, gently squeezing his belly, he struggles against it, losing the fight against the monster and the icy ocean. He doesn't need to try so hard. The Hermit raises him high, and the cliffside onlookers shriek as the last remnants of the monster's humanity deliver Victor safely to the beach.

Harold, who has waded into the shallows, whips around and screams at Victor. "What have you done?" He falls to his knees and screams in grief, scrabbling deeper into the water on all fours.

Victor yells after him, "I sacrificed a sinner." He relishes the other man's grief before asking, "Can you tell me what thirty-one minus ninety is?"

Harold freezes mid-paddle, realization washing over him. He stands, sprints, and joins Victor on the beach, but it's already over, he's already soaked. Victor looks down on him as the man collapses in the sand, his bones turning into something moldable, gelatinous, and he watches Harold become younger at an astonishing speed.

He's handsome until he hits his teen years, when he becomes awkward and buck-toothed. When he hits single digits, he begins to wail, and Victor almost feels guilty as the big-eyed child pulls at his wet trousers and begs in a high-pitched tone, unbroken by puberty, "Please, don't let me die! I don't want to die!"

Victor sits in the sand, takes the child's hand in his own, and watches it shrink into something no bigger than the tiny pebbles surrounding them. He cradles the shrieking baby with his warmth until it falls silent. He sheds a tear as it turns into something pink and underdeveloped, and as it continues to shrink into primordial putty, he digs a tiny hole for it in the sand and lays the weeks-old fetus inside the ditch. He picks up a handful of sand to bury it, but the blob turns to dust and blows away.

Victor tucks his knife into his knee-high sock, gets to his feet, feeling every hour of his twenty-three years, and faces the horrified inhabitants who still line the cliff. He knows that, like the eels, they'll let him pass.

CHAPTER FIVE

REAPING FOR MOTHER

Lucas Mann

Rain battered my face, the salt stinging the chapped lines around my eyes, weathered from years of living by the sea. I worked the burn further into the creases; it was a pleasurable pain, the kind that lets you know you're alive. The wind caught my hood like a sail, yanking it back and exposing my head to the burgeoning tempest. I didn't flinch, reveling in the chill running through me, my eyes never leaving the waves assaulting the shore.

I could see nothing but darkness and the monotonous pulsing of the lighthouse miles down the shore. I squinted, searching for the buoy floating beyond the pier. I heard the bell attached to it as it swayed to the song of the ocean. It kept rhythm with the lighthouse and the waves clapping against the pier, a percussion for the chorus of wind.

The water and I had long shared a connection, an unsettled feeling now flowing between us. Full of unbridled anger that could be abated, sometimes appeased, but never gone. The rain fell on us with a furor that seemed unnatural, feeding our souls but only leaving us hungrier.

I stepped closer, hoping to see the sign I was looking for, but it wasn't there. The rain slowed to a drizzle and the wind died, thickening the air with a briny sting. The cloud cover broke, exposing the moon's gentle glow illuminating the sea.

It was beautiful, but all it did was fill me with melancholy. Remembering the nights Mother spent sobbing while I sat alone by the window, waiting for what would never come. The sacrifices she made still weighed heavy on my heart, and probably always would.

Cloaked in self-loathing, I paused before continuing along my route. My rubber boots crunched on the rocks as I followed the familiar path. Few people came to the north point these days, and that was exactly how I wanted it. Anybody who ventured to this place, especially after dark, would meet their deserved fate.

Each time I walked the shore, I remembered the stories Mother used to tell of people getting lost and never found. The signs jutting from the sand warning trespassers to turn back stood as attestations to her tales.

I stared at one and imagined it being hammered into the ground by someone who recently lost a loved one. Heartbroken and searching for their lover or child, but finding only grief. Wondering if whatever took all these people would also come for them, selfish fear eventually ending their fruitless searches.

I broke from my musings, noticing something perched on the sign. It took flight, fluttering away toward the pier, bobbing up and down haphazardly as it led me toward exactly what I was looking for.

Two figures strolled along the shore, waves caressing their feet. The girl held up the baggy legs of her pinstriped jeans, trying to keep them from getting wet, and looked up at the boy with her head resting against his shoulder. They were young—high school age—he wore a bomber jacket with the logo of the school from the neighboring town. He dropped the driftwood he was carrying and pulled her close. They locked in a kiss, their lips awkwardly exploring each other in the way young lovers do. I held my breath as I watched, wondering what it felt like to share that type of desire and trust another person to be so close. As if taunting my thoughts, they pressed against each other, then released as she jumped away, scrambling out of the water.

"Something just touched my foot," she shrieked, pulling the boy in front of her.

"It's just driftwood, Monica" He laughed, gathering the wood he had just dropped.

"It didn't feel like that. It felt…wet."

"Everything's wet in the ocean." He laughed again, splashing water up at her.

"Don't tease me, Bobby!" She moved closer to shore. "It wasn't a piece of wood."

"I'm sorry. What was it, then?"

She blew out the breath in anger while she stared into the black water. I watched with anticipation as the water yearned for her, each wave creeping closer to her feet.

"I don't know," she whispered.

"Let's stay out of the water then." He slid his hand around her waist and led her away. "We should have enough wood for the fire."

She followed, but continued glancing back at the water as they walked away, distracted enough that she didn't notice me following. Enticed by her fear, my heart raced, beating so loudly, I wondered if they would be able to hear.

They approached the massive rocks that made the foundation of the pier. It led to the parking lot, which was vacant except for the wood-panel station wagon they had driven. Echoing voices escaped from under the pier, singing along to Bruce Springsteen playing on a boombox. There was an excitement to them, and as they came into view, it was evident why. A boy held a torch, waving it dramatically above the head of the girl next to him. He tossed it, sending the flame arcing through the air. It landed on the rocks and started to die before roaring back to life in an explosion of light. The heat caused them to shield their faces and step back. Flames rose, nearly touching the wooden planks above.

"You're gonna burn the whole pier down!" Bobby yelled.

"Yeah, Neil," Monica said. "The whole point of us being under the pier was so nobody would see us."

"*Oh, oh, oh, I'm on fire,*" Neil sang, turning back toward the fire. "It'll be fine. Just needed a little kickstart."

Bobby leaned against an old rowboat that was half buried in the sand. Monica positioned herself in front of him, taking his arms and wrapping them around her.

LUCAS MANN

"You two get tired of making out down there?" Neil's poorly veiled smile pulled at his lips. "Hey Jen, aren't you supposed to protect your little sis from creeps like Bobby?"

"Bobby isn't a creep," Monica protested, tucking a lock of dark hair behind her ear. "And she's only older by six minutes."

"She can take care of herself," Jen grumbled. "She assured me of that this morning."

Neil tossed another piece of wood on the fire, causing it to explode into a shower of sparks raining down like a firework. "Do I sense some discord amongst the sisters? I knew things couldn't be perfect forever."

Jen's mouth dropped open as she turned and noticed me for the first time. She just stared, the light from the fire brightening her skin, while simultaneously deepening the lines on her face, darkening the circles under her eyes. The corners of her mouth, highlighted by her red lipstick, began to droop in what seemed like an impossibly elongated frown until they dripped, drop by drop off her chin and onto the sand.

She fell to her knees, tumbling over, revealing the ax buried in her back. I dislodged it and wiped the blood on my tattered pants, soiled from years of accumulated filth. "Mother says we must keep it clean," I whispered.

Bobby broke free of his paralyzed shock and grabbed Monica's hand, frantically tugging her into the shadows. I turned back to Neil, who had not yet recovered. He merely stood, watching the ax spin through the air, burying itself in his chest with a thud. He groaned and fell backward, landing against one of the posts. His eyes were saucers as he stared at Jen's lifeless body, life slowly fading from them until they went dark.

I sauntered over to retrieve the ax, swaying to the music. I put a foot on Neil's chest and pulled on the handle. It squelched as it released. I groaned in disgust at the sight of fresh blood, so I wiped it on Neil, leaving a red streak across his muscle t-shirt.

Turning in the direction of Bobby and Monica, I danced away from the two corpses and the light of the fire, the crooning of The Boss slowly fading from the boombox.

Stalking the shoreline, I stopped occasionally to look behind a rock or investigate a sound that came from the sea. The footprints led me along in the sand until they turned sharply into the water. Standing there, I squinted out into the ocean, looking for any disruptions in the sheen the moon left on its surface.

"I know you're out there," I called, almost singing. "I can smell you. Filth emanates from you, penetrating my nose, nauseating me to the point where I want to vomit." The boom of my laughter echoed across the water. "Hidden in the depths, entirely visible. I may not see you, but *she* surely will."

Whispers alerted me to their location and I finally saw them, crouching deeper into the water, hoping to be invisible.

"Oh!" Monica yelped.

"Be quiet," Bobby hushed.

"Something brushed my leg."

I burst out laughing again. "I wasn't lying! It's out tonight—come to me or the frenzy will begin."

Bobby disappeared underwater with a splash. His arms broke the surface as he flailed. Monica grabbed his hand and pulled, but was only successful in pulling herself under with him. The moon had disappeared and the air, as well as the water, had become pitch black. I could hear their cries, muffled by their drowning.

I waded out into the water, unable to allow them to die this way. They had no right to sacrifice themselves. Their blood was mine to give, not be taken freely.

Bobby tried to stand, but was pushed over again. His mouth was being pried open, his jaw stretched so far it looked like it was becoming unhinged. He tried to scream, but his full mouth only allowed gurgles. I grabbed his wrist, pulling him away. The object released his mouth and he was weightless, floating through the water until he woke to sand scraping along his back.

His body erupted in a series of convulsions, vomiting and gagging on the mixture of bile and ocean water. He turned onto his hands and knees, spitting the wretched fluid from his mouth. He rubbed his eyes, trying to clear the burning of the salt away. Looking next to him, he saw Monica lying on the shore. Her body was still, no breath going in or out of her lungs.

He stared at her immobilized rib cage for what seemed an eternity before his eyes moved to my boots next to her head. I smiled as I loomed over him, admiring the moonlight gleaming in his eyes.

"You pulled us out?" he sputtered.

"It will consume, but you will not rob me of my harvest." I squatted next to him, rubbing his dusty blonde hair, knowing he was too exhausted to pull away. "She especially enjoys young lovers."

My arm swung down, followed by the ax tearing into Bobby's throat. His drowning returned, but this time, instead of sea water, it was thick, rich blood that filled his lungs. And unlike before, he would not be able to vomit or cough it back up.

The darkest part of night is when sleep eludes my grasp. Memories blend with hauntings of the past, torturing me into a state that is neither awake nor unconscious. It is the time when I'm most vulnerable, left unprotected.

My eyes opened on cue to the dimly lit ceiling pulsing from embers flickering in the hearth. My vision unfocused, I couldn't tell how far away the ceiling was, but it seemed to be mere inches from my face, trapping me where I lay.

Before I could move, the bed jolted me backwards. My left arm scraped the wall, the rough wood ripping both skin and nightshirt. I winced but remained frozen, trying to be invisible to whatever attacked me. The blanket pulled so tight around my ribs, it constricted the air from my lungs, encapsulating me in a claustrophobic panic.

My emotions were fragmented as the initial wave of fear was joined by the comfort of knowing I was no longer alone. Only she could make me feel this way—afraid, content, and unworthy—a range of emotions pulling me in multiple directions simultaneously. She fueled my every action, and I wanted to run, scream, and cry all at once, but did nothing as they canceled each other out.

A wail pierced my ears, so loud, I thought my eardrums would burst. It overpowered my mind, leaving nothing but the trance I was forced into. Then it was gone. It still howled, but I could no longer hear it. Instead, I felt it blow directly into my ear. My head jerked to the side, expecting to find a person with their lips puckered, whistling silently.

But there was nothing, only the stench of rotting flesh filling my nose and pierced deep into my gut, triggering my gag reflex. I knew it couldn't be the four dead teenagers outside—it was far too soon for their decomposition to begin.

Shadows receded down the wall like peeling paint to reveal the coarse, weathered wood that had always been there. A pale beam of light shone in from the window, chasing the shadow away, its fingerlike wisps escaping through the cracks in the floor and under the door in their eternal game of hide and seek.

My fear was gone; erased so quickly and completely I could barely remember what I was afraid of. Relaxation took over, melting me into my bed. The lumps of the old mattress massaged my aching back and hips. I wanted nothing more than to fall into a deep slumber, not caring if I ever woke.

That was when I heard the song.

I rose effortlessly from the bed, seduced by the call of the song, now the only comfort I sought. In a fraction of a moment, I was at the door and pulling it open. The stench of rotting flesh was stronger when I opened my door, but with a sweetness I hadn't noticed before. The pungency that made me want to retch was gone.

The shadow wrapped itself around me and pulled me outside. Despite the chill of the night air, I didn't resist, my legs moving but the weight of my body relieved. The moon had appeared, having sliced open the clouds. It shone down in its fullness, the voluptuous curves and craters fully visible. The sand it illuminated was my destination and I had no choice but consent to its demand.

The moon grew closer as I approached the shore, until it hovered over the water. I stared, enraptured by its beauty. The blinding brightness forced my eyes closed, to focus solely on the song playing in my head in its unashamed revelry.

An orb appeared in my mind, replacing the moon. Blood trickled in and out of its pores, dripping as if salivating. It coaxed me closer, the mellifluous melody begging me to join it. To take only a few steps into the water, and join the clouds and moon reflecting on its stillness. Unknown paradise awaited in these depths that would fulfill every desire I ever had.

I saw Mother reaching out to me. She smiled, tears running down her cheeks as she beckoned me to join her. She was happy, telling me she missed me. How handsome I had become and how proud she was of me. Of course, it had been her beckoning me with her song. How stupid I had been to be afraid. She was proud of me for getting rid of the filth and wanted to tell me.

Wait, that wasn't right. Mother was never happy to see me. I was the burden she always resented. If anything, she would be happier without me there.

I opened my eyes and everything changed. The moon was back in the sky, mostly obscured by the clouds, and only a dull lambency where it had been piercing before. The water was moving again, waves gently spilling onto the sand. The salty residue had replaced the putrid smell of rot on my tongue.

I looked down and saw the last tendril escape into the water. Tears sprang in my eyes, but I remembered the voice. My reward would come soon.

Mother knocked on the door to the office, just below the placard that read, "Psychiatrist." She opened it without waiting for a response, and I followed her into the room, struggling to keep up with her long stride, the smell of bleach stinging my nostrils.

"It's good to see you, Mrs. Weaver." Dr. Nichols smiled as he wiped his green steel desk. He had long chestnut hair and looked more likely to be at a Pink Floyd concert than practicing psychiatry in this tiny New England fishing town. "Matthew. How are you today?"

I looked at the floor, making patterns of the tiles in my mind. I could only step where there were no scuff marks, and where they connected diagonally. I slid my feet onto the safe squares before Mother interrupted by clearing her throat.

"I'm sorry, Dr. Nichols." She threw a furious glance at me. "There has been some difficulty with listening lately." She pulled me into the chair and fell into the one beside me.

"Hmm." Dr. Nichols took his own chair and steepled his fingers, slowly sliding them along his oiled mustache. "The area of his brain damaged from the fall could result in decreased attention. But he is also only fifteen years old. Have you considered admitting him, like I suggested?"

Mother ignored the comment. "Could that also be what's causing the crying?" She threw me a look of disdain. "His sobbing always wakes me at night."

"He's experiencing lability too?" The doctor leaned back in his chair. "It is entirely possible. Every brain works differently, although specific areas have commonality. But it could also be a side effect of being nonverbal. Inability to express oneself can take a toll on mental health."

"Is there anything you can do to help him sleep?"

"Why, yes. I believe there is. I just read a very interesting study…"
He lowered his hands and stared at me. It was a gaze I could not meet, and
I lowered my eyes to count the tiles again. "Matthew. Can you hear me?"

"Look at Dr. Nichols!" Mother elbowed me sharply.

Dr. Nichols held his hands up. "It's okay. I need him to be comfortable
for this exercise to be effective." He leaned back in his chair. "Matthew,
you don't have to respond, but please try to follow my instructions the
best you can."

I sat frozen, fixated on the gouge on the front of his desk, wondering
how that happened. Was it from being moved into the room, or did
something get thrown into it?

"Matthew."

I blinked and the gouge disappeared. Was it really gone? Had I just
imagined it? No, it was still there. It was growing, deepening. If I kept
looking, the leg would snap, the desk would come tumbling down onto
the floor, exposing everything in this room. Thousands of secrets would
spill out, revealing all the children that could not be helped. They would
all be screaming silently, with nobody to care what they had to say. Just
like me.

"Matthew, you're embarrassing me," Mother hissed.

I looked up, feeling the disappointment radiating from her body. I
glanced at Dr. Nichols, but immediately looked out the window, the pity
in his smile too much for me to bear.

"It's okay, Matthew," he said with the forced kindness most medical
professionals had. "You don't have to look at me. I actually want you to
close your eyes. You can trust me."

I knew I should trust him. But I didn't. Despite that, I did as he
instructed. I had been conditioned to do as I was told, regardless of my
feelings. My world darkened as my eyes shut, the green outline of the
window light the only thing I could see.

"I want you to think of something that makes you happy," Dr.
Nichols said in a soft voice. "Is there anything that makes you feel calm
and peaceful?"

I tried to think, but all I could envision was the gouge growing deeper
on the desk, opening a hole in the floor, and sucking me into it.

"Butterflies make him happy," Mother said, absent of the fake
kindness Dr. Nichols' voice had.

"Ah, butterflies," Dr. Nichols purred. "Beautiful monarch butterflies
with their vibrant orange and black. Such lovely creatures. So pure. Can

95

you see one? Try to imagine a monarch flitting around just above your head. Teasing you as if it's going to land on your shoulder."

I could see it. I was a little boy again. We had just released the butterflies after finding the caterpillars weeks before, watching them grow and spin their chrysalises. I was crying because I didn't understand why we had to let them go. Mother explained it was necessary; they needed to be free to find food and stretch their wings before their migration south. It was their purpose, and to stifle that would mean they couldn't truly be a butterfly. She was so very wise when it came to animals.

"Try to reach out and touch it, Matthew."

I lifted my arm, slowly bringing it toward the butterfly when I froze as a question formulated in my mind. *Why couldn't she let me have even the slightest bit of freedom?*

The black on the wings of the butterfly began to bleed into the orange. It started to move in slow motion, doubling, tripling in size as it hovered over me. Its enormous wings blocked out the sunlight, casting a shadow over us, before exploding into thousands of tiny versions of itself. They swarmed me, covering every inch of my skin, blocking out my vision—even the green spot where the window should be.

My eyes flew open and I saw Dr. Nichols staring at me with concern. He rose from his seat, locking eyes with Mother. My eyes followed his and came to rest on Mother's face, unable to discern her expression as embarrassment or disappointment.

I wanted to scream but my vocal cords were strangled by the vice-like grip of her stare. The room spun as my head lolled, my control of it gone. I gasped for breath, an invisible weight crushing my chest. I realized the weight was me as I curled into a fetal position, drawing my legs up and squeezing them as hard as I could.

I had to escape. My nose burned from the bleach and I could no longer stay confined in this room. I jumped and ran toward the door, barely hearing the chair clatter on the floor behind me. The sounds of Mother yelling and Dr. Nichols calling for me faded, replaced by the pounding of my footfalls as I ran, faster and faster down the hall. I burst out of the building, blinded by the bright sunshine and sound of vehicles busy in midday traffic.

The rest was a blur, my mind detached from my body, and I found myself sitting on the edge of the pier, sobbing, fresh tears dropping into the ocean, completely oblivious to the sound of a vehicle pulling up and the footsteps that approached.

"Thankfully, Dr. Nichols said I won't have to pay for that visit."

I couldn't even look at her. I wanted her to care, to ask why I ran. Maybe even give me a hug when it was just the two of us. The only time she displayed any sort of affection was in public, when she knew others were watching.

"Get in the car. We need to get home."

I stared out into the harbor, watching a fishing boat rocking on the waves in the distance.

"Dammit, Matthew. I said to get in the car!" She walked over and grabbed my arm, trying to pull me up, but I shrugged her off. "Your father used to play these same games. Always giving me the silent treatment until he finally left. I swear that's where you learned this behavior."

"Father is dead." I flinched at the sound of my own voice. It was the voice of a man I had never heard before, not a scared little child.

"I knew it!" She squealed with delight. "You've been faking it this whole time. That quack thinks he needs to calm you and make you comfortable, but what you really need is the truth. Your father is dead. He died on a boat just like that one." She jabbed her finger at the fishing boat. "Because he didn't care about me. He worked all the time because he didn't love me no matter how much I loved him. God knows how many women he brought onto that boat."

I knew that wasn't true. He worked a lot, but that was to fund Mother's expensive tastes. To make sure she had the clothes she wanted, so she could dine with the elite of Brackish Harbor.

A shadow crept across the water, slowly moving toward us. I looked at the sky, clear other than a large, dark cloud spreading across it. It reached us, cooling us from the heat. Its darkness was beautiful, its edges electrified with the white of the sun behind it. I felt its power as I tried to determine what shape it reminded me of. Then I realized: it was the shape of a butterfly.

"Your father was worthless and you're growing up to be just like him."

I flinched, my attention brought back to her.

Mother's eyes narrowed, the wrinkles that may have once been caused by smiles, now only used for hate, cutting jagged lines across her face. "You'll never be enough. Not for me, not for yourself, not for anyone."

Before I knew what was happening, I was on my feet and stepping toward her. She tried to retreat, but my hands were already under her sternum. I shoved and she flew backward into the rail, flipping over it. She screamed as she plummeted into the water, and I watched with delight as her terrified face sank, disappearing into the depths. The water roiled, sediment splashing from its surface. I watched in awe as she became one with the ocean, a creature returning to where she belonged. A weight lifted from my shoulders, giving me a freedom I had never experienced in my life. I could now migrate with the butterflies if I chose. Or I could stay. What I did was not important. All that mattered was I had the choice.

I picked up a flat rock and flung it, watching it skip across the water until it trailed off, disappearing under the surface. My routine was to come to this place and try to break my mind from its downward spiral.

The memory of what I did to Mother was a constant torment. Guilt became my only companion, following me everywhere and embedding itself into every aspect of my life that reminded me of Mother.

When Father left, he did so without a care to even say goodbye. He kissed me goodnight, but when I woke in the morning, I knew he was already gone by the sound of Mother weeping behind the locked door of her bedroom.

Brackish Harbor was abandoned, the townsfolk left in a mass exodus, fearing for their lives after multiple instances of fishing boats disappearing at sea and people going to the shore, never to return. I didn't blame them. I even wanted to go. I wanted so badly for just one person to extend an offer to accompany them wherever they were going, far away from this place that held nothing but pain. But they all left without a word, just like Father. Disappearing over the course of a couple days, leaving the town mostly vacant, other than a few stragglers that held onto hope in the same way I did. The lie that something was still here, something cared about us and wanted us to stay.

Mother never left me, even when I pushed her away. I believed in my heart she really did care, and was grateful for everything I did for her. There were times when she would go for a while but I knew it was my fault because I hadn't done enough.

I did wonder what she did while she was away. Where she went and if there was somebody else taking care of her. Days would go by without seeing or hearing anything, and I would begin to lose control of my mind. The fear of being abandoned would become too much for me and I would spend hours lying on the floor of the bathroom, the cold rotten wood the only thing that could relate to how I felt. I couldn't eat or sleep, paralyzed in an anorexic exhaustion until I felt her attention again.

My entire life I longed for her to say the words I had never heard. She always found other words to use—she cared about or adored me—but never said what I craved from the bottom of my soul. And deep down, a single truth was always needling from my subconscious: she didn't love me.

I picked up another stone, sliding my fingers across its smooth, eroded surface and recognized its parallel to my heart. I launched it into the air, watching it disappear against the darkening sky. I saw the splash in the distance, discarded without anyone but me knowing where it was or what was its fate.

The horizon lit up with a flash of lightning, exposing the storm that was fast approaching. I blinked away the tears, knowing what that meant. She was coming home, coming back to me because I was the only person that could truly give her what she needed. And I would do that willingly, even though she had never met mine.

The skies opened, a torrent of rain pouring down on me as I dragged the last body onto the pier. The wood was slick and I struggled to maintain my footing, using the rail to stay upright. I braced against the wind as it tried to push me back, trying to keep me from doing what needed to be done. But this storm was no match for the joy I felt in my heart. It fueled me, the power in my muscles endless as they strained, taut against everything I had struggled with my entire life.

Finally reaching the end, I stacked the corpse next to the others. Four neatly organized bodies, lined up perfectly, just the way Mother would have liked. I knelt next to them, my eyes burning from the sweat being rinsed into them by the rain. Lightning flashed in the distance, followed by a crack and the sustained rumble of gods impatiently awaiting their sacrifice.

I held my arms out to my sides, watching the water run down my bare flesh along the swollen veins still flooded from the exertion. I trembled, the reward of my labor about to come to fruition. This was what I was created for and groomed into. I was a provider, living autonomously in a place few others could survive. While everyone else ran, I stayed and thrived. A product of this hell that I didn't create, but helped sustain.

The water sloshed against the bottom of the pier, some of the planks bouncing against the force. I looked into the Stygian abyss angrily swirling below, begging me to begin.

I rolled the first teenager's body over the edge, watching it drop. The water seemed to part as she lurched from it, countless tentacles wrapping around the corpse and pulling it in, like a squirming bed of snakes, indiscernible where one ended and the other began. The body was consumed so quickly, not a single drop of blood discolored the water.

I repeated the offering with the other three bodies and they were eaten the same way, only quicker and more voraciously with each one.

The intensity of the storm receded, the rain barely noticeable on my skin. Lightning flashed again, lighting up the horizon, showing the storm had moved inland. The pattering of drops on the pier calmed me, knowing my job was near complete.

I looked into the water, watching the movement just below the surface, knowing she was still there, waiting for me to deliver more. To give her everything she desired.

"Mother, I feel better now," I called. "I know what a terrible son I was, but you did your best. I used to feel bad for what I did. But now I realize that I saved you. You don't have to live in shame anymore. The people that treated you poorly now satiate your anger. It's my turn to take care of you. My purpose in life is reaping for you, Mother."

I reached over the edge, and a massive tentacle emerged from the water to meet me. Its tip slithered through my fingers in a soft caress. It was cold and hard, not the slimy feeling I had expected. Rubbing gently on my wrist, nostalgia of childhood memories flooded my mind. The constant yelling when Father was home, the deafening silence when he wasn't. I felt no apologies, only explanations. So many reasons why life was hard for Mother, and how she did the best she could with what she had.

I realized no matter how much I took care of her, no matter how much I brought to her, she would never be satisfied. She could feed endlessly on the pain and suffering of others and it would do nothing to satiate her need to destroy. Because, as she made clear from the moment I opened my eyes, I would never be enough.

So, I leaned in, like the child I was never able to be, and let her take me into the water, engulfing me in her chilling embrace. The pain was only physical now, and I relaxed into it, knowing soon it would all be over, and soon, she would no longer be able to hurt me.

.

CHAPTER SIX

LOW TIDE
Nick Bennett

The dilapidated village of Brackish Harbor certainly lived up to its name, if not the faded sign's promise of *The Freshest Fish in the Atlantic.* The spray of the ocean had worn away those painted words over decades of neglect, and encrusted both the rocky shores and the souls still clinging to life there with an ever-thickening layer of salt.

For miles around its coast, the ocean was a graveyard. The freshest fish in Brackish Harbor were those whose carcasses had most recently been cast against the rocks. Those smart enough to abandon the town in years past had attributed its acrid, lifeless waters to salt deposits from the island's cliffs slowly leeching into the sea, strangulating even the hardiest fish with a saline solution too caustic to breathe. If one was unfortunate enough to find themselves moored at the docks of the forsaken village, the only sign of life would be the layer of barnacles forever affixed to the rotting wood of the pier, covered in brine and bitterly refusing to succumb to an environment unsuited for anything but a slow death. As one moved further inland, they would find the townspeople of Brackish Harbor of a similar disposition.

The one individual who did not fit this description was a boy no older than ten, dressed in ragged clothes and unable to call any of the decaying houses in the town his home. He had vague memories of his mother, but more often he saw her in nightmares where her eyes turned black as she coughed up blood and fishbones. Over the years, he had become numb to the sights and smells of death. The orphan boy eked out his meager existence by picking through the refuse of those only slightly more fortunate than himself. He gathered his nightly scraps and enjoyed them in a part of town more desolate than the rest: the square where the church once stood. The only remnants left of the building were a single stone arch which once held mighty oaken doors, and above it, the last vestige of an elaborate stained-glass window. The boy often looked through the remaining colored shards that smattered the ground in front of him with hues otherwise unseen in the faded, gray village. Sunlight cascaded through the colored window and made the dead grass shine with tinges of magenta and turquoise.

On this evening, the boy was picking the skin and gristle from a pigeon bone when a visitor approached. This was more than unexpected; the townspeople seemed to avoid this entire part of town for reasons entirely unknown to a child so young. He shrank away from the stranger's advance, for he still bore scars from when he had taken food that was not his to take.

The figure recognized the boy's fear and extended a hand from beneath her cloak, a hand that clutched a small bowl with wisps of steam escaping from under its porcelain lid. The boy took several seconds to realize the bowl was offered freely, and he took it from the stranger with trepidation. Inside was something he hadn't seen in months: the bubbling broth of hot soup. It was packed with fresh seaweed, oyster, wild onion, and prawns as big as his palm. The delicious smell graced his nostrils and freed the boy of all apprehension. He looked up at the stranger who had since pulled away the hood of her cloak to reveal her aged face.

"Go on," said the elderly woman in a soft voice. "Eat it, child."

The boy needed no further prompting. He sucked down the soup with gusto, letting the myriad of flavors dance in his mouth before swallowing it in mighty gulps. He had never tasted such exquisite food in his life, and savored every drop until the bowl was empty. He rested a hand on his stomach, reveling in the novel sensation of being truly full. His dirty face had broken out in an ear-to-ear grin that showcased bits of seaweed wedged in his teeth.

He handed the bowl back to the old woman, who spoke again in a near whisper. "I see you here often, boy. I too enjoy the patches of color in this dreary place."

The woman turned her head upward, her gaze piercing the remnant of stained glass and up to the darkening sky beyond.

The boy noticed a crescent-shaped scar running from just above her eyebrow down to her gaunt cheekbone.

She spoke again, her eyes fixed on the sky. "Did you know that a magnificent church once stood on these grounds?"

The boy nodded.

"But certainly, you're too young to remember when it fell."

He nodded again.

The woman extended her hand to him once more. "Come with me, dear boy. I'll take you to a place with more delicious seafood than you can imagine. I'll tell you the story of how the church fell, and with it, the entire town of Brackish Harbor."

The boy eagerly took her wrinkled hand and they walked the cobblestone street together as she began her tale.

Grayson Thatcher's arrival in the unknown harbor came at just the right time, for the *Tashtego* was taking on water faster than he could manage. A storm had tossed the small sailboat into a rocky shoal that punctured the hull, and the sailor's paltry repair kit had barely stemmed the flow of seawater rushing into the helpless vessel. He had lost a full night of sleep using a hand pump to keep the rising water at bay, and was close to collapsing when he spotted a speck of land in the distance. It was a miracle he had seen the island at all, as it was almost completely enshrouded by the morning mists. But as he neared, the heat of the rising sun dispelled the fog and lit his way to sanctuary.

An aged stone sentinel towered over Grayson's damaged vessel as it limped into the calm waters of the bay; the enormous glass reflector at the top of the lighthouse seemed to look down upon the boat, judging it with a single, stoic eye. The tower was situated on a promontory jutting from the mainland, mirroring a second protrusion that together encircled the harbor like a massive pincer. Save for the ripples made by the *Tashtego*, the water within the bay had a glassy serenity that allowed Grayson a clear view of schools of silvery fish moving en masse around the hull of the sailboat.

The tall masts of over a dozen similar seafaring vessels greeted Grayson as he clumsily maneuvered into an open slip close to shore. The injured leaning of the *Tashtego* did not go unnoticed by the captain of an adjacent fishing barge. The broad seaman helped Grayson out of his waterlogged boat and assisted him in tethering it firmly to the jetty with the practiced deftness of sea-weathered hands.

Once the knots were tied to both the men's satisfaction, the barge captain introduced himself to the newcomer, smiling through a thick, unkempt beard. "John Ferrelly, captain of the *Coveseeker*. Struck a reef, did ye? They'll just as soon sink ye if'n ye don't know yer way 'round the island's waters." Ferrelly turned and called to his crew, who were busy rolling barrels down a plank and onto the dock. "Acker! Redford! Fetch the patchin' supplies and fix this fine fellow's vessel, on the double!"

The two burly dockhands sat the barrel they'd been rolling upright on the dock and rushed back onto the *Coveseeker* to get supplies.

"That's very generous of you," said Grayson in a weak, dry voice.

Ferrelly nodded to the *Tashtego*. 'She's a real beauty. I'd hate to see such a fine prize claimed by the depths. Sounds as if ye could use a drink, Mister...?'

'Thatcher... Grayson Thatcher,' he croaked, embarrassed he'd forgotten to introduce himself in return.

'Well, Mr. Thatcher,' Ferrelly said cheerfully as he offered Grayson his canteen, 'let me be the first to welcome ye to the town of Brackish Harbor. It's a point of personal pride to tell ye we've got the freshest fish in the Atlantic on our humble little isle.'

Grayson breathed heavily after his long drink from the canteen. 'You're a fisherman, then?" he asked, his voice revived.

"Aye lad, with the finest anglin' crew north of Provincetown,' he boasted as Acker and Redford moved past them and onto the *Tashtego*. 'Quickly now, ye filthy swabs!" Ferrelly called after them.

The affable captain led Grayson through the town proper, which was busy with throngs of tourists and townspeople. They crowded through the streets between dozens of single-story properties, all painted a pristine white that radiated a heavenly glow in the afternoon sunlight. The delicious aroma of fresh bread and coffee wafted from a nearby café, parents gifted their children wooden toy boats from the souvenir shop, and everywhere you turned, there was a different manner of fish shop. The briny smell of cod, tuna, sturgeon—and seemingly hundreds of others—washed over the two men as they pushed through the ever-growing crowd.

Around one corner, Grayson spotted a shopkeeper handing a customer the biggest lobster he'd ever seen; the thing had to be half the length of his arm at least. The town seemed entirely unreal.

"Why have I never heard of this place?" Grayson wondered aloud.

"'Tis a true slice of heaven, this here isle," Ferrelly said wistfully. "Most townsfolk have spent their whole lives here, m'self included. The mainlanders who know of Brackish Harbor try to keep it to themselves. Most of 'em think if too many folks hear tell of our clandestine spit of land it'll spoil the place. 'Course, I m'self never mind seein' a fresh face 'round here. Stale air don't fill yer sails, as they say."

Grayson was about to respond that he had never heard that particular expression when a reflected beam of light shone directly into his eyes. He blinked hard as his vision became spotty. When his sight returned, he looked in the direction of the offending beam and laid his eyes on the single most beautiful piece of glasswork he had ever seen. The window was designed in a circular pattern with a multitude of colored panes spiraling from its center. The building that boasted the astonishing aperture was itself a masterwork of architecture; the stalwart columns at its corners terminated in twirling spires rising easily sixty feet into the sky, and the elegant brickwork of its impressive walls and buttresses drew the eye inward toward the massive twin oak doors at its center. The cathedral's complexity and sheer height set it completely apart from the humble wooden architecture of the surrounding town.

Ferrelly was quick to notice Grayson's astonishment. "Brackish Abbey. Oldest building in town, if ye hadn't already figured. The town were sort of built 'round it on the foundations of the original settlement. No one livin' knows how old it really is. 'Twas a true abbey back in the day, with nuns and such. Best we can figure, some sort of religious group broke off the mainland and settled up here. 'Cept of course, it's been so long that we can't hardly figure what they even practiced; ain't a cross, star, or nothin'. No bible neither. Nowadays, we really only use it fer special occasions. Weddings, funerals, Christmas and what have ye. Ol' Mother Beatrice keeps the place lookin' neat n' tidy. She's got it in some folks' heads that the abbey is a blessin' on the island, like it keeps the sun shinin' and the fish plentiful. No harm in believin' such a thing, I s'pose."

Grayson hadn't noticed the strange lack of iconography on the edifice. Every church had its cross, every synagogue its Star of David, but any such symbol was entirely absent from the cathedral. Grayson wasn't a religious man, but the longer he looked at the strange building, the more a twinge of fear prickled his nerves. A primal fear that all mankind shares to an extent: the fear of something more powerful than themselves. Something or someone powerful enough to control the fate of its subjects, to bring seasons of blight or plenty. Men use idols, human likenesses or any sort of representation to give such omnipotence a physical presence amongst them, to anchor their god to the mortal realm so it could be understood. Perhaps this was the sincerest religious monument on Earth, one that didn't purport understanding. It was that—the apparent resignation to the unknown forces of the universe—that raised the hair on Grayson's neck.

Gulls wheeled and screeched in the afternoon sky, high above the unpresuming town, as Grayson gazed out from the bay window of his room at the Blackreef Inn. He massaged his weary eyes; it had been well over a day since he'd slept. He drew the curtains and the room was swathed in soothing darkness. Removing everything but his undergarments, he climbed into the welcoming bed. His body ached with exhaustion, hopefully enough to allow him to sleep until the next morning. Grayson closed his eyes, and the afterimage of the spiral window flashed across his vision before unconsciousness claimed him.

It felt as if no time had passed when he awoke, but the pitch blackness of his surroundings told Grayson that the sun had long set. He groggily pulled the chain on the bedside lamp and checked his timepiece. He'd been asleep for nearly nine hours, but the aches in his tired muscles urged him to return to peaceful slumber. Grayson figured there wasn't much else he could do in the middle of the night, and was about to turn off the lamp when he heard a faint shuffle on the cobblestone road outside. He would not have paused were it the sound of only one or two people, but the clatter of footsteps belonged to a large group. He clambered out of bed and crept to the window to peer through the curtains.

The dull light of the harvest moon illuminated the view from the second floor of the inn. He could make out several people walking through the streets below, and as they moved into patches of moonlight, it was apparent that children were among them. A few couples having a late-night outing was certainly not unheard of, but with children? Even more strange was that, as Grayson watched, he realized everyone was moving in a singular direction. His curiosity overcame his weariness, and he redressed and quietly made for the door downstairs. Having a seasoned sailor's keen sense of direction, there was an unsettling certainty as to which monument would be their destination.

Grayson kept a block's distance as he followed the group, though his stealth was rather unwarranted as none of his quarry turned to look back. At one point, he thought he'd been spotted when a child spoke up loudly, but they were quickly hushed by one of the adults. Other than the child's outburst, the midnight walk had been eerily absent of voices.

Grayson's previous misgivings proved correct as the twisting spires of Brackish Abbey came into view, its pale outline instantly recognizable silhouetted against the low-hanging moon. He watched as the last of the group turned the corner toward the abbey. The moonlight from behind the building cast its face in ominous shadow—save for the stained-glass window, which was lit by a source from within the walls. The massive doors were open, receiving groups filing in wordlessly from all directions.

Standing staunchly at the doorway was a woman clothed in some form of ceremonial gown, occasionally nodding to the people entering. Grayson surmised this was the Mother Beatrice of whom Ferrelly had spoken; even from far away, her posture and slight gestures radiated an air of matronly authority. Once the last of the crowd had shuffled inside, the Mother silently followed, closing the heavy oak doors behind her with surprising ease.

Grayson waited crouched behind an adjacent building, trying to make sense of the situation. Captain Ferrelly had said the abbey was only used for holidays and ceremonies, but even the closest major holiday was months away. Surely no sane person would hold a wedding—or even something as somber as a funeral—in the dead of night. All these questions seemed insignificant compared to the one that most unnerved him: why were the children brought along? The need for what could very well be disturbing answers proved the only force that moved Grayson forward.

On the abbey's northern side sat a row of narrow windows through which he could see its dimly-lit interior. The nave of the abbey was traditionally built, with a single aisle splitting two rows of pews where the townspeople now sat. In the transept were two thick pillars topped with stone braziers, and the firelight spilling from them allowed Grayson to see the congregation more clearly: single or pairs of adults, all of whom were accompanied by one young child. Several faces he'd seen while walking through town; he even spotted the man who had greeted him at the desk of the Blackreef Inn sitting next to who could only be his wife and young son.

Mother Beatrice stood at the altar and spoke to the congregation, though from outside, Grayson couldn't hope to hear what was being said. Sweeping gesticulations made her flowing robes shimmer in the firelight. She turned away from the pews, and Grayson briefly spied a spiral shape embroidered on the back of her gown, bearing an identical likeness to the stained window at the abbey's forefront. From behind the twin pillars emerged two women dressed in similar yet less ornate gowns, each holding a large wooden chest.

After the Mother had spoken for a few more moments, the two subordinates opened the chests and passed by each member of the assembly. Grayson could scarcely make out the objects produced from the chests, but whatever they were seemed to match the number of children present.

When the families nearest the window were given theirs, Grayson was finally able to see the objects. Any seafarer would have recognized them instantly: the bleached white test of a sand dollar. In life, they belonged to disc-shaped urchins but once dead, their circular skeletons often washed up on the beach. They certainly weren't something to be used as communion wafers, for inside each one were five V-shaped bones that act as the urchin's teeth.

The Mother made a grand proclamation, her palms extended toward the masses. Grayson squinted as a member of each family broke their sand dollar in two.

For most, only the five small teeth fell from within the broken discs, but one woman held something else as well: a black, spiraled shell of nearly imperceptible size. She held it aloft for all to see.

The two assistants moved toward the woman and her daughter, and led them to the head of the congregation where the Mother waited to receive them. The girl's mother wore a stony expression, but her eyes betrayed sorrow. Her daughter rubbed her eyes tiredly in the light of the braziers, looking around the room with clear naiveté as Mother Beatrice gently laid a hand on her shoulders while addressing the assembly. Grayson wished he shared the young girl's ignorance in the face of such an abstruse experience, but all he felt was the slow, creeping dread of comprehension.

The sailor was forced to press himself into the shadows as everyone rose from the pews and silently filed out of Brackish Abbey. The parents emerging from the vast doorway seemed to clutch their children more tightly than they had before entering, and Grayson couldn't help but think that those children were somehow more fortunate than the one who'd been chosen. The crowd eventually dispersed into the dark streets enough that Grayson felt he could safely peer through the window once more without being detected.

The fires were dying, but even in the dim light he noticed that the mother, daughter, and three clergy members were nowhere to be seen. He was certain they hadn't left with the others. Before the fires were fully extinguished, he noticed a long tapestry lightly rippling against the back wall of the nave. Grayson's mind was a maelstrom of apprehensive thought. Dark conclusions jutted like sharp rocks threatening to tear away at his composure. Surely the girl would be safe with her mother...but he remembered the woman's expression, one of sorrowful resignation. The subdued ritualism of the procession only made Grayson more fearful for the girl's safety.

His awareness returned when his feet crunched against the discarded sand dollar halves littering the floor; he had entered the foreboding hall unconsciously, without thought of his own wellbeing or what the consequences might be.

Embers crackled in the braziers, but their feeble light still adequately illuminated the wall at the back of the sanctuary. From floor to ceiling, the bricks were laid into the wall in a series of crazed patterns; spirals within spirals, helical trails of stone whirling around each other in ways that were dizzying to behold. Grayson would have reveled in the stunning volutions of the architecture when bathed in daylight. But now, underlit by orange fire and surrounded by encroaching darkness, the helixes only radiated malevolence.

Grayson pressed a hand up against the tapestry and nearly fell when he failed to make contact with the solid wall he expected to feel behind it. Instead, he stumbled halfway into a seam at the tapestry's center which was practically invisible when it hung motionless.

Once past the secret aperture, Grayson found himself in a small alcove lit by four candles atop ornate stands, placed around a circular metal slab set into the floor. It was about four feet in diameter and bore yet another spiral pattern. He crouched to examine the metal plate and was met with a faint but familiar sound, one that, by all reason, should not be present at all: the gentle ebb and flow of the ocean. He moved his hand around the metal rim and felt a small hole through which flowed a tiny stream of cool air. He attempted to pry the plate free from its setting, but his fingers were far too large to fit into the gap. This was clearly the only way to gain enough leverage to move the metal disc.

How had the Mother moved such a thing?

Amid the flickering candlelight, he spotted it leaning against the wall: a long, thin metal rod resembling a fire poker with a wooden grip and terminating in a slightly hooked point. Grayson plunged the pointed end into the hole and, with a single thrust, successfully pried it from its seating. Dragging the metal plate away from the opening it concealed, he heard more clearly the crashing of waves against rock, and smelled the salty sea breeze. Seeing far past the portal proved more difficult, as the meager candlelight hardly penetrated the darkness below. Stone stairs descended sharply to unknown depths, and as Grayson stepped gingerly downward, he decided to take the metal pike as a means of defense against whatever might await him below.

The steps were taller than they were wide, and Grayson stepped deliberately, lest he slip on the damp stone. The candlelight abandoned him as the passageway twisted downward at a frightening angle into bedrock. He kept one hand pressed against the slick walls to keep his balance, the other clutching the metal rod. He struggled to imagine a town of such picturesque quality calmly sitting atop the horrors that his mind conjured. The life of a mariner was not without its perils, and as such, all seagoing men held the same necessary respect for the vast waters. The ocean was a tumultuous place prone to erratic and violent weather, its storm waves rising fifty feet or more and crushing any vessel manned by those foolhardy enough to believe they could battle mother nature and emerge victorious. The seabed was covered with the bodies of such men, and there were many times when Grayson turned back toward shore rather than count himself among them.

But now, descending into the deepness of the earth, he felt not the fear that comes from respect and experience, but one born of the same instinctive panic of being circled by hungry sharks, waiting to look into the voids of their eyes before being torn apart. He felt that helpless terror would fully consume him until he saw the steps beneath him had become

110

faintly illuminated by a pale orange light. This would have urged Grayson forward, if not for the voices barely audible against the noise of the waves, which caused him to tread more cautiously than before.

The end of the tunnel opened into a much larger cavern, the last set of stairs roughly hewn from its wall. His head cleared at the bottom of the shaft, allowing him a full view of the strange vista; a huge grotto cluttered with porous, rocky outcroppings covered in seaweed and marine flora, its floor littered with countless pools of deep water.

Navigating through the cave with minimal light proved challenging. Every surface was slick with seawater and algae, and Grayson had to take great care not to slip into the pools which, upon closer inspection, were home to hundreds of spiny urchins. Using the hooked end of the pike for leverage, he made his way toward the voices. He heard them more clearly now, three distinct voices speaking in chilling unison.

Until he rounded the final stone formation, Grayson assumed the orange glow had been the light from a fire. But it was something far more immense than a simple flame.

The huge harvest moon sat low on the horizon, its baleful orange glow reflecting off the waters spilling through the cave's wide mouth. Silhouetted against the imposing moon was the harbor's lighthouse far in the distance. It looked as if it sat atop a huge mountain, like the earth had sprung up underneath it in the night. Then it dawned on him that the tides had receded more than should have been possible, revealing hundreds of feet of rock below. It was no wonder the subterranean chamber was full of aquatic life, for under normal circumstances, the cavern would be entirely submerged. But the moon had exerted unthinkable strength and ripped the ocean away from the island, exposing its capacious secrets with a power hitherto unseen by man. In the pale light of the imposing orange sphere dominating the heavens, five figures stood at the water's edge.

Mother Beatrice and her two underlings stood at the shoreline with their arms raised, surrounding the young girl. Her mother stood like a statue several yards away, wringing her hands. Her unruffled demeanor had given way to nervous anticipation. Grayson edged closer, keeping to the shadows along the pitted cave wall. He could understand their words now, amplified by the surrounding stone.

"Tarphycerida, fathoms deep
Profundus somnus, a halted sleep

Aeternus gratia, sea and lake,
Donum multa, a soul to take"

As the repeated words echoed louder and louder, Mother Beatrice produced an emerald amulet from her robes and placed it around the child's neck. The girl took the talisman in her hands, and, as if in a trance, walked slowly into the water. She was submerged up to her waist, and when the amulet made contact with the ocean, the water erupted in an explosion of bioluminescent light. Grayson had seen this phenomenon before; certain algae would glow during the night when disrupted by the wake of a ship. But now the sea was ablaze with green incandescence, radiating outward from where the girl stood.

The echoes of the final chant faded into silence, and the only two sounds left were the glowing waves lapping against the rock and the rapid heartbeat pounding in his ears.

Far out from the shore, a long, splintered object rose from the depths, rippling through the glowing algae as it slowly approached. As it neared the shore, it revealed itself as a towering monolith of rotting wood, lengths of mossy rope and tattered canvas hanging from its splintered beams. From beneath the waves emerged the bow of a massive frigate, ascending from its grave as if to spite the forces that had sunk it eons ago.

Grayson was struck with utter disbelief. He assumed the ghost ships spoken of in whispers throughout the ages were only seafaring legends to enliven a sailor's imagination. This revelation turned from fantastical spectacle to stark terror as the ship leaned backward and from beneath it emerged an enormous, chitinous leg. The jet-black, segmented limb extended forth to dig its clawed end into the rocky shoreline, soon joined by three more of equal size. Then, in a massive upheaval, the ancient ship arose from the ocean to bare the nightmarish monstrosity within.

Grayson's blood froze and his stomach twisted agonizingly. The creature using the wooden vessel like a shell was beyond rational description.

The crab-like legs anchoring its form to the rock projected out from the armored body that was coiled inside the hollow half-ship. Glistening flagella sprang from nearly every visible surface, and larger tentacles whipped through the air, their suckers undulating like a thousand mouths ringed with wicked teeth. The eldritch creature didn't appear to have a distinct head, but was covered in bilateral clusters of ebony eyes, each with a celestial pattern as if each orb contained an entire galaxy of stars. The sound of it wetly sucking air through feathered slitted gills was nauseating, and its labored breathing caused its entire hideous mass to ripple. Grayson watched in horror as a mass of tentacles moved apart to reveal a gigantic humanoid face, sunken within innumerable fleshy folds and surrounded by wriggling, bristled appendages.

The three robed women bowed in reverence and backed away from the shore, leaving the girl gazing up at the inscrutable marine monstrosity. It met her gaze with the pupil-less eyes in its human face, and lurched slowly toward her as a set of oozing mandibles emerged from within its mouth.

Grayson never made the conscious decision to sprint forward with the metal spear gripped tightly in his hands. Mother Beatrice and her acolytes noticed too late to stop him from plunging his makeshift weapon deep into the creature's dark flesh. It spewed fetid ichor as the creature reeled back in agony.

The child's high-pitched scream intermixed with the behemoth's ear-piercing screech. One of its countless tentacles started to wrap around her, and if Grayson hadn't grabbed her she surely would have been lost. A toothed sucker had sunk deep into the child's face, blood now seeping from a sickle-shaped gash. Waves from the thrashing titan swept around their legs as Grayson hefted the child over his shoulder and ran.

The child's mother was suddenly upon them, her eyes crazed with fury and terror. "Interloper!" she screamed. "You've doomed us all! You've no idea what—"

The beast's razor-sharp legs swung and cleft her nearly in half with terrifying force. Her daughter wailed.

Grayson made for the stairway at the rear of the cave. Mother Beatrice and her aides were already ahead of him, abandoning any hope of appeasing their enraged god. One of the acolytes tripped and fell on the uneven ground, soon seized by an oily appendage and pulled backward before she could cry for help. Above the crashing waves, Grayson heard a sickening crunch; the unwitting sacrifice of a true believer. The glowing green ocean rushed in around them, threatening to pull them toward the sea and its sinister arbiter.

The water was almost to Grayson's knees and running became nearly impossible. With great effort, he managed to reach the stone steps with the child in tow. He scrambled up the stairs far enough to be free of the encroaching water, and looked back in time to see the horrible beast freeing its colossal form from the husk of the frigate, which floated for several seconds before once again sinking into a watery tomb.

Now unburdened by its makeshift shell, the creature moved with frightening agility through the luminous water. Grayson saw a glimpse of its dark, glossy carapace breach the surface before both the second acolyte and Mother Beatrice were pulled under the churning rollers to their inevitable demise.

As he climbed, he wondered if they had been as willing to give themselves to the ocean's ravenous maw as they had been to sacrifice an innocent child. Their looks of sheer terror before disappearing beneath the surface made him doubt their devotion.

The girl was becoming increasingly cumbersome, and Grayson was forced to push past the limits of his stamina to race up the slick stairs of the underground tunnel, and the spray of the rising seawater made the climb that much more perilous. Water filled the tunnel faster than he could climb it; he was submerged past his waist before he finally clamored through the exit in the floor of Brackish Abbey. His footfalls splashed on the stone floor, the sea never halting its pursuit.

He burst through the abbey doors and out into the chill of the night. The harvest moon had risen as if it too pursued him, bathing the doomed town of Brackish Harbor in its malevolent orange glow.

Grayson had just run clear of the square when he heard the abbey begin to topple behind him. He dared a backward glance to watch it almost completely collapse, the green water gushing from the rubble and out into the streets.

He stopped to catch his breath after he'd put enough distance behind him. His lungs burned and his muscles ached. The little girl was bloodied, soaked, and terrified beyond measure, but she was alive. The sound of a bell being rung in distress echoed through the night. People ran from their homes in confusion and panic, unaware of the inexorable force of a cruel universe unleashed upon their quaint fishing village. A rancorous screech drowned out the alarm bell, and Grayson knew he had to escape the damned island before it was swallowed by the ravenous sea.

When he reached the docks, the boats were being tossed about like toys in a bathtub; several had crashed into each other and were already being claimed by the water. Miraculously, the *Tashtego* was near enough to shore that it had avoided major damage. Grayson quickly dropped the girl and then himself onto the deck, using a hatchet he kept aboard to hack through the mooring lines and escape the pier. He unfurled the mainsail and steered through what was quickly becoming a graveyard of splintered ships. Two schooners lifted by opposing waves smashed into each other in front of the *Tashtego*, and Grayson had to shield the child from the explosion of wooden fragments that rained down on the deck. A fortuitous gust of wind gave them the necessary speed to break through the wreckage and make a clean getaway into the raging sea beyond Brackish Harbor.

Grayson looked back at the island only when he was over a mile away and safe in calmer waters. Flickering red lights dotted the island as fires broke out across the village. The moon was high now, and in the pitch black of the open ocean, he could see endless swaths of stars. Looking up from the vast ocean at the infinity of the universe above, the sailor couldn't help feeling crushed by his own insignificance. His experience at Brackish Harbor gave him a look behind the tapestry that separates the servants from their masters, mortal followers from their immortal gods. He wished he could have remained ignorant to the existence of beings who skulk the dark realms he now knew lay disturbingly close to our own.

As he turned his gaze back downward, he smiled at the sleeping child with her face now bandaged and body swaddled in blankets, and Grayson knew he had proved significant enough to save one earthly soul who could not have saved herself.

As she finished her tale, the old woman absentmindedly traced an aged fingertip along the crescent scar that marred her face. The orphan boy had been so enraptured by her grim story that he hadn't noticed they now stood on the precipice of a high cliff overlooking the dark ocean. The sun had set, and the stars glimmered in the violet sky.

"I returned here years later," the woman said, "with a group of mainlanders who thought they could resettle the village and restore it to its former splendor. I too had hope that my home could be salvaged. But the waters had long been bereft of the life that sustained this village, plagued by death and cursed to rob the vitality of those who try to thrive here. The sailor saved me, but in doing so, condemned the island to eternal woe. Sparing me was a mistake which good people have paid for with their lives."

The boy thought of his mother. Perhaps she could have lived to tuck him in at night and feed him hot meals as this stranger had. He looked to her; the old woman was holding out her hand to him, and he took the object in hopes that it was more delicious food. Instead, he found himself holding a necklace: a thin length of chain with an emerald amulet. Before he knew it, the old woman had picked him up with both hands.

"It was a mistake that I now hope to correct."

The boy was too shocked to cry out before his body fell to the water far below.

Brackish Harbor's lighthouse keeper dutifully scanned the ocean as the single beam of light swept slowly across the dark sea. His eyes caught a glint of green light, and he squinted through tired eyes at what looked like a ship veering too close to the shore. Before he could sound the foghorn to alert the vessel, he realized it was only a shipwreck, and he watched its bow sink back beneath the waves. The corpse of a sunken ship was a typical sight when the harvest moon rose and the tide was low.

CHAPTER SEVEN

THE GIFT OF RAKOSKA
Wendy Vogel

I always knew he'd come back for his son.

That thought swirled as I closed the window in little Edward's room, shoving down the warped sash and flipping the lock. There was no one to help me that night, and I blinked back tears that stung my swollen eye. By morning, my face would be a bruised mess, and my breath came in gasps through my burning throat, but my ribs had healed from the last time, the wrist healed almost to normal. I could do this alone. With a final check that my little boy was asleep and as safe as I could make him, I trudged down creaking stairs.

William lay where I had left him—in a pool of blood, my best kitchen knife protruding from his eye socket. I edged around his body toward the basement stairs. The kitchen overlooked the old wharf far below our cottage, and a dense fog had rolled in at sunset, like it did on so many autumn nights in Brackish Harbor. A few lights burned down there; ghostly spheres in the gathering darkness. William's fishing boat was docked there, along with the small rowboat he sometimes used when the week's catch was meager, and he'd had a few too many. I had prayed hard those nights to the old gods of the sea, silent prayers that my three-year-old son didn't need to hear. All the boats were dark now, their crews had slumped away; home to their families who also prayed when the men sailed away on the cold, gray sea.

No one likes a basement. No one is comfortable on open wooden stairs lit by one bare bulb, imagining bony fingers waiting to grasp an ankle from between the treads. No one relishes the feel of delicate spiderwebs grazing their face as they descend to a stone and dirt floor, feeling the weight of the earth around them, closing them off from the sky and sea, from sun and clouds. But there would be a tarp down there, or some old sailcloth, and rope. And there were worse things than basements.

The bulb threw shadows as I stepped onto the floor. Things skittered in the corners, fleeing my approach. Hulking, cloth-covered shapes might have been monsters of the deep, lit by the filtered sunlight fathoms above, crouched and waiting for unwary prey to swim by. But nothing moved except the water-bugs as I pulled a large tarp off a pile of old fishing equipment, the smell of the sea pungent in the confined dark. An oar clattered to the floor, and I kicked it under William's old worktable.

A coil of rope waited in the far corner like a serpent poised to strike. I knew I was being silly, imagining dangers when the real danger was finally dead, blood still soaking into the kitchen floorboards. How much blood did a man have in his body? Would it seep through the cracks and drip down here, a rain of red into my pale hair, drops splattering onto the rough, uneven stones at my feet? I glanced up, reaching for the coil of rope. Nothing above me but more spiderwebs, lacing the beams that held the house that had become a prison for Edward and me.

No more.

In the far corner, a locked door was further in shadow than the rest of the basement. William's private sanctuary. I had never passed through that doorway.

Not tonight.

I dragged the tarp and rope up the stairs, leaving the light on behind me. William stared up at the kitchen ceiling with his remaining eye, brown and unblinking, already drying as the wind whipped through the tiny space. I closed and latched the kitchen window. Mother taught me to always latch windows so nothing could get in. She'd never said what 'nothing' was, and I had never been brave enough to ask.

He still looked angry. Even with the handle of my knife poking out of his eye socket, his face still wore the frown that had been his only expression the past few years. Blood had caked in the weathered creases of his face, far too old for his years, hardened by an unforgiving ocean that no longer shared its bounty. William wore the seven-pointed star amulet my mother had given him when we married, an amulet of protection for sailors and fishermen. It had kept him alive for a decade on the sea. His final fate was found on land, when his hands gripped my throat over something I said or didn't say, and my hands found the kitchen knife that unlocked the prison that was this house, this man, this island.

I laid the rope on the floor and the tarp atop it. I rolled him onto the tarp, tucking his arms in at his sides. The edge of his new tattoo peeked from below his sleeve, and I shoved it under his body, averting my eyes. It was ugly, that squid-dark ink, an angular design that filled me with a creeping itch, like eels sliding under my skin whenever I had to look at it. *No more.*

I pulled my knife from his head and set it in the sink, avoiding looking into the empty hole it left. I wrapped the tarp and rope around him and tied it up tight, with a knot I could step into it like a horse in harness, dragging him behind me, straining at his weight. Out the kitchen door and down the two steps to the back yard. Bump, bump, went his head. I paused to lock the door. Little Edward slept upstairs, alone. I wished Mother was still alive, or that I had a brother or sister to help me with the grisly task. But there was just me, alone as always.

"Sleep, Edward," I whispered up to his room. "Mama will be back soon."

It was all downhill to the wharf. Had anyone looked down their windows to the harbor that had once bustled with life, but now sat mostly empty, the fog would have covered my passage. I stopped on the wharf, heart pounding. *You can do this. It's only a boat. You won't fall out.* Moonlight filtered through the fog as I pulled my stiffening burden across old, weathered planks, rolling William in his tarp into the dinghy and untying the rope from its metal ring. Stepping into the dinghy was the bravest thing I had ever done, my terror of the water overcome by my need to dispose of the tarp and its contents. The tide was with me as I rowed out to the deep-water channel where the icy current would carry William away.

He always wanted to be buried at sea. He made me promise that, if he died on land, I would be sure his body was laid to rest in the ocean he loved. I had prayed his ship would be lost; that some week he just wouldn't return, a victim of a storm or a whirlpool, or the grasping tentacles of some storybook monster, ripping apart the planks, pulling sailors into its hungry beak. The gods ignored my prayers. Or maybe they made sure that, when I needed it, a knife was close at hand. Either way, William's body made a chilly splash as I heaved it over the edge of the dinghy, delivering him to whatever waited in the deep.

As I rowed back toward the dim lights of the wharf, with salt spray in my face and blood drying on my hands, I remembered the only other time I had come to the sea on my own.

Mother had always warned me away from the ocean. She'd never allowed me anywhere near the crashing waves that battered the rocks below our house. She had filled my head with stories of hungry sea monsters, sharp-toothed sirens, of selloh that could masquerade as men, and of things that had no names, sharp-clawed with tattered gills and lidless eyes that had seen the horrors of the nighttime depths. I never learned to swim, and my fear of the deep currents had kept me far from the shore—yet, on nights when the fog held off and the moon lit the waves, I felt its salty pull.

The shoals around the island had once provided us with a livelihood and, when I was a child, the fishing boats would come in from a few nights away loaded with fish. My mother had brokered the sailors' catches, as sharp-minded as any of the men she worked with. One of those fishermen must have been my father, but she had never spoken of him, and I had never asked. By the time I'd married William, the boats traveled far out of sight for a week at a time, returning half-full at best. It had only gotten worse and, by the time Mother had died, leaving me alone with the man who had become a monster, William was gone for weeks at sea—longer in the autumn, when the ocean grew colder and hungrier.

The night I buried Mother, I'd come down to the sea alone. Not to the wharf, but to the secluded beach near my childhood home, where the sound of the surf had lulled me to sleep on warm summer nights. I'd sat in the darkness, salt tears mixing with the salt breeze, after the sun had made my shadow long on the sea-washed pebbles. I'd planned to walk into the churning water and never return, but cowardice had kept me on dry land, where I'd cried until sleep had taken me, and dreamed.

In my dream, a dark shadow lurked in the water, just past the breaking waves. I watched its approach, foam sliding off its back as it beached itself in the shallow surf, arching up toward the air. Scales softened to skin, webbed fingers detached from each other and, as it pulled itself onto land, its tail split into legs. It exhaled water and inhaled air. It stood then, and looked at me with blue eyes that had seen the drowning of sailors trapped in storm-battered ships, plummeting away from the light of the surface toward the endless depths.

In the way of dreams, I was paralyzed, unable to move, to blink, to breathe. This thing, this man-shaped thing from the deep, came to me on the beach. His arms were corded muscle, his chest heaving in gulps of unfamiliar air. Mother had named a thing like this but, as he wrapped me in those arms and pressed his salty lips to mine, he needed no name. He was the sea, and I was the shore, and we broke together in waves on the pebbled beach.

When we were done, he took me by the arms and tried to drag me into the ocean. I screamed and fought, and his blue eyes filled with sadness and regret. He spoke then, through lips still flushed from my hungry kisses.

"I await you in the deep."

Finally, he released me, returning to the brine alone.

It had been dark when I awoke. My tears had dried; my mother had still been dead, fresh in her grave, and my husband had been away for another blessed week. By the time William had returned, angry at the ocean for withholding its bounty yet again, I had almost forgotten the selloh dream.

And, a month later, when I had first felt the stirring of my son in the water of my womb, I'd wept again, alone.

Edward was mercifully still asleep when I returned from dumping his father's body into the channel. I scrubbed the floor, washed my knife, and kissed my son's sleeping face.

"We're free now," I murmured, and he smiled as he dreamed a little boy's dreams.

In the morning, I bundled him against the cold, and we walked the long two miles into town. The November gray was in every eye I passed, and I pulled my cloak tighter around my ears.

They know.

It was Mother's voice, but she was four years in her grave. And of course, they didn't know. Fishing season was over, the boats moored for winter. No one would miss William until spring. And we would be long gone by then.

We had to hurry. The ferry to the mainland would stop running soon, trapping us on the island until spring allowed safe passage. But the harbormaster said he was taking one last run to stock up on provisions for winter, and of course Edward and I could purchase our passage to visit my aunt on the mainland for the holidays. No, William would not be joining us. I kept my hood pulled up, trying to hide my swollen eye, my bruised throat, and I pulled down my sleeves to cover the deep scars on my wrist. I'm sure he saw, though he didn't comment; just looked away. Everyone always just looked away.

The harbormaster said he expected a break in the weather in two days, and his ferry would leave with the evening tide. I told him we would be there, and we trudged home for the last time, dreading the trip over the ocean in the small ship that would be just a speck on the vast water.

I had two days to pack. Of course, there was no aunt on the mainland, waiting to spend joyous holidays with me and my wide-eyed son. I knew no one beyond the island; had never left its shores except in the rowboat to dispose of my husband's corpse. But, as I looked out the kitchen window, there was a break in the clouds. Chilly sunshine streamed down over the ocean, its usual gray turned to deep blue—the color of my eyes and Edward's. Our lives would be hard, but I was strong. I could cook and sew, and it didn't matter, because no matter what awaited us out there, we couldn't possibly stay here in the shadow of William's anger and Mother's fears.

We needed to take everything of value to sell when we settled in a city, to buy ourselves time while I found work. I chuckled grimly as I packed. *As if there's anything of value here.* Mother had left me some silverware and a few pieces of decent jewelry. My wedding ring was real gold and I'd be happy to part with it.

I couldn't help but look over my shoulder as I opened William's closet, still feeling his eyes on the back of my neck. *Just one eye now.* I had never been permitted to touch his things, except to wash his laundry. His clothes were worthless, but there was a trunk in the back that I hoped might hold something of value. I pulled it out, heart pounding. It was a seaman's chest, locked and rusted. Still feeling like he might come charging up the stairs at any moment and beat me senseless for opening his closet, I rummaged through the pockets of his coats, then felt around the upper shelf above the hangers until I found an old keyring with two keys. Hands sweaty, I turned the lock, and the chest clicked open.

I should have known. It was too light to be filled with the treasure I hoped for. A lone book sat in the otherwise empty chest—a leather-bound notebook with a strange symbol on the cover. Written in dark ink, the angular lines dug into my vision. I saw William's arms reaching for me, the tattoo that ran down his inner forearm, still healing when he'd breathed his last.

After sliding the trunk back into the closet, I took the book to the window. I saw Edward playing alone in the yard. He was such a good boy. He loved playing on the scrubby grass, looking out over the little wharf below, watching for his father to come home.

Clouds dimmed the room as I opened the book. The first page was dated almost a hundred years ago—a journal entry. I flipped through the pages, looking for a name, wondering whose journal William would keep locked in a trunk in his closet, but every page was filled with cramped writing, scratchy and nearly impossible to read.

A large chunk of pages in the middle had been torn out. I strained to read the words scrawled on the page just before.

Do these things where the sea cannot find you. Surround yourself with earth, with no view of sky—unintelligible scratchings—*the gift of rakoska*—unintelligible scratchings.

Rakoska? I squinted at the writing, but the word made no more sense. The torn-out pages followed, and the rest of the book was blank. *The gift of rakoska.* Was that a treasure of some kind?

I thought about the locked room in the basement. *Surround yourself with earth, with no view of sky.* I had no idea what William had done in that private room. Like the chest, it was locked, and I had never wanted to unlock it. Even now, the thought filled me with dread. But why forbid me if nothing of value was hidden inside? He had spent so much time there in the last months of his life, as the anger that was once just an occasional flash took over his entire being, always simmering and ready to boil over. I hadn't cared what he did on his long sea voyages or wrapped in the dank shadows of the basement; I had breathed easier when his eyes weren't upon me. But, whatever the gift of rakoska was, it might be down there. Edward and I needed every penny we could pull together to start our new lives. For the sake of my son, I had to look.

Later that night, when Edward was tucked into bed, I took the lantern from the back porch and lit it with a long match. Armed with the keyring, I descended the basement stairs again. The same spiderwebs tickled my skin; the same quiet skittering as I clicked on the light and roaches fled into the deep shadows.

I felt William watching me as I crossed the basement floor. *Don't ever disturb my private space,* he whispered from his watery grave. *Never bother me when I'm working.* He had never told me what he was working on, and I had never asked.

The basement smelled of rot and fish, and my hand trembled around the keyring. *It's just a door.*

But it felt like the mouth of a sleeping monster.

The lantern flickered as I pushed the key into the door. With a click like the claw of a lobster grasping for the edge of the pot, it unlocked and swung inward.

The fish smell was stronger, as was the underlying stench of mold and rot. I raised the lantern, peering into the gloom. The room was larger than I had expected, open and without furnishings except an old table against the far wall. I stepped inside.

The dirt floor was hard-packed, and my shoes scuffed into a line of something dried and flaking, dark and smelling of metal. My neck prickled, and the skin between my fingers burned as I looked down. An intricate symbol had been drawn on the floor in what had to be blood. Fish blood, from the smell of it. Someone had poured the blood carefully into a pattern that seemed to waver before my eyes, as if it were just under the ripples of a flowing tide. Bile rose in the back of my throat, and I swallowed hard.

In the center was a large flat stone and, on it, were four cups like chalices with a bowl on a thick stem—all made of carved wood, the largest sat in the center, flanked by the three smaller ones. I forced myself to look at the carvings on the stems. Of the three smaller cups, one was carved

124

with what looked like the tail of a fish, one carving was shaped like a human hand, and the third looked like a drop of water. The largest of the three wooden chalices bore the same symbol as the journal and my dead husband's arm. All were empty, though the insides of the hand and the fish tail ones were stained dark. The little tableau turned my stomach, and I stumbled away, sweating in the chill of the basement.

I didn't want to look at the table. But my feet moved on their own until I was standing before it, lantern in hand. The missing pages of the journal were there, scattered over the tabletop. A small knife lay next to the pages, along with a little bowl stained black. The fishy smell was nearly overpowering there, and I peered warily into a larger bowl—one I recognized from my kitchen. It held the decaying remains of a squid, or maybe an octopus. Tentacles draped over one edge, and the body cut open. A trail of black drops stained the table between that bowl and the smaller one. *Squid ink?* To the side of the table, a bag of rotting fish guts confirmed my suspicion that the symbol on the floor was drawn in fish blood.

What were you doing down here? But my own blood hummed the answer. *Summoning. A ritual. A sacrifice?*

Rakoska. The name from the journal bounced around the room in a silent whisper.

What were you trying to summon? The answer would be in the pages, but my throat closed as I looked at them. Vision blurring, choking back bile in the rotten-fish chamber of evil—for no ritual he had been doing there could possibly be anything holy—I looked at the pages where they lay, and read their words.

Blood of the deepwater fish, poured from the raw flesh onto the hidden earth... On another page, words below the symbol on the journal's cover confirmed that the dark bowl was full of squid ink, and the knife had cut the symbol into William's arm, inking the tattoo straight from the bowl. I didn't want to read about the ritual, and some of the pages were stained with blood and ink. I saw the symbols from the three small wood cups. *Blood of man, blood of selloh, water of the sea at new moon.*

Mother had told me about the selloh, monsters of legend; fish in the water, men on land. Mother had also told me about sea monsters and bogeymen and pixies and Santa Claus. No doubt there was a fish called selloh, and it was probably one of the bagged carcasses making my eyes water from the stench. Its blood, the blood of a man—William?—and seawater were mixed in the larger chalice and consumed by the one who...

The page was blurred with blood there, but I saw the word "rakoska" again.

The stench of the room was overwhelming me. I was getting dizzy, and there was clearly no treasure here—nothing I could take to fund a new life for me and Edward. We would have to get by. And my desire to get away from this place, to board a ship and turn my back on this island, and never, ever look back, was a solid rock in my soul.

I locked the door behind me, ran up the basement stairs, and burst through the back door, taking huge gasps of clean salt air.

The next night, the ferry would take us away from this place. I looked out over the sea for the last time, taking in the view. The moon was nearly full, and the fog had yet to roll in. The ocean glittered like a jewel. Somewhere in its depths, William's body drifted, food for fish and things that crawled along the bottom, eyeless and razor-toothed. I smiled at the thought. He had taken from the sea his whole life, used its life and its water for the hideous ritual in the basement. Now, the sea would take him back—bite by hungry bite.

Edward held my hand as we boarded the ferry. Clouds threatened rain, and my heart was full of fear as we carried our meager belongings onto the deck. *Please hold out*, I prayed to whatever god controlled the weather. *Please let us depart this cursed dock.* My fingers were slick in Edward's small hand as I tiptoed across the plank, mindful of the swirling water below.

You can do this. A few hours and you'll never have to see this island again.

We were the only passengers, and we were invited below deck, but Edward's eyes were alight as he stood at the railing. I handed our bags to a young man, who stowed them below, but Edward and I stayed on deck, breathing in the sea spray as the sun set ahead of us in a riot of orange and pink. The deckhands cast off the lines, and I sighed as the engines churned to life, belching black smoke into the darkening sky. Wind whipped my hair from the pins that held it, and I let the hood of my cloak down, cool air on the back of my neck.

I looked back, watching the island get smaller and smaller. The little ferry swayed beneath my feet, and Edward laughed as a pod of dolphins leapt next to the ship. He reached out over the deck, and I held onto the back of his pants to keep him from toppling over. His laughter was music, and my eyes filled with tears as I realized how long it had been since I had heard the sound.

We're free.

The night settled in around us, and the dolphins dove away into the depths.

They say that fog rolls in, as if it's made in some kind of factory, belched out like smoke to cover the sea and shore. But the fog that night did not roll in from the sea. We were on the sea, our little ferry heaving left and right as the waves grew choppier, and my grip on the railing turned my knuckles white.

"It's all right, Mommy. The dolphins said it's going to be all right."

I tried to smile at Edward's fancy, but every wave sent up spray that seemed to hang in the air, the fog materializing around us until the stars and moon overhead were distant memories.

A sharp vibration banged through the deck, nearly throwing me from my feet. *Did we run aground in the fog?* But still the planks tossed beneath me.

Another bang, this one even stronger.

A cry went up from the ferry captain. "Rakoska! Sailors to arms!"

The three-man crew rushed past where Edward and I clung to the railing.

Rakoska. The word was ice in my blood. The stench of fish and blood washed over me and I heaved over the railing, sharing what was left in my stomach with the ocean below.

Gunshots rang from the front of the ship, and I bundled Edward into my arms. *Get below. Something is attacking the ship.* As the thought raced through me, I flushed with shame and fear. *Not something. The rakoska.* The thing that William had summoned in the basement. It had come for us.

Ridiculous. It was another ship—pirates, maybe. Or a whale, or a shark, or…

A tentacle slapped into the railing. I jumped back, pulling Edward away from the edge.

Slime dripped from the suckers as it was joined by another, and another. A hideous shape hauled itself up from the heaving sea, and I stared into a wide, lipless mouth ringed with triangular teeth in a hammer-shaped head. I froze in terror as it flopped over the railing, raising that head to look into my soul. One blood-rimmed brown eye blinked at me.

The other was missing, a puckered scar where it had been.

Rakoska.

It reeked of fish and rot, just like the basement where its ritual had been performed. But the ritual was not a summoning. This was no demon of the deep.

This was William, buried at sea, just like he had demanded, his corpse transformed into this monstrosity. It—I could not think of it as a he—roared at me, showering the deck with bits of rotted fish guts. A tentacle whipped toward us and I leaped back, pulling Edward with me.

From behind me, shots rang out. Bullets bounced off the thick, rubbery skin.

And, clinging to my legs, Edward laughed.

I tore my gaze from the monster that was once my husband to gape at my son. But Edward was not looking at me, nor at the rakoska. He was looking behind us. I turned.

The selloh strode across the deck, scales still turning to skin. He looked the same as I remembered from my dream—hard muscled, steel-jawed. But his eyes were not on my face or my body. With a roar of his own, the selloh launched himself at the rakoska.

Tentacles wrapped around him, tearing at his skin. A sailor threw a metal-tipped harpoon that embedded itself in the rakoska's hide, but another tentacle ripped it free and tossed it aside. Five tree-thick tentacles flung the selloh off the deck into the angry ocean below.

Again, the brown eye that had so recently stared sightlessly at my kitchen ceiling turned on me. With another belching roar, the rakoska whipped out a tentacle, snaring Edward around the waist. My son was ripped from my grasp and hurled over the railing. He did not scream as he fell into the sea.

Rage, white hot and foaming, boiled inside me. I threw myself at the rakoska, the monster that was my husband, beating at the rubbery skin, screaming wordless agony into its wide-open mouth. It hauled me up, tentacles around my waist, and a guttural sound bubbled from its maw. It was trying to talk, but no words could come from the horror of its throat.

As if it heard my thought, a tentacle wrapped around my neck, still raw from the night it tried to strangle me when it was still William, and squeezed. This time, I had no kitchen knife.

But I had pins in my hair.

I whipped a long skewer of whalebone from my head and plunged it into the rakoska's single brown eye.

It screamed and dropped me onto the heaving deck.

And, from the other side of the railing, the selloh leaped up, dragging the anchor chain in arms that were still covered in scales. He wrapped it around the blind rakoska's neck, pulling with all his might. Huge muscles strained and the rakoska's tentacles flailed until, with a wet, sticky splat, its head popped free of its body. Black blood sprayed over the deck and, in three breaths, the body of the rakoska lay still.

The selloh turned to me. Those blue eyes, no longer a dream, bored into my own. Frozen in shock and grief, I stood still as he took my arms as he had years before. He had tried to pull me into the ocean that night, to drown me in the merciless deep. This time, I let him.

Just like my son, I did not scream as I plunged over the railing. I felt no cold as the water closed over my head. The survival reflex tried to plug my throat, but I forced myself to open my mouth, breathing in the water. *Let it be fast.* Without Edward, my life was not worth another breath.

I felt a pull at my heavy skirt and opened my eyes in the saltwater.

Edward smiled up at me. Tiny scales covered his face, and he grasped my hand with webbed fingers. His legs had given way to an iridescent tail that swished happily as he snuggled into my arms.

Just like the night on the beach, the selloh gently removed my clothing. I did not need it. My shining new scales were protection enough. My perfect tail shimmied out of the skirt, and I spun in the water, holding my son with webbed hands.

I exhaled the last bubbles of air, reveling in the feel of water in my lungs.

Mother had never told me who my father was. But she had known about the selloh. Oh, yes, she'd known.

A huge splash thumped into the water from above. The headless rakoska, the remains of my husband, plummeted toward the bottom of the sea, tentacles spread as it sank.

The selloh took my hand and, again, I looked into his deep blue eyes.

I always knew he would come back for his son.

We turned in the water, the three of us together at last. Moonlight flashed on our scales as we dove into the warmth of the deep blue ocean.

CHAPTER EIGHT

FROM BELOW
R.B. Thorne

In a ramshackle cottage by the wild gray Atlantic, an old woman sat alone at her table with a deck of tarot cards far older than she was. Salty air pelted against the sides of her home; the familiar odors of rock and salt and damp hissed in on ocean air currents, permeating the house with all the smells of the sea. All but one. Cora couldn't remember how long it had been since she was blessed with the stench of fresh-caught fish as boats returned to the harbor.

Why did she keep doing this to herself?

Perhaps there would be peace in simply letting go.

Part of Cora wished she could finally move on; maybe even rest as time worked its relentless, destructive magic on the town. But she never would. She was beholden to it—to the rocks and sea and sky, and to those that dwelled in the deep—and she would be until her body was reclaimed by the sea.

She reached for her cup of steaming, honeyed wormwood tea, sipped slowly, and flipped the first card, the past. The Ace of Cups, a card of prosperity and joy, brought a wistful smile to her weathered face, green eyes glittering with unshed tears. When the fishing had first begun to decline, she'd known the worst was yet to come. First, it would be the fish. Then, the tourists. And, sure enough, year after year, the town would collapse in on itself, a forgotten relic of far better times. She'd seen it all coming, plain as the lines on her own palm, or the cards she laid out on her little round table day after day. She'd told the people of Brackish Harbor, but no one had believed her. Bit by bit, the village had left the old ways behind. People had given up the ancient rites and sacred covenants and thus the bounties and protections they'd taken for granted had gradually faded.

She flipped the second card, signifying the present. The Five of Pentacles slapped the table with a sharp *flick* and stared at her, defiant. Misery, misfortune, and poverty. She scoffed. So many readings, all amounting to the same thing. She really didn't know why she kept this up. She turned the last card over with a sigh, steeling herself against the pessimism and anger bubbling in her gut.

The Fool was a surprise. In all the times she'd consulted the cards since Brackish Harbor had gone to hell, Cora had never drawn a future card that wasn't bleak. This card—optimism, innocence, and new beginnings—gave her pause and, perhaps worse, hope. Something had changed in the last twenty-four hours, something that could finally turn the tide for all of them.

"They came out of nowhere."

Beth had kept repeating it, over and over, a mantra to ward off fault or anger or harm. Only it didn't, couldn't, not when the sounds of crunching metal and shattering glass still rang in Amy's ears; not with the deep ache throbbing across her head and neck and back. Black spots bloomed like mold at the edges of her vision: whether it was a side-effect of the collision, or shock, or a physical manifestation of her mind trying to cling to the here and now, she couldn't tell.

The last several hours—maybe less?—blended together like watercolors, mixing until it was all a muddy gray: The crash, a hit and run. Pain. Confusion. A police cruiser driving them onto a ferry. Resentment bubbling in Amy's chest when Beth bummed a smoke off the cop, even though she was supposed to be quitting. Air thick with salty sea mist. A rocky island appearing out of the gloom; a sad little town. A mechanic who made Amy's skin crawl when he looked at her and made her bristle when he looked at Beth. A long, long walk.

There were definite gaps in Amy's memory, leaving more questions than clear details. For one, how had their car made it to the island? Or, maybe it hadn't. Was the mechanic back on the mainland? That couldn't be right. Why would they have come to the island at all, then? But Beth wouldn't have just followed some strange cop onto a ferry without asking questions, and she did seem a lot more lucid than Amy felt. Amy had probably forgotten. So many details of the day were hazy and out of order. That was it. She'd simply forgotten.

Amy blinked, and found herself standing outside a giant, weatherbeaten house with a little wooden sign identifying it as "Seaview Inn." The Tiffany blue paint was flaking in more places than it held on to. It was colder than it had been, and the sky grew darker by the second.

The interior of the hotel was somehow more run-down. The pale seafoam paint on the walls peeled to reveal swaths of mildew and spiderweb cracks in the plaster. The lighting fixtures, white sconces shaped like cupped seashells fixed to each wall, overflowed with cobwebs; cornucopias of ruin and neglect. There wasn't a lot of dust—not in this humidity—but a layer of undisturbed grime blanketed every surface. An acrid tang permeated the air, replacing the smell of brine with something not too far from cat piss.

Amy's body tensed. She glanced at Beth, whose brows were also furrowed. But Beth shrugged as if to say, *What else are we going to do?* The mechanic had told them they'd be lucky to have their car back within three days, and they had to sleep somewhere in the meantime.

Beth reached out a tentative hand to ring a small, tarnished brass service bell.

A choked little *ding* rang through the hauntingly still lobby and, no more than a second later, a short, rail-thin woman came bustling around the corner, all smiles. She stopped a few yards shy of the pair to smooth her rumpled black dress. "Well, hel-lo!" she cried, placing a practiced emphasis on the syllables. "Officer Andrews told me you'd be coming this way. Welcome!"

Beth thanked her, and Amy stood silent.

"It's awful, what happened to you two," she went on. "Thank goodness you're both in one piece!"

The pain in Amy's spine pulsed as if in response.

They were walking, climbing a flight of stairs. When had they left the lobby?

"You'll be staying in our best room," said the hotelier—what was her name? Had she introduced herself? "It's normally for honeymooners but, as long as you don't mind sharing a bed, it'll be just fine."

Beth said something, but she sounded like Amy was hearing her through a closed door. Since the moment the other driver struck their car, she had been in a mental fog. Everything seemed so far away and like it was happening all at once.

Amy blinked, and they were standing in front of a door that had once been white, with a tarnished brass 6 hanging on by one little nail.

"Here we are," the woman sang. "My apartment is on the first floor, and you're the only guests!" She punctuated that with a weird chuckle. "So, if you need anything, you can find me there, day or night."

With a final cheerful smile that was so frighteningly wide it almost seemed forced, she was off again; her lopsided, silvery-blonde beehive hair bounced down the dim hallway until it disappeared around a corner that seemed miles off. Beth unlocked the door to room six.

In years past, Amy imagined, this town had probably been idyllic—a sweet little weekend getaway. But whatever had happened in the interim had drained it of anything resembling life. The smell of mold that had crept into Amy's nostrils in the lobby was ten times worse in the room. She nearly gagged, and wondered how long it had been since anyone had opened a window, let alone stayed there.

She didn't offer to help Beth with the bags. The pain was beyond distracting, overtaking her every thought. She sat on the mattress, barely noticing the resulting puff of dust.

"Well this place is…" Beth trailed off as she spun in a slow circle.

"I think I need to see a doctor," Amy blurted, words tumbling thick and awkward off her dry tongue.

Beth faced her. "Are you really in that much pain?" she asked, tilting her head. "They hit my side, and I'm basically fine."

"And?"

"It's going to drain us even faster. We're short on cash as it is."

Amy's brow furrowed. "Don't you think I know that? I'm in pain. We got into a goddamn car wreck. Are you honestly telling me I *shouldn't* see a doctor?"

Beth grimaced, and her brown cheeks flushed with shame. "No. No, of course not. I'm sorry, that was a rotten thing to say. Let's find you a doctor. Tomorrow, though, okay? It's late."

There was no clock in the room, but the sky was a dark, bruised purple, and the streetlamps had come on. Amy caught their reflections in the window. In her brightly-colored shift dress with her fiery red hair, she reminded herself of a small, frightened bird, blown in on an unforgiving wind from some warmer, friendlier climate. Beth stood behind her, staring at the back of her head. Her curly black hair was mussed and frizzy from the humidity, and her dark eyes were as unreadable as calm water. Amy thought she detected a small flicker of something beneath the surface—some stronger emotion Beth wasn't expressing—but she couldn't be sure. Couldn't trust what she saw. As she watched Beth watching her, she didn't notice the thin gray mist that crept along the road outside, blanketing the town.

That night, Amy's dreams were vivid and terrifying. Visions of roiling black water and fog and mad, leering faces with foam-covered rocks for teeth and little white shells for eyes. Beth was nowhere to be found, and Amy had the sense she'd been abandoned. She was balanced on a cliffside, her back to the long, long drop and, as she stared at the teeming mass of inhuman townsfolk, she could easily pick out the faces of the cop, the mechanic, and the hotelier, right at the front. Their vacant white eyes burned with desire—desire to see her fall, to see her body plummet and shatter on the dark, wet rocks below. Amy screamed, but her voice was the cries of gulls and the crashing of waves. Then, they were upon her, their hands shoving and groping. She fell.

Amy gasped as she woke, breath ragged and heart thundering. She glanced around the unfamiliar space, only remembering after far too long where she was: Brackish Harbor. Tears leaked from the corners of her eyes into her hair and ears as the memories slammed into her. She forced herself upright and stretched, turning her head slowly from left to right, trying to lean into the ache. As she did, she took in the whole panorama of the room: the door, closed and locked. The room, sparse and musty and decorated in a kitschy beach theme.

The window, open? A slight, hunched frame just outside. A wide smile that cut across the shadowed face. Jagged, yellow teeth, glinting in the darkness.

A wordless cry burst from Amy's mouth. She reached for the lamp, wrenching her spine in the process. She yelped again, pained. The light illuminated the room and the area just outside the open window. The frame was empty; nothing but a white fence and the empty town beyond.

"Whatissit?" Beth mumbled, turning over and draping an arm across Amy's lap.

Amy blinked a few times, unable to take her eyes off the perfect square of empty space. It *had* been closed. She remembered, she *knew* it had.

Hadn't it?

"I...had a nightmare."

"Of course you did. Come here, love."

"One second," Amy said. She got up, padded across the chilly room, and shut the window. After casting one more furtive glance outside, she pulled the curtain too.

Just out of her field of view, a figure shuffled around the corner of the Seaview Inn, off the property, and back toward the water.

"Why did you have to do that?" Amy demanded. She quickened her pace to keep up with Beth as she stormed out of the old colonial house that served as both residence and office for the one doctor in town. Overhead, the midmorning sky darkened as thick storm clouds moved in from the east.

"Do what? Defend you?"

"No, before that. You put your hand on my leg. You had to know he'd see!"

The old doctor's demeanor had shifted so quickly from kind and caring—if a little patronizing—to stone-cold, as though Amy's pain suddenly meant nothing, the moment Beth's fingers grazed her knee.

"*And?*" Beth whirled around, throwing her hands out. "We shouldn't have to hide just to be treated the same as everyone else, especially by a goddamned *doctor!*"

Had she been trying to prove some sort of point, then? Amy was dizzy with anger and pain and—if she was being honest with herself—leftover resentment from the crash that had sent them into this horrible detour.

"This isn't California, Beth!" she shouted. "People *are* bigots! They *do* treat us differently! And now I'm still in pain, and we're stuck in this foul place, running out of money, and it's all *your* fault!"

As she shouted, the police cruiser that had brought them to town rounded the corner and rolled slowly by. Amy stopped yelling and stood there seething. She hadn't realized she'd meant it until the words left her lips. It was Beth's fault. All of it. If she'd only have yielded at that junction, none of this would be happening. They'd be meeting up with friends in New York by now, their last big stop before the long drive home. But they were here, in Brackish Harbor, where no one cared if they lived or died.

She turned away to hide the tears threatening to spill down her red cheeks.

"Jesus, Amy," Beth said. "You really know how to make me feel like a piece of shit."

Amy didn't turn to look at her, not even when she made a production of sighing heavily and walking away, back toward the hotel.

Amy let herself cry then. Being alone in that place was no better or worse than being there with Beth; Amy could no longer hold on to everything she'd been keeping in since the accident. The shock had worn off, leaving her standing in the middle of an empty sidewalk, sobbing.

"You and your lady friend having a bit of a domestic?" The voice caught Amy off guard. When she opened her eyes to see the policeman, she wasn't sure what to think, but was very aware of how alone she was.

"I, um…it's fine, officer."

"Call me Harvey."

She felt herself shrinking back into old habits of gratuitous respect for people with the power to hurt her. She ducked her head and averted her eyes in an instinctive display of submission. "Oh, alright. Thank you, Harvey. Everything is fine. I think the day is just catching up with me. I should probably try to find my…friend."

The word felt like more of a betrayal than it usually did. It tasted sour and mean as it crawled down her tongue.

"Doc's a bit old school," said the cop, as though she hadn't spoken at all. "If you're still in need of a remedy, I know a place you can go. She's not a doctor, but she can help."

"Is it…is it legal?"

He snarled, "Would I be sending you there if it wasn't, girl?"

Amy's stomach lurched. "Sorry. No. Of course not."

"Her name is Cora. She lives by the old waterfront. Head up Main Street until you can't anymore, then go left. Look for the fortune teller sign in the window."

"Thank you, sir," she said. "Really, thank you."

"It's no trouble. Been a while since we've had new blood in Brackish Harbor. We're all a bit rusty with socializing. But she'll do what's needed. You won't be in pain much longer."

Amy thanked him again and turned in the direction he'd pointed, up the long stretch of road toward the coast.

Cora leaned heavily on her driftwood cane as she set a pot of water to boil. Harvey was the only one with her phone number, and he never called unless it was important. So, when it had rung a few minutes before, she'd known—she'd just known—it would be good news.

"You can't miss her," he'd said. "She looks like you."

He'd always been loyal, ever since the better days, when she was a pretty young thing with hair of fire and eyes that glittered like sea glass, and he was a slip of a boy with straight, wide shoulders and a shiny new badge. His father had introduced him to her family and taught him the old ways, and his part in them: conceal the rituals, at all costs.

Sometimes, Cora wondered if they'd been too thorough, scrubbing the town of its belief along with its survival instinct. No one even spoke of the Old Gods anymore, let alone prayed or sacrificed to them.

It used to be so easy. In the high season, when parties went on all night and the elders of Brackish Harbor worked together, all she had to do was wait for one fool to wander off on their own. She would do her part, and everyone else would do theirs. But, one by one, the elders had died off, and the next generation, improperly educated in the old ways, had eschewed their beliefs—superstition, they called it—in favor of new ideas.

And here they all were, trapped in this desolate, haunted, liminal space, neither part of the world, nor beyond it.

After two years of bad fishing, she had understood what was happening and tried to remedy it. A young boy, barely three years old and born in Brackish Harbor, wandered past her hut on a cool spring morning. He'd lost his mother and his way, and Cora had found him toddling along the rocks by the sea. The town was destitute, she was desperate, and the tide was coming in. She'd barely allowed herself a moment's thought.

She sighed and returned to her tea, unable to stare into the sad, dilapidated streets a moment longer. She tipped the contents of three small jars into the pot, added honey, and stirred. The girl would arrive soon.

Cora had never regretted pushing that little boy. Not when his tiny blonde head had split open on the rocks and his brains spilled like clams from a broken shell, and not when his mother had screamed and wailed at the fabricated news Cora had told Harvey to deliver, her sobs so loud and keening, they had reached Cora across the quiet town.

But, when the summer came and went and there were even fewer fish than the year before, and not a single tourist passed through their borders, she understood: The sea hadn't wanted one of its own. It had to be an outsider.

She couldn't let this opportunity pass her by. She wouldn't.

The eerie silence of Brackish Harbor gave way to a more natural quiet. Gulls screeched overhead and, just beyond the final row of houses and buildings, Amy could hear the ocean. It beat, steady and unceasing, against the black rocks, wearing them down slowly, slowly, into nothingness.

The thought was somehow calming. All things returned to the sea.

California beaches were so very different from this place. Even the smaller coastal towns had an air of constant movement, bright colors, and *life*. Here, it felt like Amy had fallen through some tear in the world and landed in a desolate place of *used-to-be*. For a moment, she wondered whether she was destined to wander alone forever among the abandoned shacks, with their boarded windows and sad painted signs, drained of their vibrance by years of sun damage and neglect.

Walking had seemed to calm her pain, somehow. But the chill exacerbated it. Ocean spray blew in on the wind, and cold flecks of water spattered her cheeks and limbs as she searched for the house Officer Andrews had told her to find. And there it was, near the end. A faded black sign with gold lettering, hanging crooked in the front window of a tiny shack with a blood-red door.

PAST ☆ PRESENT ☆ FUTURE
FORTUNES AND READINGS
$5

Amy smiled with relief and stepped up to the door. As she raised her hand to knock, it swung open with a low groan. A tall, frail-looking old woman smiled down at her.

"Why, hello," she said, voice as thin as sea mist. "What can I do for you, dear?"

"Are you Cora? Officer Andrews told me you might be able to help me. We crashed our car just outside town…" Amy trailed off, assuming the woman—like everyone else in Brackish Harbor thus far—had heard about her and Beth. But the old lady's mouth dropped open and her hand fluttered to her heart.

"Oh, you poor thing! Are you in need of a remedy?" She ushered Amy inside as she spoke. "I guess that's why Harvey sent you my way. He's such a nice man. Come here, sit. Let's warm your bones. I just happened to put on a pot of tea. Here, sit, sit. Such a lovely girl."

Amy thanked Cora and sipped at the tea. The liquid was smooth with a heavy, almost syrupy sweetness to it. She cradled the little red cup in both palms, allowing it to warm her from without and within.

"Now," said Cora, "tell me where it hurts."

"My neck, and my back. And I've had this fog, do you know what I mean? I can't think properly. Things seem to be happening out of order. Or, no. Not out of order. It's more like I'm missing pieces of time. I'll blink, and an hour has gone by. Does that make sense?"

The woman placed a cool, bony hand on Amy's forearm. "You've had a shock. A terrifying experience. It's only natural for you to feel out of sorts."

"Can you help me?"

"Absolutely. Just as soon as you finish your tea, we'll get started. And, by the time I'm done, I promise, your pain will be the last thing on your mind."

Amy gulped down her tea, pushing through the last sip of gritty sediment, and set the cup down. "I'm ready," she said. "Please, Cora, take my pain away."

Cora's smile grew, and she pushed herself into a standing position. "We'll need to harvest a few things from the area. Some sea grass; a few herbs. Come, take my arm. I'm not near as steady as I used to be, and the way is a bit treacherous for an old lady like me."

She put a large jar of some dark liquid into a weathered old woven bag, slung it across her shoulder, and placed a long-fingered hand on Amy's arm as they made their way around the back of the house and down to the rocky coastline.

"Just over here," said Cora. She leaned her weight on Amy as they picked their way across the rocks. "My grandmother planted these herbs when she was about your age. I've been tending to them all my life. They've healed far worse injuries than yours."

Cora had to raise her quaking voice to be heard over the crashing waves. The tide was coming in. Had Amy arrived any later, this path would have been impossible to traverse. She smiled in silent relief at her luck.

Beth sat in the room they shared for all of five minutes before her anger gave way to sorrow. After ten minutes of waiting at the Seaside Inn, she went back to find Amy. No matter how angry either of them were, there was no reason to split up in this eerie place. They could fight in their room, and that would be fine. At least they'd be safe.

But, when she got back to where she'd left Amy, Amy wasn't there.

Her guts twisted tighter with every new thought of possible horrors as she made her way back to the inn. Something about the place just got right under Beth's skin, from the first moment she'd met that weird cop to now, in this creepy, moldering hotel.

"Excuse me?" she said as she approached the hotelier's office. She rapped lightly on the frame, though the door was ajar.

Through the crack, she spied as Mira sat hunched over, as though she were sleeping. She straightened as soon as she heard Beth's tapping. As she turned, Beth caught a glimpse of what appeared to be the woman's more natural state. Her expression, unguarded for the briefest second, held a bottomless, resigned quality. Sadness, maybe? But it was instantly replaced with the same bright, welcoming smile as the day before. Only, this time, Beth noticed the disconnect between Mira's mouth and eyes, like oil and water. The edges of her lips were framed by deep curving creases, but no crow's feet lived in the downturned corners of her eyes, only a permanent pair of wrinkles between her blonde brows.

"Hello!" she trilled, springing up from her chair. "How are you and your lovely friend? Is there anything I can do for you?"

"I...I'm looking for her, actually." The words stuck on Beth's tongue, the wrongness of the situation blooming further in her chest.

Mira's facial muscles shifted, her smile becoming one of confusion.

"We sort of had an argument," Beth went on, "and I came back here. I thought she would eventually follow me, but she's not here, and she's not where I left her. Is there maybe a diner, or some other place she might have found nearby?"

The woman placed a comforting hand on Beth's arm. "Well, I'm sure everything's alright. Where did you two split up?"

"Out in front of the doctor's office. He was supposed to help her. She's in pain from the accident. But he didn't help her, he just sent us off." And Amy was in pain and alone in this ghostly place, and Beth was trying very hard not to panic.

"The doctor's office. Downtown?"

"Isn't that the only one you have?"

Mira's already pale face drained of its remaining color. Her still smiling lips pressed together.

"Mira?"

Her eyes darted back and forth, as though she was afraid of being overheard in the empty lobby. She leaned in. "There's...someone else," she whispered. Her smile had finally dropped, and so too did the world from under Beth's feet.

"What do you mean? Another doctor?"

Somehow, she knew that wasn't the answer.

"No, not a doctor, but..." Mira's grip tightened on Beth's arm until it hurt. "She's dangerous. You need to go get your girl and run."

"I don't..." Beth's words sounded so far away, as if she were hearing herself from underwater. "I don't understand."

142

"That witch, she took my son. Killed him. I know she did, no matter what they tell me. She's ruthless, as single minded as a shark on the hunt, and I'd bet my life that she's set her sights on your lady. I knew as soon as you showed up here. I should have said…" Mira shook her head. "Go up the main road until you get to the boardwalk. Turn left, and find the fortune teller's hut. Then you get Amy, and leave. I'll pack up your things, and I'll call Charlie—the ferryman—and tell him to be ready. He will help you, I'm sure of it. Please hurry. I'm so sorry. But she won't stop. She'll never stop. Go, Beth. Now!"

She let go, and Beth didn't hesitate for a second. She turned and ran.

"So, you were born here?"

"No, no. My mother was running an errand two towns north of here the day I was born. It was pure chance that I came into the world somewhere else. But I would never dream of calling anywhere but Brackish Harbor my home. Just over here, do you see?"

Amy squinted toward where Cora was pointing. Splotches of green and purple and white were visible all along the rocky coast and cliffside. From where they were, everything was blurry. Or perhaps it was the sea mist in Amy's eyes. Everything seemed to swim and shift the more she tried to focus on it.

"I think I need to stop for a moment," Amy said. Her legs were heavy, and balancing on the uneven rocks had made her spine ache with effort.

Cora's step quickened, pulling Amy along, wrenching the young woman's arm in her haste.

Amy yelped. "You're hurting me. Please, I need to stop."

Cora turned and glanced toward the town. Her eyes narrowed. "It's too late for that, girl," she hissed. All traces of warmth and tenderness were gone, leaving behind a menacing, stone-faced terror of a person.

"What's too late, what do you mean?" Amy asked. But, even as the words spilled from her mouth, thick and too round for her tongue, she realized that something was terribly wrong.

The old woman pulled harder, unrelenting, her strength accentuated by Amy's sudden bone-deep weakness. She struggled to keep her eyes focused. Ahead, the rock slope climbed, and the path twisted until its abrupt end at the edge of a high cliff.

Through the sound of the waves and the screeching of the gulls, Amy could make out the cry of a lone beach bird. It almost sounded like it was calling her name.

She couldn't remember climbing the narrow cliff path, but she was looking down at all the purple and green foliage, and farther—much farther—at the rocks and white foam of the churning sea. She gasped and moaned, clutching desperately to Cora's shawl and sleeves and hands.

"Please," Amy managed, her words more slurred by the second. "What're you doing? What'd you do to me?"

The old wretch laughed, a short, bitter barking noise. She did not answer. Instead, she took the arm she was holding and twisted it behind Amy's back, sending white-hot pain throughout her body. Black and silver stars exploded across her vision, and she went down hard on her knees. Through the thundering of her own heart, she was dimly aware of the woman's voice, low and fast, chanting.

"Hear me, Gods of Old. Hear me and know I am your faithful servant. Long have we waited for a worthy sacrifice, long have we wanted for the bounty of your favor. May this offering of flesh and bone, anointed with the blood and ash of our forebears, quench your mighty thirst."

Cora dipped her fingers into the jar from her bag and drew them back, coated in something slick and dark and viscous. She smeared it across Amy's forehead.

The gull cried again, louder and closer. In her daze, Amy would have sworn it really was calling her name. Maybe it was the god to whom the old woman spoke, come to collect its sacrifice.

"Take her now, and allow us to again bask in the warmth of your favor. For we are yours—this place and these people—now and forever."

A rumbling from below, loud and deep, drew her attention. Something stirred in the brine, making it bubble and roil and crash against the cliffside in unnatural patterns. And there—was she hallucinating? Or were several long, thick, meaty gray tentacles rising from the deep? A mouth, wide and gaping and terrible, opened in the dead center of the disturbance. Hundreds upon hundreds of sharp, jagged yellow teeth spiraled down as far as Amy could see into what must have been the thing's throat.

Amy whimpered and squeezed her heavy eyelids shut. She hoped whatever happened next would be quick.

"Beth," she whispered, "I'm sorry."

A sudden, final jolt of pain and the sound of body knocking against body cut off the witch's next words. Amy opened her eyes to find a struggle, two people grappling right next to her. Cora's growls were half-feral as she clawed at the face of the interloper, opening three deep slashes in her right cheek.

Beth cried out but did not relent. She swung a right hook at the old hag's face, but Cora was quick, and her dodge threw Beth off balance. Amy struggled to her feet just as Cora grabbed the front of Beth's sweater with her blood-covered hand and gave a hard shove.

Everything slowed down. Amy's scream was visceral. She lunged for her lover, falling hard as she caught hold of someone—one of them—just as both Cora and Beth tumbled, screaming, over the cliff's edge.

As the hand of whoever she held clutched her arm, Amy choked out a short, heavy sob. Had she already lost Beth? Should she just let go?

"Amy?" called a small, unsteady voice.

"Beth!" she cried. Her grip was weak, her body still swimming with whatever the witch had given her.

"There are footholds down here. I think I can climb up. Don't let go, alright?"

Amy smiled through her tears. "Never."

On the dark gray rocks below, a body lay shattered. Limbs bent at odd angles, and skin and bone split and splintered on the jagged edges, spilling blood into the sea. Her desperation drained away too, with the bright red rivulets, as she watched the sacrifice and the disruptor disappearing over the top of the cliff.

She had been the last true believer. No one else had the devotion or the knowledge or the *strength* to carry on the practice. Perhaps Brackish Harbor would finally collapse into true ruin and be swallowed whole by the sea it had long taken for granted.

Or perhaps...

Perhaps she *was* the sacrifice. All her years of caring for the town and its people; all her own personal sacrifices and hardships and *love* for the place and its gods had caused her to forget that she, too, was an outsider by simple definition. She'd been born outside Brackish Harbor, and perhaps her life had always been leading to this moment. Maybe, somehow, her mother knew what she might be called to do in service of her gods.

Something long and smooth brushed against her ankle. An exploratory stroke. The heat of it lingered on her skin. Not hot like a fever, but warm, like her wormwood tea.

Perhaps it would be painful—the embrace of her ancient deity—or maybe the teeth and tentacles would come after the drowning. After her spirit was gone and only her broken body remained. She wondered if her God would show her that final mercy. Surely, she had earned that.

With that thought, Cora sighed a final ragged breath as the incoming tide washed up around her.

Two young people who never should have come to Brackish Harbor limped west up the main road. Sand and dirt caked their knees and elbows. A dry smear of blood-soaked ash flaked off Amy's forehead like old paint. The pieces fluttered away unnoticed, carried off on the cool coastal breeze. Beth leaned heavily on her, half-dragging her twisted ankle, face red with effort. It hurt to carry her partner, but Amy wasn't going to let go for anything. Neither of them dared to look back. Exhaustion scratched at the edges of their artificial, shock-driven stamina. Soon, they would collapse. Soon, they could rest. But first, they had to get far away.

As they trudged toward the ferry, they stopped at a faded blue house with its shutters closed tight and two backpacks sitting on the front step. A small, thin woman in black passed them on the walkway and dipped her chin in wordless greeting. Beth nodded in acknowledgement and, glancing down at what Mira was holding, nodded again in grave approval.

The gas can in Mira's hand was heavy, and it slowed her pace, but not by much. The liquid sloshing inside reassured her of her purpose, and the rightness of it. The matchbook in her pocket fit perfectly into the palm of her small hand and she ran her thumb along the rough striker strip, back and forth, like a prayer.

She marched toward the coast she had grown to despise, one last time.

CHAPTER NINE

BLOOD UPON BLOOD

Mary Tait

It was a damp night on the eve of October when the first fish screamed. Seamus Lynch had returned home late that night, his boots crusted with sand and sea foam. Nothing was on but a small light in the kitchen, glowing over the table and the lone place setting left for him. His wife and daughter were asleep though, as he lay a pile of mackerel on the counter, he heard the whispering steps of his wife's feet.

Removing his boots and coat, he went to wash his face when Eliza crept down the stairs, her straw hair bound in a soft braid. "You're back late," she said. She handed him a cloth to dry his face, then worked her shawl back onto her shoulders. "Another good day?"

"An excellent day." Seamus slipped one of the striped fish from the string. "There are an unusual number of fish in the waters."

"Are they good?"

"The richest I've ever tasted." He motioned to the string of fish. "Douglas and I cooked some this afternoon while we were sorting. I brought some for you and Jenny to try."

His wife reached for them but he waved her upstairs. "I'll take care of it."

"Are you sure?"

"Yes. I'm going to cook one before heading to bed."

Her soft kiss tickled his beard. "Thank you."

Seamus watched the drifting hem of her nightgown and smiled.

She had been brave, moving from the city to such a solitary place. Men had dressed their best when they met her, tipping their hats and smoothing their collars like peacocks. She could have had her choice of the most respectable of them, but she chose the burly seaman with only a trunk of clothes and a dream.

He watched her hurry up the cold stairs on her toes, casting him a loving glance before vanishing into the dark.

Releasing the exhaustion from his lungs, Seamus grabbed a cutting board, drew a knife, and rolled his sleeves higher up his thick wooly forearms. He had aligned the blade with the throat— the fish released a shrill scream.

Nearly dropping the knife, Seamus jumped back and looked around. His first thought was that Jenny was hidden somewhere nearby, making silly voices, but she was still young and the voice had borne the depth and ripeness of age.

Peeking out the kitchen door, he saw nothing but a faint mist and the cold black sky hazed with the shrouded light of a waning crescent moon. He shut and locked it tight then went upstairs to his daughter's room. Peering in, he saw her huddled beneath her sheets, hair a scattered mess over her brow. Every muscle in her face showed the ease of sleep, and he knew she had not been downstairs since his return.

Moving to his room, he searched the dark for his wife or any trespassers. She stirred slightly, but she too slept in peaceful oblivion. Seamus watched her breathing and its familiar, gentle rhythm, allowing it to settle his heart.

He was tired. The entirety of Brackish Harbor was in a flurry to impress Mr. Langford, and Seamus had spent almost every night of the last month fishing, sorting, and presenting the hotel and restaurant proprietor with the island's finest offerings.

Yes. It was his tired mind that had conjured the fish screaming.

Taking one last look around the room, he returned to the kitchen.

The scales of the mackerel roughed his hands as he gripped the body, lowering the knife to its neck.

The fish screamed, the shudder of its breath crawling up Seamus's palm.

He dropped it.

It stopped screaming.

Setting the knife aside, he pried the mouth open with his thumb and peered inside. Nothing was there that shouldn't be. He laid the fish down and prepared to cut again.

The tip of the knife came within a centimeter of the belly.

The fish screeched, eye twitching, jaw cocked open in an expression of total and utter terror. The vibration of its voice shook its body. It began to wriggle, eye never leaving Seamus's face.

With a cry, Seamus slammed the blade through its neck. It fell silent.

Swallowing the flutter of his heart, Seamus crossed himself and tossed the body and head into the trash. He fetched another fish and set it on the counter.

He took several slow and steady breaths, shutting his eyes to clear his mind. It was exhaustion. Hunger. The sooner he had some food and rest, the better he would feel. A few moments passed before he brought the knife near its flesh.

It did not move or mutter.

Muttering another prayer, he severed its neck. The head dropped as cleanly as that of every other fish in his life had, its long-dead eye staring off in empty lethargy. He slit its belly and prepared to clean out its innards—but hesitated. His eyes went to the fish in the trash, its lonely face staring at him.

Huffing and muttering to himself, he did another round of the house, even searching cupboards and nooks for anything that could be hiding. He found nothing.

On his return to the kitchen, he snatched a pan and placed it on the stovetop. He began to gut the fish when he happened to look down.

The head of the first fish lay on the floor, mouth agape, its eye fixed on him.

Seamus did not sweat or swallow. Only his breathing tightened—as if a momentary restraint of air would reign in his imagination.

Taking up the head and body of the first fish, he cut it open and gutted it, prying through its organs for any anomalies. Its head watched him, silent.

Unable to find anything unusual, Seamus took the fish and its innards to the dying fire in the other room. He stoked the flames, keeping an ear toward the kitchen in case an intruder showed his face. Once the blaze was aglow, he tossed in the fish, bracing for a scream.

Only the logs groaned, wondering why they were being burned at the late hour.

Settling on his haunches, he poked and prodded the head deeper into the flames. There he sat for well over an hour, watching the scales char and drip. His stomach forgot its hunger— his muscles, their weakness. And, in the dark and silent watch, the nightmare burned away with any memory of the morning.

Seamus woke as if he had never slept. It was a cold first of October and, even as thick and hairy as he was, Seamus shivered. Poking at the fire, he found the bones of the burned fish. They were no different from any other fishbones, but something about the empty sockets of the fish's skull dropped weights into his stomach.

He gathered the ashes and bones and wrapped them, setting them by the door to dispose of in the sea on the way to work. The scent of the day-old fish drifted through the house, their salty stink wafting Seamus awake. A splash of cold water finished his waking ritual, and he shoved on his boots in preparation to leave.

Eliza appeared in the doorway, her cherry-red shawl gathered up around her neck. "Seamus, did you sleep out here last night?"

"I sat down by the fire and fell asleep."

"Are you headed to the docks?"

"Yes. Mr. Langford will make his decision today, and we want to be ready for him."

"Is he interested?"

"It's between us and McCann."

He found the knot on the sack of ashes worked open and a skeletal head peering out. Shoving it back into the sack, he tied the knot tighter and slipped into his coat.

Eliza started a new fire. "I had a strange dream last night."

He froze. "What was it?"

"I dreamt that there was something coming up Willy's Maw and that the waves were coming in twos."

"Twos?"

"One wave after another, but side by side as if two great legs were stirring them."

Seamus studied the sack, dark eyes searching the floor for any remnants or bones left behind.

"Are you disposing of the fish?"

"Yes. Didn't want them stinking up the house. This is the one place where I can get away from them."

"Shall I expect you late again?"

"Perhaps. I hope not."

Seamus took up the bag, wished her goodbye, and made straight for the water.

The town of Brackish Harbor spread from the sea onto the hillside like the paw of a mighty wave, with its finest establishments and homes nearest the harbor, and the poorer, more forgettable facilities adorning the fringe. Seamus's home sat on the fringe, but only halfway up the hillside to the east, making it a relatively respectable but modest place to abide.

There were no other homes to the east, save the boarded shed that once resided on the property of William Peterson and his family. Old Willy, as they used to call him, had purchased the island in 1895 and fished it for over two decades, amassing a fortune with his sales. Eventually, he invited others to settle on its shores and Brackish Harbor was born.

Willy had burned his home down nearly twenty years ago, after his wife and son were swept from a ship by a spindly wave. He had lived in his shed until, in the process of being shipped to an asylum on the mainland, he leapt overboard and was lost at sea. No one had bothered to resettle the land and Seamus, who had arrived at Brackish Harbor a year later, was the only one who would pass near the property.

Shuffling downhill, he made for the lowest part of the island where he could meet the ocean unseen. Once he arrived, he yanked the knot tight one last time and hurled it and the spoiled fish into the sea. After ensuring that it sank, he hurried to his dock in the harbor.

The sky blistered with thick white cloud cover, the kind that made Seamus squint so hard he looked furious. The wind danced about the men and crates scattered along the docks, carrying with it a certain cold that promised a bitter and sedentary winter.

Seamus found Douglas, the co-captain of his fishing boat, poking around their crates, muttering something about presentation.

"Douglas?" Seamus said.

Douglas spun around, small onyx eyes blinking. "Yes?"

"Has Mr. Langford come around yet?"

"Not yet, but word has it he's left the hotel. We made fine work of the ship and our crates yesterday. All that's left is to show him the catch."

Seamus helped a crew member carry a large crate of mackerel.

"Fine luck we've had with the fish lately," Douglas said.

"Have any of the others?" Seamus said.

"I sent Bill to check the other ships yesterday. Everyone caught more fish than usual. Some said it was almost as if they were driven into the nets."

Seamus glanced at the mackerel, lifeless and expressionless in their crate.

"Do you think," Douglas said, "That perhaps Brackish Harbor's got the blessing of the Lord on it?"

"I'd like to hope so."

It wasn't more than half an hour later when a man in a clean wool suit strolled down the walk. The cigarette squeezed between his fingers trailed a fine line of smoke behind him like the banner of a tiny parade. Only a few people marched in his entourage—the most notable being his daughter, dressed in so many furs she might have been mistaken for an animal. Were it not for her soft dark eyes and gentle smile, Seamus would have attributed it to the same self-importance in her father's bearing.

"Mr. Langford, you're early," Douglas said.

"Yes, I am." He grinned with half his mouth and tapped his cigarette, dusting the dock with ash. "I hope you boys are ready for me."

"Of course, you can see yesterday's catch." Douglas brought him over to the crate.

Mr. Langford fit the cigarette in his mouth and examined the mackerel. For all his opulence, he was one of the few suited men whom Seamus had ever seen stand as near to fish as those who caught them.

"Hm, and you say they are not as popular this time of year?"

"Yes. Although we can provide a hefty catch of mackerel multiple times a year, their numbers dwindle in the colder months."

"It's perfectly fine. What matters is that the fish sell and that they taste as delightful as they look." He bent down to examine one fish, gazing sadly up at them. "I say, look at him. His mouth is so curved he looks like he's about to—"

The fish wailed, its mouth open so wide its voice blew back Mr. Langford and snuffed out his cigarette.

All those near the harbor looked in the direction of the sound, and the other fishermen stopped their work to watch. Seamus seized up the fish and hurled it into the water where it fell silent.

"Which one of you thought of that ghastly trick?" Mr. Langford said, brushing back misplaced strands of hair.

"Neither of us, Mr. Langford. It's—"

Another fish wailed and another, and another, until all the boxes rattled with their groans.

"Well, if that is what your fish are like, I will take my business elsewhere." Mr. Langford walked to the next dock while Douglas, Seamus, and their crew scrambled to stop the noise.

Each mackerel bore the same expression of agony and flapped their sleek blue bodies against the hands and faces of their captors.

"Are there any good ones here?" Douglas shoveled fish out and kicked them over the dock.

"I don't know." Seamus braced his shoulder against the crate. "Dump them over!"

Even as they pushed, the tone of the fish changed. They grew higher, shriller, louder. They beat the boxes with their tails while their wild eyes rolled in a maddened fury. The men scrambled along the dock, pushing and shoving in whole boxes as fast as they could. Each crate's tumble ended with a splash and sudden silence.

The last crate fell, and all was still.

Fish cluttered the harbor waters, floating dead and motionless.

The bewildered fishing crew searched the faces of onlookers for pity, but they were only met by unsympathetic glares. Seamus looked to where Raul McCann displayed his catch with confident flair, expecting to hear screams.

There were none. All the fish in the harbor were silent.

Bitter disappointment boiled in Seamus's chest as he watched Mr. Langford shake hands with McCann.

"So much for the Lord's blessing," Douglas muttered. "Pack it up men, we're not going out today."

A part of Seamus thought that he should say something about the first fish, but he kept quiet. The crew concluded that they had fished in bad waters, and he agreed. There seemed no other natural explanation.

The others headed home, but Seamus went west to the center of the harbor to visit Willy's Maw.

The Maw was the shallowest length of the harbor, plunging into the landscape as if a giant jaw had taken a bite of the island's crust. The town wrapped around the edge of it, giving the impression that it had avoided something unpleasant. Despite that, the rim of the Maw was the most accessible patch of sand on the island and was often crowded with children and tourists.

Seamus stood atop the tall boardwalk, watching children play. The position provided a clear view of the rising hillside where Brackish Harbor's one and only church, First Church, nested at the town's crest.

Turning, he looked out to the waves splashing at the Maw's gums. They rolled in as they had every other day he'd seen them—to the steady beat of the ocean's heart.

He watched for several minutes to be sure there was nothing strange then departed for home, rehashing the day's events in his mind.

Why had his fish, and no one else's, screamed? Had one of his crew dabbled with the devil, or was there some grave wrong he'd committed? Perhaps it had no supernatural cause at all but was some trick invented by McCann to ruin his chances of earning Mr. Langford's contract.

But theories offered little condolence, and he went home in silence.

The fish, however, weren't finished.

That evening, Raul McCann celebrated his new contract with Mr. Langford over a lavish feast at the Brackish Harbor hotel. The menu featured all of the island's delicacies, and the proprietor's specialty stargazy pie, served for Mr. Langford with all the pomp of a coronation. A pastry crust covered the fish-filled dish except where the heads of six sardines peeked through, eyes turned towards the heavens.

Mr. Langford raised his glass in a toast to honor their good health, and the servers began to cut the pie. Occupied with his cigarette, Mr. Langford didn't notice the eyes of the pie-baked fish roll in his direction. Neither did the server, who placed a hefty slice on Mr. Langford's plate.

One of McCann's crew had just told a joke, and Mr. Langford was laughing when a squeakish sort of laugh came from his dinner plate.

Looking down, he found the fish in his pie staring at him. He withdrew his cigarette, replaced it, took up a fork and—

It laughed.

Langford's cigarette nearly jumped from his mouth, and he drew the fork away.

It laughed again, stretching into an uncomfortable squeal like it was being squeezed.

The other heads in the stargazy pie joined it, wiggling in their butter crust pockets. Their squeals leapt octaves as the unsettled diners left their seats.

The stargazy fish screamed, as did the rest of the fish in the restaurant. Whether roasted, fried, or preserved, every bit and piece of fish made noise—even their flesh cried out, hoarse voices roaring between flaky layers like stifled mouths.

The servers rushed to clear the tables, only to hear a din rise from the kitchen. The noise trickled down the halls and into bedrooms as every fish in the hotel moaned and shrieked. Bones left over from room service squalled. The waste bins rattled with the flesh and discarded innards, their bellows echoing down the halls.

Servers and staff rushed to empty the building of fish, piling buckets on trolleys and racing to the shoreline. Some tried burning the bodies, but that only made things worse, as the fish screeched like they were in hell.

Mr. Langford and the other guests had fled the table, and he shut himself in his room until morning.

Under the sliver of moonlight, the staff worked for hours to quell the cacophony, loading and emptying boxes and buckets into the sea. As had the fish on the docks, they stilled when they hit the water, maintaining their silence as the waves piled them onto the shore.

They finished in the dim morning, the stink of the raw flesh filling their nostrils. One of the cooks quit, and there were rumors that the remaining guests had started packing.

Four hours later, Mr. Langford emerged with a brief declaration that the contracts were canceled, and that if they had any complaints McCann could write his lawyer. Both Mr. Langford and his daughter departed that afternoon on a ship to the mainland, along with all the other guests from the Brackish Harbor hotel, who had decided that they had seen and smelled enough fish to last several lifetimes.

That was, of course, a crushing blow to Brackish Harbor's economy, and Mayor Barnum did his best to assure Mr. Langford that it was a most peculiar incident and would not happen again. Mr. Langford didn't listen, and the entire town watched helplessly as the ship filled with the bad report carried off the last of the year's tourists.

McCann, who received the brunt of the blame for the lost revenue, went after Seamus and Douglas, who returned the blame to him. Neither crew claimed authorship of the event, nor did the hotel, and all parties retired that night in fuming restlessness. That night, the moon waned, the wind paced, and the waves rolled steadily into Willy's Maw.

The next day broke with a bright sun, a spot of clouds, and a wind as crisp as a fresh apple.

Invigorated by the autumn light, Mrs. Orman, who lived on the other side of town, rose to make herself breakfast. She hummed to herself as she prepared her toast and had just produced a jar of jam from the cupboard when a plinking tickled her ears. Peering into the pantry, she noticed that the can of her finest sardines—well-aged and on reserve for a special occasion—was quivering. She blinked and adjusted her spectacles to ensure she was seeing correctly. The cans quaked and squeaked, and she withdrew a moment to catch her breath.

Telling herself that it was simply a mouse in her pantry, Mrs. Orman slowly reached in and took a can. It wiggled. She dropped it. It burst open. A dozen tiny fish flew out in a spew of oil, yelping and squealing, tiny eyes bulging.

The other cans followed suit, hurling themselves out of the pantry and onto the floor. Sardines gushed across the tiles in green pools of oil. They bounced and flailed in a small swarm, their squall rising like the shrill warble of a radio signal.

Scrambling for the door, Mrs. Orman was hardly outside before she heard her neighbor screaming for her husband. He shouted too. Then the house beside theirs erupted in screams, then the one beyond that. Soon, the air was filled with the sound of humans shouting and bellowing in fury and terror.

Seamus woke to Eliza screaming and helped her and Jenny in a mad search for all the fish on their property. They emerged with a blanket full of wriggling, chanting beasts and joined their neighbors in the mad rush to purge the land.

Behind it all, like an ambient orchestra, rose the sound of squealing fish.

At first, it was a shrill wail. It bled into a screech, then a scream held all at once and in such unison that even those on the mainland heard it, as a whisper. Then, one by one the screams subsided and boiled into a seething chatter.

The people of Brackish Harbor thought it was the jaws of the fish clicking, but it soon took on a deeper tone. It carried a rhythm and variance too purposeful to be flesh and bone.

It was a language. It rose and fell in an ancient dialect known only to those who breathed the sea. It poured from the mouths of hundreds of fish, uttering, wailing, and groaning as they tumbled from buckets and carts back into their home.

The town labored from dawn to noon beneath a shrouded sun, each man forgetting the grievance against his neighbor for the shared goal of peace.

When the last—the very last—fish was propelled back into the deep, the entire town stood on the shores of the harbor in complete silence. The clamor of the last several hours haunted their ears as they waited for some sign that it would return.

It was then that the people did what most humans do when faced with the unfathomable. They went to church.

The First Church of Brackish Harbor was a humble building of dark wood, worn from frequent lashings of the sea winds. Attendance had been spotty at best, so many of those who pilgrimed on the hillside entered those heavy but silent wood doors for the first time.

Few spoke, mostly in pardons and whispers as they filled the dim and sacred space. Nearly the entire town cloistered there, standing or sitting in every nook and crevice. Even Mr. Farley, who had never sat on a pew in this life, glowered in the corner, upset that the supernatural would so rudely interrupt his perfectly rational life. Seamus and his family managed to find space behind their usual pew. He narrowed his shoulders, doing his best to give Eliza and Jenny a little more space.

Father Latimer took his place at the front of the church. He would later admit that he had prayed for the growth of his congregation, but was a bit unprepared for the flock that filled his fold. Seamus couldn't help but notice him fidgeting with his clerical sleeves, stained with fish oil from the town's purge.

Clearing his throat, he led them all in prayer to start the meeting. Then, as Mayor Barnum had nothing to say about the matter, Latimer briefly reviewed the mentions of fish in the scriptures. None of them were very pertinent, except God permitting man to eat fish.

"Why then," hollered Mr. Farley, "Should those damn fish be yelling so much?"

Father Latimer swallowed and coughed into his wrist. "I don't know," he confessed.

The room swelled with whispers. A cold descended upon the people, and Seamus stifled a shiver.

McCann stood up, removing his cap to reveal the large bald patch on his wispy blond head. "Father, I think Seamus and Douglas might have some answers. They were the first to see a screaming fish."

A murmur rippled through the crowd, and all eyes fell on Seamus and Douglas, who muttered a curse at McCann then asked God to forgive him.

Seamus stood up, removing his hat from his dark curly head. "Douglas and I have no answers. We thought it was bad waters, but after today I don't think that is true." A lump formed in his throat. He swallowed. "Father, are you sure the good Lord said that we may eat all the fish in the sea?"

"Yes. After the great flood, God gave man all beasts to eat."

"Then perhaps," Seamus swallowed. He worked the hat in his hands as if he were wrapping rope. "Perhaps these fish don't belong to us."

A hush rippled through the crowd.

"Who would they belong to then?" said Father Latimer.

"If they do not belong to man, then they must not belong to the good Lord either. Father, I think that they belong to another god."

The people exploded into whispers. Seamus took his seat, face burning. He returned his cap, asking God to forgive him.

Mrs. Perkins, the second oldest resident of Brackish Harbor, raised her wrinkled hand from her seat in the far corner pew.

Father Latimer quieted the crowd. "Yes, Mrs. Perkins?"

"It's Old Willy, Father," said the petite woman. "Before he was carried off to the asylum, he spent his days wandering the island and muttering about fish. He claimed they could talk." Her squinty eyes searched the room, landing on Seamus and his family. "It would make sense why Seamus's crew would see the first fish, his home once belonged to Willy's servants. I believe you may find an answer in Willy's shed."

"I say Seamus goes," said McCann.

Many uttered their approval.

Seamus's temper boiled. "Why me?" He felt Eliza's touch and tried to soften his fists.

"Because you're the one closest to Willy's place."

Seamus tried to protest but McCann spoke over him. "Who thinks Seamus should go?"

Nearly the entire room raised their hands. Betrayal sank Seamus's soul. He stared at the stark, fear-ridden faces, many of them unable to look him straight in the face. Even Douglas. Only his wife and daughter, Father Latimer, Mrs. Perkins, and a few others withheld their vote.

McCann led a group of people out of the church and across the hill to Willy's shed. Seamus was obliged to follow, and Father Latimer walked with him.

"Father, stay in the church," Seamus said. "There are still plenty of weary souls in there who need your help."

Latimer gripped his hand. "May God protect you, Seamus," he whispered.

The Father released him and Seamus was swept up in the current of bodies moving across the hillside.

Clouds masked the sun in a white veil, casting a stark, pale light over the landscape.

They arrived at Seamus's house. The crowd stopped with the road, gathering as if to watch a performance. Seamus fetched a lantern, telling Eliza and Jenny to stay near the house. Lighting it, he stepped out onto the field that stretched between his home and Willy's shed.

The crooked heap of boards sat like a disheveled tramp on the hillside; its lone window staring out to sea. A notable board on the face with the window had come completely loose on one end, giving the shack a slanted mouth as if it were recalling something.

He spotted Douglas on the road and went to him. "Come with me."

Douglas wet his lips with his tongue and swallowed. "I'll go with you to the shed, but I won't go inside."

Seamus sighed. "All right but, if something happens to me, you will watch over Eliza and Jenny for me, won't you?"

"Of course, Seamus. But what do you think is in that shack that could harm you?"

"What is in that shack that keeps you out?"

They stared at one another, neither able to say. Their answers were in the language of nightmares and shadows, dark dreams that had no parallels in the waking world.

They made the silent trek across the field to the shed's weather-worn door. After a muttered prayer and a quick cross, Seamus headed inside.

Due to the large window, the shack was surprisingly bright. Rain and wind had infiltrated the slats and scattered leaves and papers across the floor. A pile of blankets, marred with dirt and stains, marked the final night of Willy's rest. A creaky crate served as a table for a chipped bowl and tin can.

Papers and drawings covered the wall opposite the door, tacked to the wood with pins, nails, and shards of glass. Below, papers and notebooks littered a fine leather chest that had served as Willy's desk. Several stunted candles lay around the room in various stages of decay, but it was the wall beside the door that made Seamus stop.

Mounted in incongruous splendor was a great blue marlin, its glassy eye glinting at Seamus in the lantern light. Arched as if frozen in an elegant leap, the spike-nose fish was the lone relic of Willy's fishing prowess.

For some time, Seamus held his breath, staring it down, expecting a shrieking voice.

The marlin, however, was silent and still.

Setting down his lantern, Seamus began to sort through the papers on the floor. Strange marks filled them, the most frequent being a thin horizontal ellipse atop a half-moon pierced with a vertical line. There were drawings of fish with songs coming out of their mouths. The lyrics were old pub songs and shanties frequently heard around the harbor, offering no answers to the questions at hand.

Finally, taking one last glance at the marlin, Seamus sat down before the chest and sorted through the journals. The pages were a mad haste of rarely sensical scribbles and marks. The entries jumped around without narrative order, offering a fragmented preview of his working mind.

Some days, he had recalled his wife and son. Other days, he'd raged about how they'd been stolen from him. A few entries recounted specific conversations that had frustrated him but, scrambled in-between, in flashes and phrases, was the story of the island.

William Peterson had purchased the island for cheap from a fellow who had been "very eager to sell." When Willy had landed on its shore, he'd discovered near-barren waters inhabited by skinny, sickly fish. He had been about to give up the island as a loss when he'd received a "rare opportunity" to revive the waters.

He'd taken it.

The ocean had cleared and been teeming with life. Fishing had improved, the island had grown, and Willy and his family had enjoyed the luxury of his position until he'd remembered the blood.

The blood. It ran through everything. Sprinkled in sentences and scrawled in margins Willy had rattled on about how much it had cost him. What it had done to him. How it had bound him to him.

Him.

The unnamable thing breathed through the pages. It was behind every word and syllable. Willy claimed he was the reason for his wealth and the source of his sorrows.

I was a fool when I bound myself to him, he wrote in one entry. *But blood given demands blood in return. His kin for my kin. Their lives for mine.*

Seamus's fingers trembled as he turned the page and found the entries ended.

I tried to save them but he took them anyway. He will take them all in the end, I suppose. Shame, there are so many children. They will be grown when he comes.

Several lines were empty, nicked and smeared by the attempts to steady a weary hand.

I tried to break the stone but it cannot be broken. No one can stop him. He is coming.

"Poor Willy," croaked a deep voice behind Seamus.

Every hair on Seamus stood on end. He slowly looked over his shoulder at the marlin.

"Poor, poor Willy," it said. Its head jerked in his direction, dry scales crackling.

Seamus stood, gripping the journal.

The marlin screamed, its jaw thrown wide. Its massive body thrashed against the bonds of the mount and battered free, crashing to the floor. Its dry hide creaked and snapped as it thumped and flopped its way toward Seamus. Seizing the lantern, he slammed it against the marlin and fled out the door, bolting it behind him. Inside, the deep beat of the marlin's body melded with the gradual hiss of fire and the fish's extended scream.

Douglas helped Seamus away, and they watched the shack burn.

The scent of oncoming rain mingled with that of the smoldering shed. Gray clouds covered the sky, and the wind grew fangs, biting the cheeks, fingers, and ears of those who watched from the road. Eliza and Jenny stood apart from the crowd with their arms clasping one another's.

"Are you all right?" Douglas asked.

Seamus showed him the journal. "Willy made a bargain with someone for his fortune."

"What was it?"

"The blood of the fish he caught would be paid back by the blood of his kin."

"That's why the sea took his wife and son." Douglas removed his cap and wiped his forehead. "But why are the fish acting up now?"

"The deal has expired. Willy said it would happen when the children in town were grown." Seamus glanced at the crowd. "The kin Willy spoke of wasn't just his family. It was mankind. Us. We're Willy's kin. Something is coming, Douglas, and it is coming for us."

"Oh God." Douglas went white behind his dark beard. "Oh Lord have mercy."

Seamus turned to the crowd. "Has anyone tried to leave the island?"

"My crew did. No one could get off," McCann said. "Everything pushed out to sea is pushed right back. There's no rowing either—the current's too thick." He eyed Seamus. "What did you find in that shed?"

"Willy made a bargain with someone who made the waters prosper. It was an exchange of blood for blood, and now payment is due."

"What payment is that?" McCann said.

"It's us," Seamus said.

The crowd chattered and snapped, their din rising like the fish's cries. Seamus noticed Mrs. Perkins watching him. He turned to the final page as he hurried over.

"Willy made the pact on a rock somewhere on the island," he said. "Do you know where it is?"

Slowly, her eyes traveled to the crest of the island's hill. "He tried to destroy that rock many times." Her eyes fell on Seamus, hard and gray, absent of light and hope. "There is no way to undo what Willy has done. The blood is too strong."

"We have to try," Seamus said. He turned to the crowd. "Everyone, gather the strongest tools you have and meet me here."

Men scattered to their homes, each taking up their heftiest tool. They regathered as a small swarm and barreled up the hill through the wind.

From the height of the island, Seamus looked out to sea. The waves at the lips of Willy's Maw curled into the harbor with more than their usual strength. They were not rhythmic as in Eliza's dream, but their belching rise and fall made his stomach sink.

They found the flat gray stone at the very peak, half-covered in moss. Upon it was the symbol Seamus had found in the shed, written in blood as red and vivid as the day it had been painted. Douglas tried to scrub it off, but it only stained the cloth.

Seamus crossed himself as McCann took a large sledgehammer and smashed it against the rock. It made neither dent nor crack. McCann struck again, and again, each swing growing in fury and fear. Four men, then five, then six, battered the stone with hammers and chisels, their blows drumming a deep dirge.

In the midst of the din, Seamus noticed that some moss had been pulled from the rock. Pausing the others, he asked Douglas to help him peel it off. The entire stone was covered in marks, each drawn in brilliant red blood. Some bore the scratches of hatchets and blades, others were smooth as if someone had tried to wash them off over hundreds of days. One, buried deepest, was drenched by a large dried pool of blood. The symbol blazed through the faded puddle in bright red agony.

Then Willy hadn't been the first to bargain with this beast or to regret his choice. But each and every mark was a spit in their faces, the testimony of countless others who had tried to break the curse and failed.

Seamus went numb. McCann and several others took to the rock with greater fervor, screaming and shouting with every strike. The wind snuffed their cries, raising its own voice above them all.

Every man in Brackish Harbor spent the night on the hill. Seamus understood why Willy had gone mad. The monument was too hard, too deep for mere mortals to shatter. It was entwined with the very fabric of the island, the very firmament of the earth.

The island then was not an island, but an altar to an unknown god.

Douglas took hold of his arm. "Seamus. It's no use. I'm going home. If I'm going to die, I want to be with my family."

The lantern cast his face in flashes and shadows, and Seamus saw his friend's eyes were swollen. "I suppose you're right," he whispered.

Only a handful of desperate souls continued the fight. Those who returned home were shells of the men they had been that morning. There was no moon to guide them. No words for comfort. All that was left to them was howling October wind and the unsettled sea.

Seamus stopped outside his house and listened to the tumbling waters. Whether tonight or tomorrow, he had little doubt that it all would end.

The town of Brackish Harbor woke to the chorus of crashing waves.

Seamus looked out of his window and saw, beneath the gray sky, hundreds of thousands of fish leaping and thrashing in the sea. Having slept in his clothes, he tore out of the house and ran to the shore.

Every type of sea creature rose and dove beneath the furious waves. Whales, jellyfish, sharks, and fish alike were battered to and fro, each ignoring the other in the desperate rush to flee the current.

The great sloping gutter of Willy's Maw splashed with sea foam and twisted mangles of seaweed—their long, slimy tentacles swaying with the rhythm of the waves. They came in twos, one after another. It was nothing Seamus had ever seen on the ocean, only in small tide pools when a child waded through with the water at their knees.

It was then that he saw it—a dark mass on the horizon, its towering body stretching from sea to sky. He ran back home and found Eliza and Jenny dressed.

"It's coming," he said. "The waves, they've changed. He's coming." He drew his wife and daughter in, kissed and held them, wishing he had more time.

Eliza went to the window and looked out. She trembled. "Lord. Oh Lord, what do we do?"

Jenny looked out too, though Seamus tried to stop her. She turned pale and slowly retreated to her father.

"Come," he said. "Let us go to the church. If this is our last hour, the best we can do is make right with the Lord."

They rushed to the church, the wind tearing the hats from their heads and yanking coats off their shoulders. All the while, the ocean teamed with the frightened fish, wailing and crying in their animal voices. Waves rammed up the beach, slamming sea life against dock and ship. They screeched, trying to return to the sea, but the current always drove them back.

At first, Seamus wondered at the reason for their terror—was not their king, their god, coming for them? But, as he observed their frantic writhing and helpless abuse by the waves, he understood. Their god was not a savior, but a ruler who bartered the blood of his subjects for the chance to shed that of humans. They screamed because they too were sacrifices who could not escape.

The god was nearer now. Seamus could make out its blue hide, worn and crusted like that of an ancient whale. What they could see must have been the body and some of the legs, as the shoulders and head were above the clouds.

They fled into the church, Seamus forcing the door shut behind them. Only a few people sat inside, but Father Latimer was tending to his fold, speaking gently with each person, though his eyes were wild with worry. "Seamus, Eliza, Jenny. Welcome. I wish I could offer you more than a seat."

Mumbling a thank you, the family took their places in their pew. Father Latimer proceeded around the room, carrying bread and a cup for those who wanted their last rites. Seamus received the elements. The wine seemed more bitter this time.

The wine. The communion wine was the blood of Christ. The blood of God.

"Father, do you have more wine?" Seamus said.

"Yes," he said.

"Where is the bottle?"

"It's up in the front."

Seamus ran to the front and found the partially emptied bottle of wine behind the altar. Grabbing it, he ran for the door.

Father Latimer followed. "Seamus, what—"

"Let me do this, Father." Seamus turned to his family. He kissed them, said goodbye, and rushed outside.

The waves slapped the side of the island, battering the homes nearest the waterfront and vomiting fish into the streets.

Something creaked in the sky, and Seamus looked up.

An oblong head. Bulbous knees, knotted and twisted like an old tree in some dank patch of forest. Feet like the roots of a long-seated oak, raised and sprawling out in all directions.

Despite feeling his legs melt, Seamus raced up the hillside to the rock.

The beast was at the shore now, its tentacled toes snatching up every bit of debris and manmade item and hurling it out into the waters.

Seamus reached the crest of the hill and saw the sea was the same in every direction. All the sea creatures screamed.

Finding Willy's mark, Seamus stood and held the bottle up toward the beast. "Here! I offer you the strongest blood we have. The blood of man and the blood of God!"

A rumbling deep-throated chuckle pulsed through the air. The god reached out to him with a hand of spindly, twisting fingers leech mouths on their ends.

Seamus screamed. The bottle fell from his hands, shattering on the stone. "Have mercy," he whimpered, collapsing.

The toothy mouths chittered and chanted in the language of the fish. They mocked him. Smacked at him. Seamus curled into a ball, clutching his head. What a fool he had been. Now he would die alone.

The wind stopped, and the fish went silent. Seamus rose.

The ocean was as still as glass, the fish staring at the open sea.

The beast looked over its shoulder and turned.

On the horizon, a wall of black cloud swelled. It curled in on itself, rolling forward and gathering speed like that of a thousand horses. Its darkness extinguished daylight like a candle. A noise like the wind followed, stretching into a wailing sigh caught in some great throat.

The god stood before the oncoming cloud, releasing a guttural claim of its prey.

The cloud thundered back. It rushed the sea god, consuming the fish, the water, the god, the island, and all that Seamus knew. Darkness swirled around him. Wind and thunder mingled with the screams of the sea god, growing ever distant and faint.

Something hummed above him, sparking and staticky like a lightbulb. Peering up, he saw two white eyes in the sky, piercing, glowing like two great furnaces burning with the breath of a million stars. They looked down at him without blinking, staring at the man and stone of blood. The depths of those eyes never ended. Seamus was unable to look upon them. He fell flat on his face as if dead. A voice whispered in the wind.

Stand back.

He scrambled away from the rock. Out of the darkness came a great finger drenched in brilliant red blood that shuddered and flickered like fire. Down the finger went into the stone, plunging deeper and deeper into the earth, yet it never ended, so great was the hand.

Out came the finger and its great red stain. Seamus looked down into the hole and saw earth and core and earth again and then blackness. And he knew that the being of the cloud was not just there, but wrapped around the planet as a cloak, like some great skin meant to encase the earth.

Heat from great lungs lashed Seamus's face and arms, and he knew that he would burn. The wind swirled around him, threatening to tear him from the earth.

Seamus clutched the grass until his knuckles ached. He knew who had come. This was the one who had breathed time into existence. The being whom the very stars served. The one to whom his soul belonged.

A melody broke through his lips. Seamus uttered a tongue he did not know, thoughts that he could not explain.

The dark and the heat wrapped around him, and he heard the being breathing. Then, a sigh.

And all was silent.

Seamus opened his eyes. The sky was pale and bright. The sea was calm. There was no beast in the ocean. No fish lay upon the land. Only the houses and boats bore the scars of the great root feet, smashed and scattered like matchsticks upon the hillside. He could hear people crying and calling out for those who were lost in the debris.

Beside him lay the great stone without blemish or spot, the shards of the wine bottle scattered across its face.

Brackish Harbor was never the same again. Seamus and his family left for the mainland with several others. It was very well too, for the fish populations dwindled and grew sickly. By midwinter, they were not enough to sustain the island. Little by little, month by month, the people abandoned Brackish Harbor.

And the stone rested upon the crest of the island, waiting for another to find it.

CHAPTER TEN

THE SILENT SONATA
Matthew Siadak

The night began the way most things did for Jacobs: with a sound. Most of his life—or as much as he remembered—things began with a sound. Sometimes, it was the mundane sounds that came from living in Brackish Harbor; someone screaming, or playing music in the distance, perhaps, or, when the cock crowed with the rising of the sun each morning. Whether already awake or just going to bed hardly seemed to matter none; he always noticed the sounds. Most of his fondest memories were tied to what he heard.

Some of those noises went back to a time before he'd even been born. His mother chatting to him, his father's sing-song homecomings, he had memories of those.

After receiving a few of *those looks*, Jacobs quickly learned to not talk too much about the sounds, whether it was the ones he remembered, or the ones he still heard sometimes. Because to remember noises from the womb? That scared people, yes it did, it unsettled them something fierce.

As he'd grown up, the earliest sounds stayed with him. Mother still talked to him, father still sang, but there was something beneath it all. Something buried beneath the rooster's call, beneath the music Old Lady Winthrope played on her radio, loud enough to wake the dead, as if she were playing a concerto for the entire town. She hadn't played her own music in more years than could be remembered—she'd often lament about that—but nevertheless, he remembered it.

Even so, like clockwork every evening, her house lit up and the radio became a lullaby welcoming the day's passage into night. Jacobs had grown to appreciate the music much as he appreciated just being able to hear. That ear infection back in the summer of 1909, when he was but a pup prone to swimming often, had scared the dickens out of him. Both ears, clogged up tight and painful enough, he was sick from it—but that wasn't the worst of it.

The most distressing aspect was the distinct deafness. His stomach still twisted when he remembered the world coming through a muffled filter of pain, if it coalesced at all. That was when he realized he missed the sound, the one that had always been there and, he thought, would always be there. A creature of habit, he had found comfort in it, even as a child. Even after he learned to not talk about it, keeping it safe within his own heart. Even though its presence was a constant, the sound itself changed from time to time. It remained his secret happy place—made of, occasionally, a low, electrifying hum—that he closed his eyes and lost himself in. Other times, it was like the sudden crackle of ice remembering what it was to not be frozen, of nature waking up, of life. Or maybe it was little more than the promised words of a loved one, spoken from afar, as if calling to him.

Every so often, the sound drew him along, and Jacobs found himself ready to chase, if only he knew where to run. But he knew, if he dared try, that it would fall silent, a cricket's chirp teasing him for the attempt. As ever-changing as it was, he knew it when he heard it. It was a constant companion when nothing else in life remained, unchanged. If there was a time when he didn't hear it, it wasn't due to its absence; usually, it was because he'd failed to listen.

Tonight, the prevailing sound was the sharp clank of glassware being jostled discordantly, close enough that he could hardly ignore the din meant to wake him. And yet, beneath the harshness that assaulted his ears, he heard it—*his* sound—ever present and ever pleasant. It carried like an echo he could barely remember, soft and serene, one that tried to pull him back to sleep. And it might've worked, had he been anywhere else.

"We're closing up here soon, Mister Jacobs." The voice was tired and stank of the brackish drinks served at the bar night after night. Brought out of his reverie—out of the warm embrace of the sound beneath the *tink, tink, tink* of clearing glass—and silverware before closing—Jacobs looked at Sal behind the bar.

"Already? Wasn't but half past ten a few moments ago." Jacobs slurred as he spoke. He heard it and hated it. But it did little to lessen the sound that waited, as always, between each syllable. Neither did it stop him from swallowing the last of his drink without another word to Sal. Little more than dregs and salt, but he drank it down all the same. In the silence, he heard Sal's impatient waiting, from the tap-tap cadence of the man's fingers against the bartop, to the way the floorboards creaked under his shifting weight. The man never stilled when he was ready for someone to leave. Jacobs had occasion to note it more often than he cared to.

"Yes, sir." Sal's morose voice broke through Jacobs's train of thought. "It's but two moments to midnight now. You best be getting home while it's still safe. You know well as I do that nothing good happens past the last bell's tolling. I'd have woken you earlier, but truth be told, as silent as you tend to be some nights, I plumb forgot you were here. That all said, there's a nasty storm brewing. Best we both be getting home."

Sal seemed beside himself that they were still in the bar. There was a hitch in the man's voice, in the way he looked nervously towards the windows each time a shutter caught the wind, but Jacobs waved him off and looked into the depths of his cup, as if that might cause one more swallow to appear. The sound swelled in the silent emptiness of his drink, like the howling wind outside. He ignored both as he waited for his head to stop spinning. "No reason to worry here, none at all. I'll be moving along and out of your hair, quick as I can," he replied, trying to keep the words crisp and clear. Against his wishes, the words continued to slur out of his mouth. Before Sal could respond, the church bell clanged away like it was noon rather than midnight. No one bothered fixing the timer on it, reversing day to night and night to day, and it had been broken long enough that the town had ceased caring.

Jacobs used it as an anchor whenever he closed his eyes to drown out the world. In the arms of slumber, he let the sound in. It echoed like crashing waves, and he welcomed the warm cradle of its sweet, melodic embrace.

He wouldn't be lucky enough to make it home for that comfort. Not that night. And so, the sound remained distant.

"That'll be two dollars for tonight's tab." Sal wasn't in enough of a hurry to forget about that. Jacobs sighed. The bartender's hand was stretched out and waiting, fingers worn, tired, and almost as polished and smooth as his bar was.

Jacobs muttered and fished around in his pocket, listening to the rustling of his own worn clothing. *Not that one*, he thought to himself. *That* one had a hole in it that he'd been meaning to mend. From his other pocket, he produced the three dollars earned from the latest trip fishing, his fingers still sore from hauling heavy nets, slick with grime and stinking of salt and fish. Shaking his head, he laid two down for Sal and returned the last bill to his pocket.

Jacobs wobbled from his stool and shuffled towards the door, Sal escorting him. He yanked the handle and the door lurched open, unstuck from the warped wood frame. Instinctively, he braced himself against the noise lurking just outside, ready to pounce as soon as it could. Then, gone was the relative silence of the bar, empty but for him and Sal, and he bathed in the waves of sound that washed over him.

There, on the ocean-laden air and almost too faint to hear, Old Lady Winthrope's radio assaulted his ears like the cries of a forlorn, forgotten lover. Almost a counterpoint to it, the church bells rang a few more times, not quite drowning out the music, but commingling with it. Beneath the competing noises—a concert of chaos—he heard the one constant in his life.

The sound greeted him with open arms and, ignoring the other noises of Brackish Harbor's midnight melody, he gladly lost himself to it once more.

Beneath the stars that blotted out the darkness of the sky, he heard the sound loud and clear enough, it reverberated through him.

For a moment, before he stepped over the threshold of Sal's and into the thick night air, he paused, hesitating, his foot halfway out, hanging in the air. The words were on his lips, a question burning in his mind as he turned to ask: *Do you hear it too, Sal?*

"Good night, Jacobs. Hurry on home now, and mind it's past midnight," Sal answered the unasked question and gave Jacobs a gentle nudge out the door, which promptly closed behind him.

The sound played against the clanks of the locks being drawn, of the door being sealed tight. Jacobs shook his head and shuffled off the small stoop that hugged the crooked building. Sal had been saying, for some time, that he would fix it. Not that there was much point with how the ocean struck vengeance against anything new that encroached on the town.

Leaving Sal's Bar behind, Jacobs set off into the night, his footsteps echoing almost playfully as he made his way to the street.

Soon, the church came into view, hard to miss as it rose above the town, mostly white but where the weather had stripped it down to its brown bones. By then, the bell had gone silent, its last tolling little more than a memory, a silent warning that echoed Sal's words. Not that the night itself was quiet, far from it. On the storm-heavy and salt-scented wind, the waves crashing against the shore, the creaking of the ships at moorings, and the call of a lone bird roused from slumber brought the night fully to life.

The soundscape of Brackish Harbor almost always felt like home.

Wary of the time and putting a little pep in his step, Jacobs turned left at the small, dented street sign that loomed over the crossroads, and headed for what served as home.

The route led him closer to the widow's house. Every other shack and building had long-since gone dark with the coming of the witching hour, but not there. Never there. Not for as long as he could remember. Even if he did not know where to go, the music called to him, dragging him closer. Any thought of home eroded beneath that pull.

The widow's window, thrown wide open, allowed as much light to escape as the harmonies that issued forth. He recognized the song as Beethoven's *Moonlight Sonata*. He paused to marvel at how little the snarl and crackle of static interrupted the song. The radios were often beset with interference enough to drive listeners mad, broadcasts fading in and out and sometimes coming through in a language that was, at best, tangential to recognizable. Somehow, the widow always had the best reception, and that night was no exception.

Before he knew it, Jacobs stood in front of her large window, bathed in that light. There, inside, in the arms of Beethoven, the widow danced and swayed with someone he could not see. The sound waited for him; he heard it in her movements, a pattern that boggled his mind. It crept from the shuffle of her feet against the hardwood floor as she twisted, turned, and twirled.

The sound within her movements, the light dancing from her window, all of it drew him in, drew him closer. As much as he hated to stare, he could not stop himself. It was only when a stick snapped underfoot, threatening to give him away, that he ducked out of the sudden swerve of the widow's attention. He waited for her to scream.

Only when no such noise split the night in twain did he breathe again. "You're a damn fool, Jacobs. Damn fool." He chortled, and the sound echoed an almost chittering laugh.

He froze, still as a statue. Not because he did not want Old Lady Winthrope to notice him, but because that was the first time the sound was something *else*, something other than what he knew. As much as it shifted with his moods, or the world around him, never had it done *that*, whatever *that* was. The closest comparison he had was that it had chuckled, but that was where explanations fell to pieces. Now that he knew it had laughed with him—or at him—he could hardly label what it had been before; that low, incessant, thriving hum that radiated through him wherever he went, whatever he did.

And when it laughed, he realized he had, too. He was quick to cover his mouth and skitter away just as the widow leaned out. Blond hair with little gray in it swirled, caught in an eddied breeze of salty air, whipped this way and that. Her eyes did not turn downward, and for that, he gave thanks, but rather lifted skyward.

Whatever words she spoke fell away as Jacobs dove beneath her hedges, scraggly as they were, and closed his eyes. The sonata on the radio went quiet, replaced by something more modern. Trapped in his hiding place, Jacobs had no choice but to listen. Not that he minded.

"And when temptations press thee near, awake to watch and pray." The widow's voice lifted in a singsong cadence, following the words on the radio, carrying hauntingly out into the night. The song dwindled, as did the widow's mournful voice, as the window closed with a quick, quiet *snick* of the lock falling into place.

Silence fell once more, unbroken except for the sound. No longer laughing, but still waiting to embrace Jacobs with its familiarity. The hum grew, infused into every bone in his body, and drew him on.

And yet, something felt different.

Something had *changed*.

What, though, he had no idea, and for the first time in as long as he could remember, he felt afraid. Fear crawled through him, a visceral twist of his stomach that threatened to empty itself. Maybe it was the horror of change, maybe it was the rotgut he had been swallowing faster than a fish gulping for water back in the bar. Maybe both.

Whatever the source, Jacobs swallowed hard against the rising bile and stumbled away from the widow's window. He meandered onward until he felt the timbers of the town's winding walkway solid beneath his boots. The sound followed, accompanying every clomp of his feet against the wood. His legs roiled, as if he were out on the ocean, still struggling with the squirming piles of fish, shiny and panicking as they flopped and gulped against the air, hauled from the ocean, thrown into the stale, briny water in the hold of the ship. Jacobs couldn't help but wonder how the fish perceived that, and yet there were always more to be caught.

Or, there had always been more. These days, there were fewer and fewer waiting to squirm in the nets, and no one spoke to what that meant. Everyone in Brackish Harbor knew it—those that were left—but no one addressed it. Or at least, not out in the open, and not where he could hear. No, he kept his head down and he did what he did best. Every morning, or night, or when the mood struck, he found his way to his boat and puttered back out into the frigid, waiting, welcoming waters. Out there, the sound was the strongest, the calmest, and almost warm. A vibration through the soles of his feet that seemed to rise from the water to the heavens.

Now, as he wandered the streets in fading Brackish Harbor, the need to be out on the waves struck. Hard. He felt their pull and the unfettered purr of the sound calling to him.

Jacobs staggered under the heavy need to feel swaying beneath his feet. To feel a solid foundation on the water, more real to his body than the crumbling earth ever could be. In the space between, as his heartbeat quickened and his feet pattered clumsily against the rickety walkway, echoing through the night, the sound waited. It laughed again, and then keened mournfully, calling to him. Drawing him on, and in.

Bleary-eyed, and not only for lack of sleep, Jacobs looked down at his hands. Surprise flared as he found himself standing on the ramshackle dock, his small boat bumping against it with every errant wave. Its creaking hull and mooring ropes, tied to disintegrating buoys, echoed the sentiment of the sound.

Hurry.

It became a growling call that made his innards quiver and threaten to turn into jelly. His body was no longer quite his own as it moved, like a puppet in a children's show, to the tune of someone else's song. For a moment, unmoored in his own mind and body, he felt the warmth of the widow Winthrope, as if he were dancing with her again, as he had dared that one night, eons ago.

"Come join me, sailor man." The widow's voice had been quiet, low, pained, as she touched his shoulder in Sal's Bar. That night had been one of rarity, when she had left her house, letting her radio's silence reign over what was left of Brackish Harbor. She had found her way to the bar. There had been nary an empty seat in the place, but she seemed to mind that none. That was back when people still bothered to show up on the good, clear nights. Or the ones that followed a good haul of fish.

Those nights remained distant, broken memories. And yet, Jacobs found himself mired in the remembering, hardly able to escape even as he climbed into his boat, cast off the moorings, and rowed further and further from shore. Some part of him recognized the meaning of the land dwindling away. The rest of him was fixated on that memory, of the widow standing expectantly in front of him.

"Ma'am, I'm—uh—I'm hardly a sailor anymore," Jacobs had stammered out. The words echoed in his ears as he uttered the remembered words to the emptiness of his boat. Much like the wind or the rain cared naught for human woes, she paid his resistances and excuses no mind. And, as if on cue, the music started up around them. He'd been struck, in that moment, by how quiet the bar was. Those who remained in the village, out late enough to see, watched them with eyes shining in the dim light. He remembered dancing with her, the frailness of her body had made him afraid to hold on, to move. Within a few steps, she had coaxed him into swaying to the rhythm of the music. They had danced to whatever song was playing, and beneath all of that—in her timid heartbeat, in the scrape of their shoes against the beer-and-salt sodden floor—he heard it.

The sound echoed from that remembered night to his wavering now, sitting in his boat. The sounds were one and the same, a harmony of what he heard and the widow's sway, not unlike the swell of a wave rocking his boat.

Like a lover, it waited for him, both then and now. And like an unfaithful fool who spent too long away, he returned to it. Never far apart, never able to stay. Sometimes he could resist its pull.

That night, Jacobs chased the sound. Lost between the memory of the dance with the widow and the frolic of the ocean, torn between two nights. The only constant that connected them was the sound. With the alcohol souring in his stomach, with his eyes shying away from what little light remained of the moon, he lost himself in the swelling of the waves. This, if nothing else, was where he found home. Accompanied by the sound, embraced by it, he sighed and listened. Here, in the quiet of the night, amidst the cacophony of remembering, it swelled like an ocean's wave, threatening to capsize him.

The sound was there, much as it always was, but that night? That night, it did not chime alone.

No, he and the sound were not alone.

It came with an entourage of its own; the hum within the water, and the slap of his oars against its rippling surface. Something alien lingered in the chorus of noises that came together to join the sound. He heard it all, everything that had ever been paired with his constant companion. His mother's gentle, story-telling voice, and his father's singsong lullaby that protected against howling winds and thundering storms. The clinking of glass in Sal's, the widow's radio, the rooster's morning call, the screams, the crying. So much crying.

A hurricane of noises inundated Jacobs, but he kept rowing, pulling oars through the water, pushing it out of the way. With every straining movement, his shoulders heaved, and his stomach calmed even as the water churned more and more the further he ventured. Brackish Harbor was nary more than a distant pinprick of what little light remained, while the clouds swallowed the moon whole.

Out there, rolling with the waves, the laughter was unmistakable. Unfamiliar, new, alien. Hiding, but no longer hidden, within the sound. When was the last time laughter, genuine laughter, had graced this forgotten little village? When was the last time he'd really laughed about something, with the bliss of mirth spilling from his throat? And yet now, he felt it burbling up inside. A trickle of a giggle at first, and then a bark of humor, followed by a chortle from the very depths of his stomach. Tears came as he threw his head back and laughed.

The sound laughed with him. Commiserating in one another's joy, it embraced him, coursed through him like the current that spun his boat. He almost felt complete.

The wood vessel moved in a lazy spiral against the buffeting waves as they carried him further from shore. Long gone was the noise of land, replaced with the eerie echoes that flitted across the surface of the water. Ignoring the ache in his hands, blisters ready to concede their battle, and the pain flaring in his back, he grabbed a handful of the heavy net as he lurched towards the side of the boat.

With a heave that almost took him along, the net spun through the air and, with a series of thudding plops, landed, and sank beneath the surface.

He could hardly see in the darkness. The clouds, which had yet to sate themselves on the moon, devoured the stars, too. And yet, beneath the surface and the waves waited a light. It glimmered, so far below, pulsing in time to his continued laughter. Not just his laugh, but that of the sound, and the echoes of both drifted along the ocean surface, and dipped below, as if swallowed by a large fish.

With every expanding wake from the sinking sounds, a distant light flashed in the depths of the water.

Rope unfurled at his feet as the nets sank further and further, deeper and deeper. He paused and listened to the sound within the cable as it scurried against the rough wood side of his ship. While his attention was caught, the sound's laughter subsided. His guffaw faded, at least for now, and with it, the merriment of the sound declined, too. And like any good laugh that's gone on too long, it became something else entirely; tears welled and spilled forth freely.

As if the sky felt his surging sorrow, it, too, opened its heart, and he felt the first raindrop against his forehead. A cold shiver ran through his body as a wind picked up, and a second drop was not far behind the first. The third was a little slower, but with it came friends. Dripping from the sky, the rain came fast enough that he hardly had a moment to care before it was simply too late.

Water ran down his face, washing away the salt of his tears so that, perhaps, they might flow into the ocean. Like called to like, and once more, he felt at home out on the water, despite the torrent that threatened to drown him. In the pattern of falling raindrops, the sound built, louder, higher, and worked towards what he could only imagine was its warm, humming crescendo. His heart raced as it tried to keep pace, his breathing labored as if after a hard run. He screwed his eyes shut, but that did little to stop the sound, or the sudden bursts of light that he tried to ignore.

Curiosity warred with caution. When Jacobs could no longer resist wondering what broke the darkness of the night, he peeked with one eye, surveying the ocean. Out on the water, with each raindrop, there came an answering light from within those brackish depths. Tiny flares, like fireflies, flashed and flickered.

Transfixed, Jacobs barely noticed the reflection in the water. In the mirrored, shifting surface, a counterbalance lurked; as every drop met with a flash of light, the depths stole from it. As the ocean became a bright fabric of glistening drops fighting against the backdrop of an unknowable nothingness, and without the stars to light it, without the moon's warm glow, the sky ceased to be.

Whether looking skyward or to the bottom of the ocean, his stomach twisted and turned in an attempt to remember how to breathe on land. Under water. Which was which? He was no longer certain, even as the boat rocked beneath his feet.

And yet, the sound grew, becoming all-encompassing as the rain twisted back around; as though tired of falling, it bled back toward the sky. Jacobs tried to understand what he was witnessing. As the water flew up, he reached out to touch the dark droplets. They were warm against his skin. In a flash of lightning that cracked through the sky—or was it the water—the image of something looming burned itself into his eyes—no, deeper, into his very mind.

The sound had taken on an edge as lightning crackled through it and the star-ridden water. The light in it changed as well, rupturing and breaking into a halo of indescribable color. Nor did he have words for the shape in the clouds. For the briefest of moments, he found himself hoping that all of it was nothing more than the alcohol in his veins muddling his mind.

Or that, like a child's fancy, the shapes were his mind's way of interpreting them. There, an elephant with too many tusks, and over there, a figure with more hands than arms, or the one that looked vaguely like Mother in her Sunday finest. Or maybe it was the image of his father, before the bottle cracked open. Back then, when there were happier times, long before the Harbor had harbored so much pain.

That hope—that these were just fanciful imaginings lending shapes to the clouds—died when the sound did. For the first time in as long as he could remember, silence fell harder than the raindrops. Since before he was born—when he was still between wherever came before and this small little town—he had heard it.

Until now. Until this very moment when silence swallowed him whole.

The burgeoning lack of sound, the fading whisper of the waves, scared him. More than the figure so far above him, so alien, his mind scrambled to find some semblance of familiarity to latch on to. He tried, but the surface of understanding was as slick as the sodden boards beneath his feet.

Distracted by the silence, afraid of it, he let out a scream.

Or he thought he did. Maybe. His teeth rattled in his mouth, his lips—chapped and wind-burned by the cold—split, and he tasted salt of a coppery sort, and he screamed again. Silence engulfed him to the point he could not hear himself.

Jacobs *knew* he was screaming, but he did not—could not—hear himself. In the awful silence, he did not hear the sound, nor the gentle words of his mother, the lullaby of his father, or the sigh of the old widow during that stolen dance. With the absence of the sound, all of that was gone, too. It left him dazed and wondering if he had ever truly *heard* before.

Lightning brightened the sky again, casting the crawling figure in the clouds in an almost bas-relief. But no resounding thunder broke. There was only the light splitting open the canvas once again, painting it in vivid, bruise-like colors; mottled green, deep, dark, scattered purple, all threaded with red. Like broken blood vessels filtered through torn flesh, whatever loomed there crawled out of the rent in the heavens. The state of the sky scared him, but even that horror paled in comparison to deafness.

Jacobs wept, warmth leaking from his eyes as he tried to shield his eyes from the horror. He screamed again, and again, until he was not certain if he fell silent to the bursting of his vocal cords, or if he still made noise that his ears could not register. Might be that he'd never know, the permanence of the silence unknowable. Not that it mattered. His mind could not comprehend ever having been able to hear, nor could he fathom hearing again. If he had once thought the quiet of that ear infection had been impossible to bear, this was so much worse.

The silence became absolute.

The presence above had more eyes than he could count, more everything than he dared even try to understand. He recoiled as it opened its mouth in a mirror image of Jacobs's scream. What came out shook the very ocean beneath him.

A sound unlike anything he had ever heard. It ripped through him, leaving his senses numb as visions poured through his mind.

The jumbled snippets of his life filtered through what little was left of his mind, assaulting those parts that had not retreated from the horror in the cloud, like a wounded, whimpering animal.

He was frozen. This alien world, full of what structures that defied any laws of physics he had run afoul of in his lifetime. Surrounded by creatures innumerable, nigh indescribable. Teeth and wings, sometimes together, flesh that slurped like water. He barely grasped what they looked like before his brain reminded him none of this was possible. Worse even than the sights before him was the realization that he could once again hear, even if he did not want to, not the sounds these creatures made, anathema to his constant companion.

The horrible realization settled on his shoulders, that their mouths moved not in *making* noise, but in consuming it.

And the sound, *his* sound, drew their hunger towards him.

He looked around their world, tried to find purchase in this nightmare so that he might find his way back home, but wherever he looked and whatever he gazed upon made his mind falter, so like a motion picture after the reel had degraded, everything came in one frame at a time. Some repeated, stuck, shifted, blurred together.

With each stuttering movement came a static-filled crackle that was infinitely worse than any broken radio. Somewhere between the silence and the presence of so many beings, he realized they were *speaking*.

To him.

Too many arms—or were those slithery cephalopod-like appendages tearing at one another?—and innumerable eyes looking across time, reaching out.

Toward him.

The ground was barely solid beneath his feet, the air twisted and burning in his lungs as he strained his neck back, and up, until he gazed upon constructs encircling those that had first caught his attention. Once again, he tried to make sense of their buildings, and once again, they seemed to defy any logic. And yet, the only thing he knew for certain was that their world and its inhabitants were in tatters.

And in his fear, he tasted their hunger.

"Beware, beware," the multitude of chittering voices called out into the void, their voices stretched long and thin, until it reached his ears far below them, where he stood on the broken crust of their world. Like angry fire ants, the words crawled into his heart and bit into his brain, alighting there an entirely new sensation of pain. The struggle to breathe threatened to first dim then blacken his vision, but he could not draw in that next breath, no matter how hard he tried. Nor could he tear his gaze away from the towering beings.

And then, just like that, he was on his own again.

Gone was the oppressively heavy air that refused to seep into his lungs. In its absence, Jacobs found himself retching hard with the need to breathe. His body betrayed him, refusing to listen, until at last he gasped, like a fish out of water submerged once more. His hands had found his tackle box, somehow. Throwing it open, he found the flare gun, and pointed it directly toward the creature lurking in the clouds.

With a soundless sob, he pulled the trigger.

As the signal gun exploded its fiery star, he listened for the whistle of it screaming through the air.

Silence reigned supreme.

It lingered, looming like the others, until a cacophonous tendril reached across the vast darkness—of the sky, of the ocean—and popped the bubble of silence. Another sob racked through him as, bit by bit, the lack of sound receded like a tide. The first noises came from his own body.

Jacobs's own scream finally reached his ears, loud enough that it overrode the roar of the ocean. The thunder blossomed as lightning struck across the sky. He recoiled as the resurgence of sound threatened to tear him apart at the seams, to render him down to the basest components. He felt his fingers become little more than motes of dust, followed by his arms and legs, just as eager to join this dance of disintegration.

He almost succumbed to it. Almost let it take him, until he realized what the faint noise that had burst the quiescence was; another voice had joined the fray, and chaos receded enough for the world to take on a semblance of reason once more.

Turning, Jacobs saw that, somehow, against all reason, the waves had pushed the boat closer to shore.

Closer to home.

Closer to land, and yet no further from the horror that followed.

Waves sloshed before his boat, and Jacobs wanted nothing more than to hear the sound again. *His* sound. Laughing at the absurdity of that, he scratched at his hairline, dug in, and tore at his scalp. With a lurch, the boat collided with the docks, where Old Lady Winthrope stood against the driving winds and the needling rain, her arms held toward the sky. She threw herself into the song, becoming a moonlight sonata in and of herself.

Her voice lifted in refrain, belted out incantations.

And through it all, she danced.

Oh, how beautifully she moved beneath the light of the revealed moon, as if she'd coaxed it out of hiding. The silk of her shift sodden from the rain became part of the dance, circling her as the raindrops ceased falling. Not that the rain ended. No. Rather, the droplets froze, hovering in the air as her voice grew louder, until it was loud enough that Jacobs felt the pressure of her presence even with the distance between them.

The widow let out a primal scream, without missing a step in her graceful movements. In her dancing, she had gathered the moonlight like a web around herself and the small pier. She extended it over what buildings remained in Brackish Harbor. The water pushed away from the shore, leaving the docks bare, and exposing their mucky, green legs to the air. The boat drifted further from her, too. As much as he loved being out on the water, how quickly the shore receded spiked more primal fear inside of him.

Beneath the dark sky, within the boat upon the starry ocean, he was torn between the siren's call of the widow's song and the impossible, large hand that clawed for the boat, threatening to draw him back out to sea. Back to *their* world.

But the hand stretched and shrunk, flickering in and out of focus as the being dilated and stretched, even as it shrank. The boat lurched, the salt-slick surface sending Jacobs sprawling this way and that.

Until the inevitable happened.

As futile as it was, he windmilled his arms, as if that might stave off what he knew was coming. Every sailor, or fisherman—or anyone worth their salt on the open ocean—knew, whether by experience or instinct, when a boat was about to capsize.

Jacobs reflexively swallowed as much air as he could, sealing his lips against the brackish water as it collided with him, hard as a brick wall. Unlike a brick wall, though, the water parted, accepting him in its saline embrace. The water stung his flesh with a burning chill. And yet, he welcomed the sensations as he kicked hard, a violent motion meant to drive him further from the depths tendriling to meet him, and back towards air. There, lurking just above the surface, whatever had crawled through the abscessed, wounded heavens froze, and for a moment, for the briefest of heartbeats, the surface became a mirror.

In a face that was not his own, he recognized the anguish and loneliness in the multitude of eyes boring into his flesh. It lanced through him, threatening to chew up his very soul. The ocean burbled again as the thing spoke: *beware, beware.*

That, too, receded as the moon burned bright through the clouds, shaking off whatever blanket of blackout remained. Haloed by lunar luminescence, the widow Winthrope walked out onto the dock and reached into the water. Wiping away the reflection of that face, she reached for Jacobs. Her fingers, long, wiry, and soft, wrapped into the front of his shirt, and hauled him out as if he were no heavier than a babe.

He laid on the wooden boards, staring up at her as she stood over his body and faced the sea. She screamed again, and again, and again. Each sound tore at the water, driving it and its inhabitant further and further from the shore. And all the while, Jacobs wept, for the sound increased with every yell, suffusing through him as he curled in on himself, fetal and safe. But he could not close his eyes against the sight of the wave that rushed back to greet him and the widow both.

The ocean that approached them bore no resemblance to the gentle kiss of a tide returning to shore; it was a rebounding tidal wave crashing into the earth and spraying into the sky. Droplets, rivulets, and the spray spread with the recaptured light of the stars, tossing them back into the void so far above. Each thrust of light returned to the sky diminished the looming darkness, pushing back a writhing mass of limbs, of what might be hands, of what moved like a worm, of what boggled the mind.

Cast in starlight, with its wounded sky quickly sealing, the horrific form fled.

Jacobs collapsed, but he could not tear his gaze away. The storm raged on and the rain washed over his face. He knew fear again, this time of paralysis, until the widow's face appeared, upside down, over his. Leaning, she pressed a kiss to his brow and murmured a series of words. With them, and her touch, the sound returned in full.

In the feel of her lips, in the crest of the wave, he heard it. *His* sound. In the whispered words he could not comprehend—not unlike the way his mother talked, and somehow eerily similar to the lullaby of his father— Jacobs found himself lulled, calmed, awash with pain but hardly caring.

Darkness came, but one that was familiar, as he faded into the land of dreams. There, like a boat on the ocean, he drifted, oblivious to the world.

Sometime later, dawn broke. The rooster's call shattered the silence of the night, and Jacobs rolled over. Forgetting for a moment that he was not in bed, and hardly noticing the way his body wracked with shivers, he nearly spilled right back into the murky waters.

"Told you to go home, Mister Jacobs." It was Sal's voice, terse but worried all the same.

Jacobs lifted his head, groggily scrambling to hold onto the memories from the night before. He could only remember watching Old Lady Winthrope dance, and the swell of darkness in the water.

"Shame about your boat, but I did warn you. Glad you made it through the storm last night. Come with me. You look like you done seen a ghost. I'll make some soup and tea to warm you up." Sal helped Jacobs to his feet, half carrying him towards the actual solid ground.

Jacobs stumbled once they reached earth, his legs betraying him for the want to be out on the water. Mourning his boat, he shot a sidelong glance to where it lay in shattered pieces. One of the last boats still good for fishing, and there it went.

He half-listened to Sal's ramblings as the man wrapped him in a blanket. The boards of the town walkway creaked and squelched beneath their muddied boots. Through it all, Jacobs heard the call of the sound, distant and thundering. As Sal opened the door to the bar, Jacobs saw the widow standing on her stoop, wrapped in her shawl, staring at him.

And she smiled.

CHAPTER ELEVEN

THE ORIGINS OF CORA DEERING
Teagan Olivia Sturmer

ATTN. DR. JONATHAN ESTRA, UNIVERSITY COLLEGE LON-
DON, MARINE SCIENCES –(STOP)–

WE ARE BEING HUNTED BY A SEA CREATURE OF UNKNOWN
ORIGIN AND ASK YOUR DEPARTMENT'S ASSISTANCE IN
IDENTIFYING THIS TERRIBLE BEAST AND PUTTING IT TO
REST –(STOP)–

BRACKISH HARBOR

The boat arrives at precisely eleven o'clock in the morning. It is a
strange little thing, all rotting wood, leaky rudder posts, and oars that
seem time-worn and wave-bitten. A woman emerges from the hull, two

ragged carpet bags clutched in white-knuckled hands and an old steamer trunk with brass buckles leaning against her heels.

She watches the town come into view—all salt-washed shingle and gray rock—as the waves lap the boat closer to the rickety dock. The town is unfamiliar to her, *a cold place*, she thinks, as the wind rushes off the vast ocean to rocket against the white-stone shores. Her fingers tighten around the handles of her bags, brine-bitten face set in determination. She has endured cold places before, other unknowns. In fact, they are what she has always thrived upon, and she does not see this island as anything different.

A dock boy runs along the creaking wood, one hand to the wool cap set upon wisping curls, the other catching the thick rope tossed his way. He wraps it in, around, and through a metal cleat, expertly tying off a knot before straightening to offer his arm to the woman aboard.

She does not need it.

Her heels click against the wooden slats as she nods to the steamer trunk still bobbing on the deck.

"You can have someone take that to the Avalon Inn," she instructs, voice resolute. "Attention to Ms. Cora Deering."

The young man nods and, before he can inquire anything further, she sweeps away, eyes set on the landscape ahead. She can feel the paper rustling in her jacket pocket, but she does not need to read it to know what it says. She has memorized the forty-two words—could recite them forward and backward if someone asked. But no one has. In fact, everyone else who has seen the telegram thinks it a joke, some hoax made up by the strange, isolated citizens of the island.

But Cora does not. The moment she heard the other students laughing about the ridiculous correspondence their professor had received that morning, she was the first to volunteer. The others—all men—raised eyebrows over cups of lukewarm coffee and wished her the best of luck through sneers and half-smiles. She knew what they thought of her— still does—just another woman trying to make her way in the world. She grinds her heel into the gravel as she makes her way up the hill toward town.

And they were exactly correct—in everything but their use of the word *try*. She will not *try* to make her way in the world.

No. She will succeed.

The road leading to the only inn on the island is long, narrow, and hedged in on both sides by tangles of thorny, bare bushes and piles of smooth, gray rock. Cora passes only a handful of wrinkled, worried faces, each bent against the wind that rushes in off the savage sea. She is an outsider here, an unfamiliar face, and she feels it in each brush of eye contact, each half-swallowed whisper. Gray-faced and stony-eyed, they mill about their business in quiet, isolated clumps. No one bothers to offer a welcoming smile or a raised palm—only sideways glances and suspicious murmurs held on oily tongues. She tries to ignore it, to form a shell against the curious inhabitants of the island.

If she is going to call this inhospitable spit of rock home for the next few weeks in hopes of an aquatic discovery, she cannot let the bitter-faced townsfolk get in her way. Her grip tightens on the handles of her bags, and she forces herself forward.

High above the ocean, set into the rocky cliffs, the town awaits. The square is nothing more than a few shops and a fountain in the center, ringed by moss-laden cobblestones. She stops to get her bearings. Perhaps she should have waited for the dock boy, jumped on the cart, and rode up to the inn along with her trunk. Now, it seems, her belongings might arrive before she does. She sets her bags down on the lip of the fountain and pulls out another slip of paper, this one less creased, the ink fresher.

THE BLUE ROOM, AVALON INN is written in her familiar, hurried handwriting. There was no address given, no details, just a place—a place she has no idea how to get to. She's about to pick up her bags and march into the nearest shop demanding directions when she hears boots scuff the cobblestones behind her, and someone clears their throat.

"You're looking a little lost, there."

Cora turns to see a man, dressed in fisherman's attire, with violet stains under both eyes. His hands are thrust deep into the pockets of wool trousers, a coil of rope wrapped around one shoulder. She heaves her bags from the fountain, narrowing her eyes against the stinging wind.

"Do I have that look about me?" she asks.

A smile hints at the corner of his lips. "We don't see many tourists on the island."

"Oh, I'm not a tourist," Cora explains. "I am a marine biologist from London." She drops one of the bags to the cobbles and fumbles with the paper in her pocket. "Someone from your town requested I come and help uncover what creature it might be causing all the trouble around here."

"You?" The man's face lengthens with shadow as he takes the paper from Cora, eyes snagging on the words. For a moment, he doesn't speak, and Cora thinks he might get angry. She watches his jaw tighten, his fists clench, and then he hands the paper back and shoves his dirty palms into trouser pockets.

"Right, well, I wouldn't know much about that."

She eyes him, cautiously, studiously—how she's been taught—to study and dissect, to peel back outer shells to see the blood and bone and sinew beneath. She crumples the paper back into her jacket and picks up her bag.

"Perhaps if you could just point me in the direction of the Avalon Inn, then," she says, trying to lighten the tension coursing between them.

The man scratches at the red hair tangled around his jaw and points behind her. "Take that road there. It will lead you to the inn if you stick to it." He goes to turn and swivels back. "If I were you, miss, I'd be careful. You're all alone, and there's no telling who you'll run into in this town." He flashes a too-bright smile and tips his hat. "Just remember, don't...don't stray off the paths. And don't go into the sea alone, not for any reason."

Cora is about to tell him how ridiculous he sounds, telling a marine biologist not to wander into the ocean, but he is already walking away, disappearing amongst the decaying clapboard buildings. *Never mind*, she decides, she has never been much for listening to the words and warnings of men anyway. She spins on her heel, focusing on the white gravel road licking higher up the rocky island cliff.

She will take any path she pleases, thank-you-very-much, and to hell with the rest.

The Avalon Inn rises from the rock and mist like some monument of a bygone era. Its stone walls are choked with the dusty remains of summer's ivy—nothing but frost-bitten vines and shriveled, gray leaves. Though it is nearly March, there is a bitter chill to the air that Cora cannot shake despite her wool dress and many petticoats. Dr. Estra had told her the expedition was foolish. Besides her being a woman, the ocean itself would be a brutal beast. Ice shoves made their way inland from greater depths to melt against the shores and lace the shallow waters with piercing cold. But she was determined and, as she looks to the crashing waves far below, she still is.

She will unveil whatever it is that plagues these shores and give it a name. They will celebrate her return as she presents her discovery, treating her—finally—as one of their own. She can already taste the champagne, light and bubbly on her tongue.

A door slams shut ahead, pulling Cora from her daydreams. A woman stands on the front porch of the inn, her dress as drab and gray as the landscape. She lifts a hand to her brow, eyes narrowing as the wind whips white hair around her wrinkled face.

"Are you the lady scientist?" she calls from the porch, voice like crackling seagrass.

Cora hoists the bags tighter in her palms and breaks into a jog toward the inn. The old woman raises unkempt eyebrows as Cora reaches her.

"Bit young, but I thought you might be, come along inside."

The inside of the inn is hollow with cold, and the damp scent of mildew hangs in the air. Cora wrinkles her nose, eyes following the crown molding gone black with mold.

"You'll find your room up those stairs, third door on the right. Your trunk has already been delivered," the older woman states, pointing behind Cora. "Wasn't sure what time your boat would be arriving, so I've only now instructed Della to start a fire, might be a little cold."

Cora smiles and moves toward the stairs, trying to settle the nerves pressing against her heart, threatening to overturn it in her chest. She turns back. "Before I forget, for research purposes, do you know of anyone who has seen this creature mentioned in the town's telegram?" She swallows, throat suddenly sharp. "Anyone who might be able to assist me in my search?"

The older woman moves behind a desk, fingers digging into her hips. She blows a hiss of air from her lips, eyes suddenly flashing dark. "Telegram? Well, I might know. Only one to see the thing and still live to talk about it is Tom Seward, a local fisherman." She reaches for a teacup resting on the desk and takes a swig. "Though, Tom's never been much for talking since his wife died." The older woman's lip twitches as she takes another sip of tea.

Cora notices a strange sickle shape on the bottom of the porcelain cup and nods, making a mental note. *Tom Seward, fisherman, wife deceased.* "Right, well then, thank you, Ms.—"

"Beckett. Ruby Beckett."

Cora smiles and tips her head again. "Ms. Beckett." She adds the name to her growing list as she climbs the stairs. *Ruby Beckett, innkeeper, origins unknown.*

Cora has been doing that ever since she can remember, cataloging things in her mind. Her father found it strange but blossomed with pride when she was accepted to university. The first class of women marine biologists, she told him, wasn't he proud? And he was, until influenza had turned his lungs to ash.

She pushes the memory away and fits her palm to the brass knob of the third door on the right. What awaits her on the other side, she doesn't know. And it thrills her—the unknown, what brought her here in the first place. She turns the knob and flings the door open to reveal a room hanging in moldering blue damask wallpaper, adorned with the same strange sickle pattern on the bottom of Ms. Beckett's teacup. Cora ignores it, focusing on the trunk beside the bed. A smile hints at her lips. She will take the rest of the day to relax, warm up, dig into her plans and equipment and, tomorrow, she will uncover whatever it is that keeps this town so quiet, so isolated—and she will make it her own.

The sound happens sometime in the early hours of gray dawn, breaking Cora from her sleep. For a moment, as she clutches the bedcovers with cramping fingers, she reminds herself of where she is, what she is there for. *An island somewhere off the coast of Massachusetts...to discover what sea creature plagues the town...*

Again, the sound rips the morning air, and Cora feels a shiver run the length of her spine like spider silk. She tosses the blankets off and sets her feet on the thick blue rug beside the bed. Her head feels heavy as she looks about the room, eyes snagging on the strange pattern in the damask wallpaper. Despite the cold, sweat beads on the back of her neck.

Something is not right.

She hurries to the window and throws up the pane of glass, the salt-tinged breeze licking her face. The world smells of sea and what is left when the tide goes out—churning seaweed, broken shells spilling clammy viscera, fish bones, driftwood, and little chunks of smooth glass. Cora's eyes train on the docks; she can see fires lit in lampposts, their orange light flickering on the wavering sea.

That noise again, bitter and sharp and altogether unholy. Cora's hands tighten on the windowsill as goosebumps prick her arms and the back of her neck. Without thinking, she dashes to her trunk, throwing it open and dressing in the first thing she sees—a smart wool skirt and jacket, sturdy boots, and a knit cap. Something is wrong out there in the water; she can feel it, and she is sure that whatever it is has something to do with whatever she is looking for.

She takes the stairs two at a time, out into the dim light spilling into the inn's lobby, highlighting a strange trail of puddles from the door to where Ms. Beckett is sitting at her desk. She is dressed in a white cotton nightgown and sipping tea from her sickle-patterned porcelain. Cora half makes up her mind to ask the woman what the symbols—the sound happens again, farther away, but loud enough to make Cora's flesh crawl.

"There'll be a body I suspect," Ms. Beckett says, staring out the windows that look over the cliff face.

A wind rattles the bubbled glass panes. "How do you mean?" Cora asks.

The older woman sips her tea, shoulders slack. "There's always a body after those sirens. You'll come to understand the ways of this island, Cora Deering."

Her eyes flash at Cora for a moment and then she slips from her desk through a door, shutting it tight behind her, dripping dark water as she goes. Cora feels sweat collecting in the lines on her palms and swallows, throat suddenly raw. She faces the door to the porch, the only thing between her and whatever it is waiting outside. Her stomach boils, but she bites down, feels her teeth, like she's going to grind them down to dust. She's here for a reason, to prove to those stuffed shirts back at the university she has what it takes. She remembers Ms. Beckett's words.

"Lady scientist, indeed."

She flings the door open.

The walk down to the docks is cold, wind biting at Cora with iron teeth. She shivers beneath all the wool, beneath her own layer of skin, tissue, and fat. Nothing can stop the cold from sinking claws into her flesh and breeding there in the spaces between marrow and bone. The huddle of shops is quiet as she walks across the cobblestones, not a soul out at this time of day. Not a soul braving a world ripped in two by the shrieking sirens from the water's edge. It isn't until she reaches the dock that Cora sees another living soul.

The man from the day before is standing outside a small clapboard shack, wiping blood and fish innards on a cloth hanging from his belt. He looks up when she approaches, face darkening. "Good morning," he says, reaching into a barrel at his side and slipping his fingers around a fat, slimy fish. He slaps it down on the table in front of him and slits its stomach open, viscera spilling out like tea from a kettle.

"Same to you," Cora replies, trying not to let her stomach turn from the smell rolling up from the lacerated scales. She is used to being around dead things, used to the smell of blood and the ocean, but the way the entrails stain the table like crushed rose petals still makes her skin crawl.

She watches his expert fingers remove scale and bone, dropping them into a bucket at his feet. He does the same to three more fish before she gets up the courage to ask the question blooming on her tongue.

"Do you happen to know a Tom Seward? He's a fisherman, and I'm wondering if he might help me in my research."

The man does not look up from his fourth fish, and Cora watches as the knife slips through dermis like melted butter. "I was worried Ruby might slip and give you my name," he says, the peculiar hint of a wry smile on his voice.

Cora startles, hands wringing her skirt. "Oh, I—I didn't realize."

He looks up then, flicking damp hair from his face with the back of his hand. "You couldn't have, Ms. Deering."

Before Cora has a chance to respond, voices rise from beyond the docks, in the harbor. Through the haze, she can see men in dark coats, the waves lapping at the shine on their boots. They are huddled around a figure—just a mound of gray and white through the mist collecting on the rocks.

"Did you hear it?" Cora asks, not turning her face back to Tom. "The sound this morning, it wailed three times."

"I heard it," Tom replies, slapping another fish onto the table.

Cora's hands tingle as she watches the men on the shore pull a body from the ice-laden waters. From where she stands, she cannot make out a face, but she watches a clump of frozen, dark hair fall across it, and knows it is a woman.

She turns back to Tom. "Is this what the telegram was about then? Whatever creature you all believe is stalking the waters?"

He doesn't answer for a moment, but Cora notices the way his cuts become sloppier, more jagged, and quick. "You'll never find it," he says, finally, sliding the fish over to join the rest of the eviscerated corpses and thrusting the tip of his knife into the wood.

Cora matches his gaze, the tilt of his head, the grim set of his lips. "Won't find what?" she asks. "You saw it, didn't you? Ms. Beckett—"

"Ruby talks too much, should be minding her own part of the—" He stops himself, eyes glinting dangerously in the early morning sun. He rips the knife from the table and scoops up the last remaining fish. "There are people in this town, Ms. Deering, who would skin you alive if you found out the truth." He threads his words carefully between his teeth. "And you'll never find it because they—*it*—doesn't want to be found."

Cora feels a shard of ice embed itself in her stomach, shooting roots into her chest until it feels like her heart will stop. "You saw it though, didn't you?"

Tom does not look up. "It doesn't matter what I saw that night on the Sound; what matters is that we keep to ourselves, allow it to be so it allows us to, and the few times it rears its head and leaves a body on the shores, we bury it in the churchyard and keep on living our lives."

Cora's head spins. *The Sound, the churchyard, bodies on the shore. Tom Seward, fisherman, wife deceased.* She studies him, the way his fingers make quick work of the fish, and she can't help but feel as if he is keeping something from her. "It killed your wife, didn't it? Whatever is out there?" She juts her chin in the direction of the water.

The knife slips, blade slicing across the pad of a finger. Blood presses out against his flesh, beading like rubies. Cora startles, reaching out but not knowing what to do.

Tom only wipes it against the cloth hanging from his waist and keeps cutting. "Yes," he says, voice deeper, darker. "It killed my wife, just like it killed that woman they'll be bringing up from the shore any time now."

Cora does not have to turn to hear the boots scuffing against stone behind them. She and Tom stay quiet as the group of four dour-looking men walk by, a makeshift stretcher slung between them. They are silent, faces grim-set, and Cora watches as they make the ascent into town with a single, white hand dripping from between blanched sheets.

"Don't you want to know—"

Tom's knife sinks deep into the wood again, his eyes sharp. "I don't. The Scylla doesn't want to be found and, if I were you, Cora Deering, I'd be careful in my search for it."

Cora wastes no time. The strange name on her tongue, she returns to the Avalon—only to leave with the necessary equipment and dressed in something warmer. Trousers, to be exact. Everyone in town eyes her strangely as she marches past, a configuration of binoculars, a microscope case, a camera, and enough jars and vials to make her sound like a traveling circus.

Before leaving the inn, she asked Ms. Beckett about the Sound and received the expected response.

"Met Tom, didn't you?" Ms. Beckett said, eyes glinting. "Tragedy what happened with his wife and all, I'm surprised you've decided to venture there yourself."

Cora said it was all in the name of science and progress but, the farther she ventures from the town's cobblestones, the less sure she becomes. Cold mist still clings to the rocky shoreline as she makes her way toward a strange strip of land that curls through the ocean like a barren, gray tongue. The tide has washed out and the air swims with the sick, sour smell of seaweed spewed up with the dregs of the sea. Cora's boots sink into the fleshy mounds of thick, frosty green tangle as she inches her way toward the shore of the Sound. The water is dark here, deeper than she expected at low tide. She deposits some of her equipment on the rocks, edging closer to the lapping waves.

There is something strange about the water—as if, were she to fill a jar with it, it would be black rather than clear. The smell becomes something more than the rot of seaweed as she bends to press the lip of the jar against the pooling liquid—there is something else, too. Something like putrefied flesh, like an ancient thing has been unearthed there, turned out of its burial shrouds to play witness to the sun once more.

She feeds the water into the jar, lifting it quickly as she watches something dark slip into the glass. A shelled creature settles to the bottom as the silt and sand swirl in the murky contents. Cora studies its unfamiliar shell in the sun, but the water is too dark. She takes a sieve from her pack and pours the water through until all that's left is the mollusk. Slime coats her palm as she tips it out into her hand, fairly certain she's never seen anything like it in any of her books or charts. The shell is black, almost obsidian against the sun. Her chest thrills. This might not be the thing plaguing the town with the bodies of dead women washed up on shore, but it is a discovery all the same.

Settling back onto the rocks, Cora takes out a sketch pad and lays the creature on her knee. She examines the lines in its shell, the clear film that secretes across the wool of her trousers. It isn't until the tide comes back to lap against her boots that she stops sketching the thing and lets it back into the jar. A face stares back at her, flickering on the waves. A human face.

She screams.

"That's not the reaction I was anticipating."

Cora scrambles up, the pad of paper almost tumbling from her grasp as she turns and catches her ankle in a cleft of stones. Tom's fingers wrap around her arm before the rocks can bite into her knees. The air is thick with salt—Cora's lungs close against it as she catches Tom's eye and steadies her footing. Between them, tension grows until Cora is almost sure that if she opens her mouth and bares her teeth, she'll feel it cut against her tongue. Her skin charges as his fingers drop away, shoved back into his pockets. She straightens, brushes nonexistent dust from her trousers.

"What sort of reaction were you expecting, sneaking up on a lady like that?" she asks, placing the strange specimen into the satchel at her feet.

One eyebrow arches on his weather-worn face. "Truth be told, Ms. Deering, I've never seen a *lady* wearing trousers."

"Welcome to the 20th century, Mr. Seward," she says, snapping the buckles on her satchel, and slinging it up around her shoulders. "You're going to have to get used to a few more things besides a woman wearing trousers." She picks up her camera and focuses the lens to the deepening waves cresting with angry, white foam. "Is there something I can help you with?"

Tom drops his gaze to his boots, watching the dark water lap against the rocks. "I thought I told you to be careful Ms. Deering. And now I find you out here, on the Sound—I mean."

Cora looks over her shoulder. "And when did you get the impression I do as I'm told?"

Her attempt at humor goes unnoticed as Tom's face twists. "The things out there." He juts his chin in the direction of the open ocean. "They're no laughing matter."

A sick and salty wind blows off the waves, and Cora almost chokes as it passes beneath her nostrils. Her skin flares against it, throat seeming to swell.

Yes, she thinks, *yes, but aren't they beautiful?*

Once more unsnapping the buckles on her satchel, she brings out the jar and holds it up to the weak sunlight.

"Do you see this?" she asks, letting the water fall away from the black shell inside the glass.

Tom steps forward, face souring.

"I've never seen anything like it." Her awe is palpable, the wind catching it as it brushes her skin. "The way the light seems to disappear against the shell, as if it's sucking it all away, making everything else dark around it." She swirls the inky water around in the jar, watching as the mollusk clings to the glass, leaving trails of slime. "It's beautiful."

Behind her, Tom snorts.

She whirls around, cheeks flaring warm. "I assume you don't agree?"

Tom shrugs, kicks at a rock with his boot. Cora watches as it tumbles toward the water, sending ripples that heave against the waves. Silence stirs there, so deep Cora can hear the way the ocean retracts on itself like a thin blade. The wind hollows out her ears.

"What was that for?" she asks, not taking her eyes off the waves that now seem to stretch long toward the horizon like sprawling fingers. She crouches low, reaching toward the ocean, but Tom is quick at her side, wrenching her away.

"Don't," he says, voice rushed. "Don't touch the water."

She wants to ask why, feels the word on her tongue, but she crushes it against her teeth as a strange, dark mist moves in against the Sound. "What is that?" she asks, voice barely above a whisper.

Tom's body is hot at her back, his fingers digging into the soft flesh of her sides. "That is what comes before," he says. "Before the Scylla rises from the water and slits claws across skin, Ms. Deering. And, if you know what's good for you, you'll run now and you won't look back."

The words singe Cora's hairline, turning the wisps of mousey curls there to smoke. A chill cuts through her as she watches the mist undulate against the wavering surface of the deepening water. Her chest twists, breath halting. "And what happens if we stay?" Her voice is no more than vapor coiling from between her lips.

A twinge in her sides—Tom's grip tightening. "They'll be pulling your body from the waves in the morning."

Cora's thoughts turn to the university students—the men, faces polluted by self-absorption and the desire to see her fail. Her muscles tighten, cords of sinew stiffening with resolve. "I'd like to see them try." She breaks away from Tom, gathering her equipment in sloppy movements as her feet struggle through rocks further up the shoreline.

The wind swirls up, bitingly cold as ice shoves quiver in anticipation. Cora hurries from the water's edge with Tom on her heels. She slips behind a damp-stained stone, large enough to cover a tomb, and fumbles with the bellows of her pocket kodak.

Tom slips behind her, eyes spitting fire. "You're going to get us both killed."

Salt sweeps in off the sea, stinging Cora's skin as she fumbles with the focusing screw, her fingers cold and clumsy. Her heart races, seemingly not aware that it belongs in a cage of ribs, of sinew and flesh, as it pounds viciously against its confines. Wind rushes in heavily, blowing the hat from her head. She nearly drops the camera. Her eyes drift out to the waves, where the swirling mass of shadow grows thicker, closer, as the scent of rotted seabed slicks the air like oil. Her breath escapes in short, brittle puffs.

A brush of Tom's hands at the curve of her waist. "Cora—"

His words are too late, half-swallowed in the tempest blowing in off the guttering, ice-choked waves. It starts in the water, a thin ripple as if a stick has been tossed into the sea. It licks around the edges of the shadowed mist, spreading out until it touches the shoreline. That is when Cora feels it, deep in the hollow of her chest—a fear that threatens to shatter in bloody lines across her face, like cracks in China. The camera feels like ice in her hands as she watches the water churn and undulate, writhing like a bed of thick, black snakes.

Tom says something, words inaudible, as the *thing* rises from the sea. At first, it seems like a large wave, curling up from the depths, but then it stretches out and Cora sees it for what it is: a monster, all scales and flailing tentacles that lick through the water, reaching toward the shore. Wild eyes, pupils like ebony gashes click open and shut, open and shut, as it turns its heads, sickle-shaped horns glinting like pools of midnight oil in the weak sun.

Cora wants to scream, wants to tear her mouth apart until it cuts bloody across her face as the sound rips jagged from her throat. But she can't even force a breath between her lips as the thing in the water turns to her, smiling with six rows of needle teeth. A scent fills the air—more than salt or sand. It burns Cora's nostrils, keen and hot, as if someone struck a match against red phosphorus. Tom's nails dig into the small of her back and she can feel his breath hot on her neck, but nothing can take her eyes from the creature.

"It's beautiful."

The words leave her mouth in a breath, and she knows it is strange, to be face to face with something that should not exist, to be filled near bursting with a fear that tastes of the Devil, and still find the thing beautiful. The monster—Scylla—ripples forward, its slick, scaled body gliding through the water like a great vessel of war.

"We need to leave." Tom's words are rushed, running into each other like a drunkard's. "Now."

But Cora is too busy adjusting her focus, too busy to notice the Scylla now lingers only moments from the lapping shore—thick, sinewy tentacles reaching for stones. Breath hitching, her finger grazes the shutter. Then Tom is pulling her back, farther up the bank, as the monster slaps slime-slick limbs against the stones and rends the air in twain with a cry that curdles Cora's blood.

It is not until Tom is wrenching her across the threshold of his clapboard home that the words on her tongue turn to cracking laughter, a tangle of nonsense and half-finished sentences.

Cold sweat clings to Cora's skin. The light is dim, sneaking in around the boards haphazardly placed against the windows. Tom leans against a table, sleeves rolled to his elbows, smelling of washing soda, citrus, and coffee grounds. His thumb rubs against the smooth wood grain, eyes pointed down. The photograph flutters in Cora's hand as she stares blankly ahead, eyes unfocused. Her heart beats, but it feels far away—as if someone has ripped it from her chest and set it to pound a rhythm in somewhere Cora cannot reach. Her mind feels blurred, hazy; her gut swims with nausea. She looks down at the picture again, hoping—praying—that it will be different.

The sickle-cell horns are the first to turn her prayers to ash. The image is blurry—taken in a moment of skin-boiling fear—but she can make out the beast all the same. Dark lines of scales, a triad of tongues and teeth and roving, lidless eyes. Searching tentacles slithering out against the black, angry waves. Cora's stomach sloshes, presses against the back of her throat, and before she can stop herself, she's spilling white lines of sick onto the rotten boards of Tom's kitchen.

"Shit, fuck." Tom fumbles with the patched, ragged cloth on his belt, slimed with blood, bending down as Cora empties her stomach onto the floor.

It burns like acid up her throat, and she can do nothing to stop it. Her body shakes, her mind cracking along its own fissures. Spittle slips from the corners of her mouth. "You've got to tell me if I'm dreaming, Tom," she says, voice haggard. She grasps his shoulder, fingers sinking into thew. "Tell me that I'm dreaming."

But he only stares at her, eyes vacant—pupils so dilated they might be black holes sucking her in. She reels back against the chair, wiping vomit from her lips. The photograph still flutters in her hand, but she cannot look at it, not now, not when her very blood seems to boil, her skin wanting to shred itself on her jagged bones. She wobbles to her feet, skin goosing as she turns to the door.

"Where are you going?" Tom asks, breathless.

"I—I..." Her lungs sputter and fizzle, like the motor of a broken automobile. There is so much she wants to say, questions she wants to ask but, as soon as the thoughts become words on her tongue, they crumble like dust in her mouth, turning her throat to sandpaper. She swallows, wincing at the raw sensation clinging to her skin like pincers. And there's nothing to say—not now, not after what she saw, because nothing makes sense. She fits her fingers around the iron latch and swings the door open, stepping out into the gray mist as Tom's cries bite at her back.

When Cora reaches the Avalon Inn, the sea has started to consume itself, a black snake swallowing its own tail. She watches it from the crest of the hill, limbs rattling at the sight of the great, hungry thing as it cracks violently against the rocks. The Scylla is nowhere to be seen, but she knows it is out there, can feel it...waiting beneath the waves. Waiting to run its clammy tentacles over her skin, to open her up with its claws and taste her on its teeth. She shudders, trying to conjure the resolve, the determination she felt when her boots hit the dilapidated docks only yesterday.

Wicked, dark clouds bite along the western edge of the horizon, and Cora knows what she must do—what she came to this wretched spit of rock to do.

She must prove herself.

The inside of the inn is devoid of life. Mildew drips from the ceiling, and Ms. Beckett's desk is deserted. In the shadows, Cora notices the sickle-patterned China cup sitting overturned beside a piece of white paper. She crosses to it, her fingers fumbling with the fine, clean edges, and turns it over. It is blank, save for a single smear of red in the shape of a crescent moon. Cora's heart drops to the soles of her feet, beating hot rhythms against her skin. She lifts it to her nose.

Blood.

Of course, it's blood.

She has no time to think, no time to list out her thoughts, categorizing and cataloging them in accordance with logic, with reason. Because there is no logic and reason anymore. On this island, there is only madness seeping up from the sea, and it is already sinking deep into her bones. She can feel it, worming its way through the seams of her skull, to grow roots in her brain—roots so deep she feels her head might explode. But she needs answers, that deep desire to prove herself still settling firm in the muscle and sinew of her shoulders.

She goes back outside, feeling the cold mist whip at her face. The ocean crashes angrily below the cliffs and, as she stares at it, gaping before her like some gray-matter maw, her jaw goes slack and a smile creeps along her lips.

"Unknown origin," she titters to the wind.

The thought should have sparked fear and trepidation but, for her, it had only sparked curiosity. Now, though, even that has turned to ash, and her gut swims with knowledge—true knowledge. She pictures the Scylla and realizes that there is nothing in the world with a known origin. Even she herself is an unknown, just a sack of meat and bones drifting in a vast sphere of mystery. In a cosmos of—

"Cora!" Her name rings out above the din, and she spins to see Tom cresting the hill, coming up from the sea, the blood and sick-soaked cloth slapping at his side. Before she can stop him, his fingers are on her face, peeling at her skin, eyes crazed and wild and filled with salt. "Cora, we must get out of here!"

His voice cracks across her face, breaks her from her thoughts. "Why?" she calls over the ripping wind.

"This storm, you've got to understand, this storm is not natural. There are things," his fingers dig into her shoulders. "There are things about this island, Cora, about these people—"

But his words stop halfway up his throat, as though invisible fingers have plucked them out—bloody roots and all. Cora moves a hand to touch his rough-hewn cheek, wet mist making her fingers slippery and unsure.

"Show me," she says. "Show me the rest of your secrets."

They hear the chanting before they reach the sea. It spills along the wind, just whispers at first, strange vapors of sound. Cora's heart capsizes as it reaches her ears, brushing thinly against her skin.

"What is that?" she asks, the noise rattling her teeth.

But Tom doesn't stop, dragging her forward toward the Sound. That is when she sees them—all in white, chanting with raised arms in the shallows of the mighty, ice-bitten sea. Their bodies sway back and forth, back and forth, in a rhythmic display as their left arms stay rigid until their right ones swing over their heads, making the sickle shape over and over and over.

"*Veni ad nos, o magne*," they sing. "*Veni ad nos, daemonium abyssi.*"

And, though Cora has never spoken a word of Latin in her life, she studied it enough to know what they are saying.

Come to us, oh great one. Come to us, demon of the deep.

A shiver licks up the back of Cora's spine before wrapping around her neck and settling deep into her shoulders like a thing with scales and teeth. She feels Tom's hand brush the small of her back.

"Who are they?" she asks, voice barely a whisper.

For a moment, Tom does not answer, just keeps his damp eyes on the undulating mass of white-robed figures as they form a circle and sway in the shallows. "The Cult of Scylla has been here since the island was founded, hiding in the shadows, keeping forked tongues behind their teeth." The words drip hot and angry from his lips. "They recruit few to their numbers, but birds are always flying into nets, aren't they?"

Cora remembers the mention of his wife, of her death at the hands of the Scylla. "What was her name?"

203

A pained expression crosses Tom's face, all hard lines and hot tears. "Elizabeth, Elizabeth Worley. A girl from Boston who was too blinded by love for a fool to see the trap he was leading her into."

Cora turns to face him, trying to make sense of his jagged jaw, his water-logged eyes, the way he watches the undulating water with fear so strong she can taste it on the wind—like bitter brine and rotten fruit.

"But it wasn't your fault, Tom. How were you to know her fate? You didn't know what you were doing."

He looks at her, so dark, so filled with shadow that it makes her skin goose. "Can't you see, Cora?" he says, voice ragged and raw. "I thought you could save us, but don't you understand? It's...I have no choice—" He turns his hands over, tears streaming down his cheeks. "I'm doing it now."

She barely has time to scream as strong limbs wrap around her arms and waist, carrying her away from Tom to the open ocean. She fights them with biting nails and gnashing teeth, but their hold is too strong, too tight against her failing limbs. She feels the water, cold at her back, and then hands—she doesn't know how many—press her deeper, until the ocean fills her mouth.

No, no. This wasn't how it was supposed to go. This wasn't how it was supposed to end. She can taste the champagne still, souring now on the back of her tongue. She thrashes, clawing at the robed faces bending over her.

"Stay still, little fool, or you'll ruin the meat."

No. She knows that voice. Through the stinging salt water, she blinks up at the wrinkled face of Ruby Beckett. "You." The word is half-drowned as they press her deeper into the churning waters.

"Yes, me, my darling. A lady scientist, indeed." She bends closer, so close Cora can smell the tea rotting on her breath. "I was angry at first, when I heard about the telegram. But then you," she laughs, a lilting, stunted thing. "You were perfect. Just the sort of thing the Master commands—sweet meat—and I thought, why not? Why not let you play your little game, collecting shells and seaweed. But then Tom told me of the picture—poor thing, has a hard time keeping things from his mother. So, I gathered my sisters and conjured our god."

Cora's stomach convulses, searching for Tom in the sea of faces, but he is nowhere to be found. Nothing but a coward with blood on his hands.

A mighty roar rends the air, and Cora's heart surges, the fear cascading through her.

Ruby looks up to greet the swirling, shadowed mist as the Scylla breaks through, sending sprays of ice and rotten seabed. Her voice rings out against the preternatural storm. "We have brought her, oh Great One. We have brought her for you, another bride to join you in the deep."

Cora kicks and searches with her open, ocean-filled mouth to bite at the hands clasping her under the waves. Her heart pounds. She wants to taste champagne, she wants to hear cheers and salutations, but they all turn to muddled, bloody cries on the wind. The sky darkens and, in a moment, the women in white fall away.

She looks up, gaze snagging on the slits of dark pupils that stare unblinkingly down at her, its mouth with rows of spiny teeth opening, shutting. Opening, shutting. Her skin crawls. The Scylla slides greasily through the water, its hide slick with mud and bloody scales of eviscerated fish.

Tom's fish.

Tom—just a pawn, a plaything compared to the cosmic beast that rends the sky above Cora, dripping black water and blood. A great head rips from the waves, spilling slime from its teeth.

Unknown origin.

The words pop effervescent against the roof of her mouth. The scent of upturned seaweed and rotting flesh fills her nostrils. There is nothing known in this world, not anymore. Her skin grows hot, flushed, ripping itself like the threads of a tapestry. A smile breaks across her lips, scratching bloody at her throat. The Scylla's head dips toward her, tentacles thrashing, sickle horns glinting. Cora opens her mouth, laughing, turning her face to fissures of rotten inky pus as the monster sinks venomous teeth into her flesh.

She is not afraid. She welcomes death—lets it slip hungrily around her body and pull her beneath the darkening waves. Because death is just another unknown and, perhaps, Cora Deering has been dying all her life.

ATTN. DR. JONATHAN ESTRA, UNIVERSITY COLLEGE LONDON, MARINE SCIENCES –(STOP)–

I REGRET TO INFORM YOU OF THE DEATH OF MS. CORA DEERING, WHO WASHED UP ON SHORE SOME DAYS BACK AFTER SUFFERING WHAT APPEARS TO BE AN UNFORTUNATE RESEARCH ACCIDENT –(STOP)–

YOURS TRULY, THOMAS SEWARD

CHAPTER TWELVE

UNFETTERED GREATNESS

William Bartlett

Asylum for the Insane, somewhere on the east coast, 1918

A woman with chestnut hair, oiled, slicked back, parted, and cut short like a man's, waits in a stiff metal chair. Stacked cinder blocks, painted hospital white, make up the walls of the stark room where she is contained. Her button-up shirt and slacks, clean and pressed, bare no signs of lower-class filth and display all evidence of a wealthy man. Her posture is perfect, proud, and powerful. She waits with closed eyes until the large and heavy metal door opens, and the institution's head doctor enters.

"Good morning, Eleanor." He is followed by an elderly woman clutching a notebook and a pack of pencils.

"Pardon me, Doctor, as I have corrected you countless times before, my name is Walter Cunningham. Dr. Walter Cunningham," the woman says as she opens exquisite hazel eyes.

"Yes, of course," he dismisses. "Let's pick up where we left off yesterday, shall we?" He sits opposite Eleanor, setting his things upon the cold metal table. "So, you were talking about your late husband."

"I was talking about her late husband, yes. I have her memories stuck inside me, as well as my own."

"For the record, you mean Eleanor? You have Eleanor Weatherford's memories inside of you?"

"Yes. She and her husband were dealing with the emotional turmoil that accompanies two miscarriages and a stillborn child. They were suffering. Instead of comforting one another, he chose crime and she chose isolation."

"When you say he chose crime, do you mean the illegal purchase and consumption of alcohol?" The doctor looked at her over his glasses.

"Yes. It led to suicide."

"After he died, what happened?"

"Eleanor spent a year recovering…"

"Dr. Cunningham, for the sake of simplicity, would you be willing to speak as Eleanor in the first person?" the asylum doctor asked in exasperation.

"Why? So you can begin the process of indoctrination? Convince my subconscious of her identity, and rid me of my own?"

The doctor sighed. "Not at all. Please just humor me, at least to simplify the recording, so that my superiors do not have to battle with extra confusion."

"Fine."

"Please continue."

"She… I…spent a year recovering from the suicide. I was devastated. I was poor. And I was angry with God. Until one evening, a car pulled up to my house. I lived in a neighborhood where the houses were small, but lovely. Our home was our only inherited possession. Now I'm sure you can remember, cars were not as common seven years ago as they are now. I was blown away. And there was a woman driving it! I couldn't believe my eyes. She was dressed so elegantly. Clearly, she came from wealth. I invited her inside, but she refused and insisted she must be on her way. She was to deliver an invitation and had a dozen others left to deliver. I could not believe that someone would invite me to anything. I had no friends, and my family lived out of state. I had never even met someone of wealth, much less a socialite."

"Who was the invitation from? And what was it for?"

"The invitation was for a dinner being held on an island not far away from here. It was for the country's most distinguished academics and scholars. I couldn't help but think there was some kind of mistake. But the letter listed my full name: Mrs. Eleanor Ruth Weatherford of the late Mr. David William Weatherford. The invitation stated that a car would arrive in a week's time to pick me up."

"And who was the invitation from?"

"Well, from me of course. Dr. Walter Cunningham."

Brackish Harbor, 1911

The island was simple and quiet, seemingly uninhabited save for a few simple structures. The buildings were worn down heavily by decades of abrasive breeze. Eleanor inhaled the salt-enriched air as she stood at the ferry's port bow. They approached the eastern edge of the island where a massive lighthouse adorned a rock cliff. The lighthouse itself was old and worn, the paint long peeled away. Everything man-made on the island seemed to have lost its paint, the salted air abusive to the harbor. The docks were made of tarred wood and moss covered stone. The negative energy of the overcast sky embraced Eleanor like a wet blanket.

The ferry's deck was littered with the other dinner guests. No one made an effort to converse with her. She observed they were all dressed in their finest. Men wore expensive coats and top hats of finer quality than the solid gold railing of the ferry itself; the women with fur as sheen as a duck's back. Eleanor looked down at her own modest clothing. Her dress had been gifted by one of the ladies at her husband's church. It was silk and of fine quality, but it was old and stained. One of the socialites even asked her for another glass of champagne. She laughed when Eleanor explained she was not a crew member. Their shoes clicked upon the polished hardwood flooring, an added extravagance to the expensive boat.

The guests pinched their noses as they docked. The smell of the sea had grown pungent and unforgiving.

"I see where the island gets its name," a woman remarked. "This is all very brackish indeed." The other women laughed in the pretentious way the wealthy seem to do effortlessly.

"I have always enjoyed the smell of the sea and all that it has to offer."

Everyone turned to look at Eleanor as they crowded the ferry's gate.

"It reminds me of when I was a child," Eleanor continued, undeterred. "I would wait hours for him to return from his fishing trips. My mother and I would have lunch prepared for him."

The privileged said nothing in reply, struggling not to expose their condescending thoughts, though it was quite obvious.

They were escorted down a stone slab trail leading up the massive lighthouse's main building. Eleanor's shabby shoes lost traction on the wet slate and a staff member caught her. She realized the staff wore tuxedos or dresses of quality finer than any of the invited guests. They wore white silk gloves and strange hats that almost resembled that of a chef. But the strangest of all, were the white painted faces. Every staff member's identity seemed protected by thick white paint covering their faces entirely, including eyebrows and eyelashes.

Eleanor realized her skin was soaked, the air heavy with moisture. She wiped her face with the back of her hand and smeared her cheap lipstick. She quickly used a handkerchief to absorb the saltwater from her brow and used it to remove her lipstick entirely. She chastised herself for caring what these people might think about her, but the feeling of not belonging was too evident to ignore.

The building at the base of the massive lighthouse was much less impressive than its facade. It was a one-story building full of portable wall dividers to make up temporary office spaces. It reminded her of the Baptist church she once attended regularly. The only difference being its eerie feel. Cobwebs matted everything. The other guests held their dresses up to avoid the filth. They followed the staff to an old lift with rusted metal caging. They were lowered into a sublevel in groups of four. Eleanor was in the final group. The lift rattled and squealed. The oxidation of the cage matched the ghostly appearance of everything else on the island.

The lift took them deep into the earth and opened into a long hallway that curved. The space was adorned with electric light, the first Eleanor had ever seen in person. Complaints traveled through the hall as they walked. Some of the female guests removed their uncomfortable heels.

"This better be worth the hassle," one of the male guests grumbled. The hallway eventually ended at another set of stairs that led to a single heavy metal door, which was opened by a gorgeous staff member. She entered a grand and capacious ballroom. Another captivating staff member took her coat. The staff members seemed to be hired as models. Everyone had a perfect physique. The males with strong jawlines, attractive musculature, and a confident demeanor. The female staff members flirted with the male guests with their full lips, wandering caresses, and voluptuous figures.

A crystal chandelier so enormous that it could have only been assembled there, hung from the vaulted ceiling. The walls were lined with exquisite marble and gold trim. Polished and stained oak decorated the walls and ceiling. The staff delivered champagne to everyone as beautiful music filled the area. There were small round tables, hand carved out of solid wood with elegant filigree edges, spread out all over the ballroom floor. Two massive staircases flowed down from a second and third floor and united at the room's front. Expertly polished marble covered the floor and stairs. The energy of the crowd immediately flipped to joy and excitement. The ballroom was the absolute opposite of the building's exterior. The island was desolate and ravaged by the unrelenting sea.

Everyone mingled for the better part of an hour, inquiring about one another's professions, achievements, and successes. There was a famously beautiful actress from Hollywood making jokes and conversing with the others like a regular person. There was a renowned surgeon who was famous for saving the former President's life when he was still Governor of New Jersey.

Eleanor did not consider herself gifted or talented by any means, but she did take pride in her knowledge of current affairs. She enjoyed reading about politics and issues of national and global value. She recognized many people here as strong and powerful figures in the United States. No one took the time to approach her, but she didn't mind. She hadn't stopped swooning over the ballroom's decor since she arrived.

No one seemed to notice when a tall, young, well-groomed man descended the staircase and stood at the marble base. His eyes seemed to sparkle, complimenting the chandelier. His hair was long on top, but combed back and played nicely with the tapered sides. His suit was exquisite and striped. His shoes were as polished as the solid gold handrails. He kept the currently popular appearance of inner-city smugglers. He was clearly a man who knew how to spend his money. The smile he revealed as he tapped his glass of champagne with a gold utensil was the cherry on top of a delicious ice cream sundae. Everyone quieted and lent him their attention.

"Welcome, distinguished guests," he said in a booming voice. "I am beyond honored to be in the presence of such prestige. I am quite pleased with the ninety-five percent turnout, a natural way to weed out those who did not deserve this honor. You are all here because of a specific talent or expertise. A round of applause for your success."

Everyone clapped and cheered, long and loud.

"Enjoy that praise, for it will be the last, should you accept my invitation."

The guests exchanged glances.

"I have a proposition for each of you. I offer you unfettered greatness!" He lifted his outstretched arms dramatically.

The guests looked nervous, but provided obligatory clapping.

"I am Doctor Walter Cunningham, entrepreneur, investor, and most importantly, scientist," the man continued. "I have a hypothesis that I know to be plausible and lucrative. But the governing forces of this world—specifically that of morality and religion—seek to prevent that which is inevitable. I am proposing domination over the magic the universe uses to create!"

Everyone clapped to hide their confusion.

"Immortality," Eleanor muttered.

The room turned their undivided attention to her, and it was accompanied with reverent silence.

"Mrs. Eleanor Weatherford." The doctor brightened. "Welcome. Your wisdom does not disappoint. You are correct."

"Immortality?" the Hollywood actress questioned.

"Of course," Eleanor answered. "The oldest human obsession."

"Indeed," Dr. Cunningham confirmed. "It is possible. I have proved it through twenty years of calculations that have been triple-checked and counter-challenged!"

"Millions of people have been murdered in the pursuit of immortality. The Holy Quest for the Holy Grail. A fictitious object. The spear of destiny. The arc of the covenant. Jesus Christ himself. It is all fantasy!" Eleanor exclaimed.

"Exactly," Dr. Cunningham said excitedly. "Religion is the root of morality. Morality too, is fantasy! All that is real, is that which is tangible and physical. Science! Here, we will work, free from the binds of morality so we can be free from the binds of mortality!"

Everyone applauded sincerely.

Eleanor tapped her glass. "That is beautifully poetic, and I do apologize for the interruptions, doctor, but before you waste any more breath on me, I cannot help but wonder why I am here. Surely, you are mistaken in choosing me. Everyone here is distinguished in some way. I am a childless widow, living in poverty. I have no honor, talent, or knowledge."

She heard a woman mutter, "How forthcoming..." It was audible enough to stir some chuckles.

"Mrs. Weatherford, society has led you to believe that," Dr. Cunningham replied. "If you drop all that fluff, you'll see yourself as I do—the absolute most important guest here tonight. Unrecognized talent is not synonymous with untalented. I did not choose everyone here because of their recognized talent. I chose them for their usefulness. It just so happens that everyone here has been cut and polished. You are a diamond in the rough, and you are the largest diamond of us all. You, my dear, are the guest of honor."

Everyone clapped through their confusion once again.

"Do not patronize me, Dr. Cunningham, and do not call me Mrs. Weatherford. My husband is dead. I may not be educated like you, but I am smart enough to know when someone is making fun of me. How do you plan to keep this all secret? Do you really think the government will not find out? Thank you for the eventful evening, but I must be returning to my home."

She ignored the giggles and murmurs as she moved through the crowd as quickly as she could, struggling not to bolt for the door at full speed.

"Eleanor, wait! I was being literal. Your expertise is invaluable."

"What expertise?" she snapped.

"My dear, you have felt the fabric of the black curtain."

Eleanor froze. "The what?"

"You stood in death's shadow! You have been to the other side! You have a firsthand account of death unlike anyone else here."

The crowd murmured as she slowly turned back to face him.

The doctor's voice lowered. "You see, this physical life we experience through our limited senses—only six to be exact—perceives only that which we are allowed to see."

"Forgive me sir, but there are only five senses, are there not?" a stiff old fool from the crowd chimed in.

"The mind, Dr. Cent. The mind is our sixth sense. The mind not only governs the other five senses, but it works as a tether to the great beyond."

"The great beyond?"

The doctor grew excited once more. "The world our senses perceive is everything on the stage of a play. Everything we are allowed to see!

Everything we are meant to see! But behind the black curtain lies everything behind the scenes—the stage crew, the equipment, the technology, the director! The great beyond! This is the technology we will reverse engineer to make ourselves gods. But first, we must rip open our consciousness— the sixth sense—just like our dear Eleanor already has."

The crowd applauded loudly, cheering excitedly without cease. Everyone gazed upon Eleanor in a whole new light. They smiled at her, truly believing her to be whatever it was Dr. Cunningham believed her to be.

"And don't worry about the specifics of our discretion," he assured them. "Everything will be done here, underground, where I have created miles of laboratories, offices, and housing areas. All under the guise of a simple lighthouse. A lighthouse surrounded by a new town that will actually house fishermen, families, stores, and a warehouse to export and import the necessities of life. Welcome, colleagues, to Brackish Harbor."

Brackish Harbor, 1917

A chill slithered through the darkness of Eleanor's quarters and wrenched her from slumber. The room was normally quite warm. Her bed was more comfortable than anything she had ever slept in before, making her permanent stay here easier to accept. She sat up and caught her breath. She felt quiet energy. The energy of another person.

"Dr. Cunningham," she said as she turned on her Persian lamp.

"Astonishing."

"Why are you watching me sleep again?"

"You knew I was here without seeing or hearing me?"

"It isn't difficult to know the presence of a mouth breather."

"Ha! Excellent," he said with glee.

"Is this the purpose of my stay? For you to watch me sleep? For the rest of my days? What are you watching for? Are you simply waiting for me to die? To study my surroundings as I pass?"

"Oh, but you have already died."

"What?"

"Once before, years ago, alongside your husband."

"I-I…"

"I know, my dear Eleanor, I know. I know about the pact you made with your husband."

Eleanor jolted to her feet and fetched her robe. "You go too far, Dr. Cunningham."

He moved to stop her. "Eleanor, it is okay. Rest easy. I, too, know the pain that comes after losing a child."

"I—you—"

"My wife, Barbara, committed suicide shortly after the accident. I know that pain, Eleanor, so believe me when I tell you I understand why you wanted to leave this world. That is why my work is so important! I don't want everlasting life for selfish reasons, I want to endow the world a victory over death! So that no one will ever have to suffer such horrible pain, again!"

Eleanor was speechless, and nearly persuaded.

"Eleanor, I enjoy watching you sleep, because it is during slumber that we are closest to the black curtain. And when you sleep, it must be within reach. The thought of that fascinates me. That is all. But today, my dear, is a very special day. I'm finally ready to show you the lab and the fruits of our labor. Come with me, please. I will take you there myself."

After a long walk of locked doors, armed security guards, and walls lined with heavy metal pipe, they arrived at a set of double doors made of iron. There was a staircase that led into a sizable room. Dozens of scientists scurried about busier than war generals amongst large chalkboards covered in mathematical formulas and equations. Papers were scattered everywhere. Half the scientists studied clipboards, while the other half scribbled down notes. Some argued with each other. The room had a long window that ran its length, but the busyness of the scientists shrouded the view on the other side.

"Don't mind them." Dr. Cunningham had to raise his voice to speak over the chaos. "They are just triple-checking everything before the procedure takes place."

"Procedure? What procedure?" Eleanor matched his tone to be heard. He grabbed her hand and led her through a second set of double doors on the room's opposite side. They walked down a hall with a long glass window that ran the length of it. The window gave view of a spectacular sight.

The laboratory was a massive oval, the walls were lined with countless pieces of technological and medical equipment. The center of the room resembled a surgical operating room, complete with enormous bright lights, an immense mirror fastened to the ceiling with gurneys underneath, and a steel table with clean instruments and tools already laid out. Thick cables like elephant trunks ran along shallow gutters that encircled the room. From the gutters, braided copper strands ran up the walls and connected everything together. Two scientists quieted as they entered.

Eleanor observed two bedded gurneys in the center of the room.

"Eleanor, welcome to my laboratory." Dr. Cunningham waved his arms with a flourish.

"Dr. Cunningham..."

She was interrupted by a finger in the air. They all waited for a long and uncomfortable moment. Then, the laboratory doors opened, and four guards entered with two bound men. Eleanor was so confused; she could not think of a question to ask. The men both wore black cloth over their heads.

"Please remove the hoods and liberate them of their binds."

As the guards proceeded to do so, Eleanor felt slightly more at ease.

"Gentleman, I apologize for the crude manner in which you were brought here, but as you already know, the experiment for which you volunteered requires the utmost discretion."

"Yea, yea, no big deal. You pay me what you promised, and I'll let you shove whatever you want up my ass," said the young blonde man.

Eleanor snickered at the comment, but quickly composed herself after seeing everyone else's disgust.

"I don't agree with this man's brackish mouth, but I too agree to cooperate if you deliver on your promise, good sir," the older brown-haired man admitted.

"Perfect. Your compensation will be doubled if you continue to cooperate after the procedure."

"Now you're talking!"

"Please, lay down on the gurneys."

"Dr. Cunningham," Eleanor began. He lifted a finger once again. The guards strapped the men down quickly.

"Hey! What's the big idea?"

"No cause for alarm sir, these...restraints...are simply for your own protection."

"For our own—"

The guards quickly shoved padded gags into the men's mouths.

"These gags are so you don't bite your own tongue off," the doctor explained.

Panic crept into Eleanor's chest. She glanced back at the double doors to find the other two guards standing in front of it.

"Don't worry Eleanor, they will be unharmed during the procedure," he assured her before calling, "Doctor Patel, please, let's not waste any more time. Flip the switch."

"Dr. Cunningham—" Eleanor tried again, fear rising inside her.

"Eleanor, please step back and put on these protective tinted lenses. Please hurry."

A frightening buzzing vibrated the walls of the laboratory. The ground seemed to shake. Lights suddenly spread over top the massive copper braids that ran across the ceiling, down the wall, and up to the gurneys. It looked like tiny lightning, glowing earthworms wriggling through the copper.

Dr. Patel flipped the switch back to its original position. The lights dissipated as quickly as they burst to life.

"Guards, please liberate the men," Dr. Cunningham ordered.

"What the hell? I said 'up my ass,' not down my throat!" the older brown-haired man said.

"What in God's good name—What have you done?" The younger blonde man stared in disbelief at the man across from him.

Eleanor glanced at Dr. Cunningham incredulously as he only grinned. It was the first truly menacing characteristic he had shown up to that point.

"It's...me..." the blonde man said as the older brown-haired man finally found himself. "You're...me!" The blonde continued. "You're me! You're in my body!"

"Holy shit. You're right. This...is madness!"

"All right, doctor, you had your fun, go ahead and change us back now! We'll take our money and we'll be on our way."

"Yea! I don't wanna be stuck in this old man's body—you just stole years of my life!"

"Exactly!" Dr. Cunningham exclaimed, his sudden outburst startling Eleanor. "Subject 56," he said, referring to the now blonde man, "I just gave you an extra twenty years of life. This, ladies and gentlemen, is how we become gods!"

The other two scientists, as well as all the people in the busy room with the large window, applauded and cheered.

"Are you kidding me?" the now brown-haired man exclaimed. "Change us back now!"

"This brings us back to my offer. Double the compensation if you cooperate after the procedure."

"Cooperate? You mean stay like this? Are you mad? No. No way!"

"Do you refuse my offer?"

"What? Are you serious? Yes, I refuse! Put me back!"

Dr. Cunningham nodded at the two guards still standing behind the men. The guards un-holstered their pistols and pointed them at the men. The now blonde man put his hands in the air. The other guard pulled the trigger and shot the brackish man in the head.

Eleanor screamed.

Dr. Cunningham moved to soothe Eleanor, but she shoved him away and bolted for the door. The two waiting guards grabbed her by the wrists and restrained her.

"Release me at once, Dr. Cunningham!"

"Eleanor, forgive me, please," he said as he nodded to the other guard. A second shot killed the other test subject. The guards brought her over to the gurney.

She screamed as they restrained her, while the others dragged the men's corpses away.

"I know you and your husband took your own lives, together," the doctor said. "You didn't want to live in a godless world. Because only a godless world would allow a child to die. I know that pain, Eleanor! I also know the pain of being left here alone. I wish I could have gone with my beloved. I wish that, too!"

"Let me go!" she screamed.

"But that is why we must do this work. We could stop people from dying! Those who deserve to live will occupy the bodies of those who don't deserve life."

Eleanor sneered. "You're trying to steal my body? To give yourself more life? You think that's noble? Selfless?"

The doctor shook his head. "No, Eleanor, no. I want you to show me the black curtain."

"What?"

"Show me how you did it."

"I-I didn't do anything. I don't know how I came back. I just did."

"Of course you don't remember now, the black curtain is closed. Only when it is open can you remember your way back."

"What are you talking about?"

"The memory is there! The mind records everything! But only in the transfer can we get a glimpse of the other side. Dr. Patel, crank the voltage all the way up and flip the switch."

He laid himself upon the second gurney while Eleanor shrieked, realizing the hopelessness of her situation. The switch flipped and the walls buzzed and shook violently. A towering glass tube burst, and voltage arced across the laboratory floor and ripped through the other scientist, as well as a guard. The power crawled across the floor like spider legs, eventually reaching the gurneys.

Pain ripped through them both, and Eleanor squeezed her eyes shut, as they were jolted into another existence.

Darkness spread from her clouded peripherals accompanied by a white flash of pain searing her flesh. She focused on the floating specs under the laboratory light. The world around her slowly faded to black, until the floating specs morphed into distant stars. Her last breath escaped. Then she floated in what could only be outer space. It was unfathomably quiet. It was not cold, in fact, it was perfectly comfortable. Inexplicably comfortable. It was a state of perfection not from our world. There was no need for breathing here. This was, without a doubt, death in all of its glory.

Eleanor became overwhelmed with nostalgia and familiarity, like an overdose of ecstatic déjà vu. She mimicked swimming motions that seemed to be successful. She remembered being here before. It did not seem long ago. The realization hit her like waking from a dream. This was true existence, not the physical world. She remembered how long she was here before, with her husband. It felt like a lifetime of swimming and exploring. She remembered how she pushed herself forward by sheer force of will, as opposed to physical movement. She let herself glide through the void, savoring freedom. The glide was as unstable as her thoughts. She remembered to focus on linear impulses to balance her movement, like the recent surfing craze. Her husband had learned and taught her before they started trying for a baby.

Dr. Cunningham came into vision, tumbling through the void, out of control and barely conscious. She intercepted his path and grabbed hold of him. "Dr. Cunningham, try to gain control of your thoughts. Focus on me."

He came to, and held on to her tightly. They spun together through the void.

"Dr. Cunningham... Walter...you need to calm yourself."

"W-Where are we, what is happening?"

"We are here, Walter. We are in the Great Beyond. But we can be easily lost here. Control is achieved through your thoughts."

He flailed his limbs as if treading water.

"Walter, you don't have a body here. Only consciousness."

"W-Why can I see your body? Why can I see my own body? And we're clothed?"

"This is how our mind perceives ourselves. It completes what isn't there as a defense against madness."

"I don't understand."

"Walter, you were right!"

"What?"

"You were right! I remembered everything upon returning here. But you must know. This is not the afterlife like you believed it would be. Our bodies are not yet fully dead."

"Then what is this place?"

"Hmm. How to put it. My husband and I called it the in-between. In your analogy, this is the actual curtain. We are currently passing through the black curtain."

"Amazing!" the doctor exclaimed.

They spun rapidly through the void again.

"Walter! You must remain calm. Movement comes from emotion, but your thoughts are what steers the movement. If you let your emotions flare, we could be lost here. Trust me, I learned that the hard way."

"Well, let us proceed to the other side!"

"It does not work like that, unfortunately. Not while our bodies are still alive. You see, once you pass to the other side, there is no return. We can only return to our bodies. When I was here with my husband, we waited for what seemed like multiple lifetimes until our bodies expired. While we waited, we explored."

"Fascinating! Let's do it again! Show me your favorite places!"

"Walter, be calm. Listen to me. This place is not what you think. Humans are not meant to linger here. During our...explorations...we discovered..."

"What? What did you discover?"

"The natives."

"What?"

"The native inhabitants of this realm. I believe they are the guardians of this place. They exist on the fringes. They ensure nothing passes."

"Eleanor, you must take me to see them! This is where the answers to all my questions lie! I must see them!"

They spun wildly again with his excitement, pushing them rapidly through the void.

"Absolutely not. You know not what you ask."

"Who are you to deny me this request? I have traveled successfully through death to arrive here. Take me to the natives at once!" His commanding voice shot them through the void like a bullet out of a firearm.

"No, Walter, please! You don't understand." Eleanor's fear rose like the tide. "I can't—I won't!"

"Eleanor! You must not deny me this! This is for the good of mankind—this is the entire reason Brackish Harbor exists!"

"Walter! Unhand me at once! You do not understand what will happen! Unhand me!"

"Eleanor!"

She used every emotion she could muster, and shoved herself away from him. As they separated, their movement came to a sudden halt. Silence resumed control. They stared at one another for a brief moment. Then a deep and reverberating breath filled the void around them. The illusion of Eleanor's face went pale, and her eyes opened wide.

Walter searched for the cause of her surprise. "What?"

The blackness behind him moved as a gigantic eyelid wriggled.

"Walter..." she whispered. "Quiet and calm..."

He turned around slowly, but his emotions got the better of him as he bumped into the living mass. The monstrous eyelid peeled back slowly to reveal an impossibly large eyeball, the color of the blood moon. His fear shoved him backward and away from the eyeball. An unsettling rumble, like rolling thunder, tore through the serenity of the void.

Eleanor grabbed ahold of Walter and pulled him away.

"Wait," he protested. "I must attempt communication!"

"Walter! We must leave! This thing is not a god!"

"GREETINGS!" the mad doctor screeched.

The pupil of the hulking eye found them both and narrowed. The eye lifted upward, far and out of sight. Then an even larger eye opened. Then three other smaller eyes opened below, all focused on the tumbling humans. The rumbling evolved into a growl, and the void itself trembled.

"Walter, what have you done?"

Countless eyes continued to open. Tentacles sprang into existence and reached out for them. Eleanor grabbed the doctor and pulled him away from the fringe as fast as she could. A few tentacles detached from the creature and shot towards them at an alarming speed. Eleanor grabbed her fear as if it were tangible and used everything she could to fly back to where they entered. It was not fast enough. One of the hundred tentacles caught up and wrapped itself around Walter's leg.

He screamed in terror. The emotion shot them both through the void faster than could be comprehended. A flash of white light came over them both, blinding, but comfortable.

Total body soreness plagued Walter as if he had been asleep for years. His joints ached and his muscles were stiff. A guard removed his restraints as he stretched, wincing in the blinding overhead light. He sat up on the edge of the gurney, his body sluggish.

The walls sparked and machines sputtered. Both scientists and three guards were dead. Only one survived. He seemed to be injured, limping as he brought a glass of water that he had just stirred some powder into.

"Here you go, sir, drink this."

"What is this?" he asked in an unusually soft voice. He cleared his throat.

"I'm not sure, sir. Dr. Patel instructed me to give it to you upon waking up."

"Ah yes, of course. Why is it so difficult to remember things?"

"What the hell have you done?" A voice just like his own asked. He spun around and saw himself sitting up on the edge of the gurney.

Walter glanced down at his new hands to observe them younger, smoother, and more feminine than ever before. Eleanor clutched her belly and screamed in agony. He watched himself grit his teeth and moan as if being burned.

She ripped the bedding off the gurney and found her reflection in the metal underneath. She hyperventilated as he struggled to adapt to the bizarreness of watching his own body scream in pain and shock but not feel any of it. The pain seemed to come in waves until she suddenly screamed with a man's voice at the top of her lungs.

Dr. Cunningham, the guard, and the room full of scientists watched silently in horror through their window as the screams from his old body were muffled by a group of tentacles forcing their way out of its mouth. Walter struggled to keep his heart rate down as he watched his former body and face split and tear. The bones snapping echoed as its blood spilled to the ground. Eleanor, trapped in the destroyed carcass of his old body, lay dead, permanently. The cosmic horror that escaped the folds of the black curtain, stretched its limbs and opened its eyes, a dozen at a time.

The creature leapt at the guard, wrapped itself around him, and squeezed. The man's screams ceased before the crunching of his bones did. Loud sucking sounds filled the space between Walter and the beast. The guard's body seemed thin, and the creature seemed to double in size. The monster emitted a loud screech as it scanned the area for more.

Walter bolted for the double doors, clumsily, as he struggled to adapt to his new female body. The creature leapt for him. He rolled his thin ankle and tumbled. The creature smacked against the door. He picked up a metal plate and heaved it at the long window, shattering it.

He dived into the hallway, narrowly dodging the creature's second attempt to grab hold of him. He couldn't help but appreciate the energy and stamina that came with Eleanor's young and healthy body. He found himself grateful amid the terror of the chase.

He flung open the double doors leading into the room full of scientists just in time to dodge another of the monster's leaps. The room froze and no one dared to even breathe loudly. The creature slapped a slimy tentacle on the nearest metal table and pulled itself atop it. Frost spread across the skin of the slime as well as on the table. The creature emitted only the sound of nasally breath as it scanned the room.

Its tentacles spread out, fell to the floor, and grew in length as they stretched and reached the edges of the room. The slimy tendrils thickened between everyone struggling to remain still and quiet. The creature's center mass opened what could only be a mouth, and out came a tongue covered in eyeballs. The eyeballs themselves had tiny mouths where the pupils should have been. Then its tentacles closed in around the scientists, with a swiftness that was impossible to counter.

Walter watched helplessly as the nation's most distinguished academics were torn to pieces right before his eyes. A tendril grabbed a scientist's foot and tore it from its body as easily as a child with a toy. Other tentacles choked and wrapped its victims like boa constrictors.

A screaming male scientist stabbed one of the slimy appendages with a broken beaker repeatedly. The lacerations opened and more worm-like tendrils spilled out and fattened as they slithered in unison into their prey's open mouth. Another scientist was grabbed and pulled out from underneath a table and decapitated by a constricting invertebrate. A female scientist broke a lit bulb and set a stack of papers on fire. She waved the blaze through the air but the monsters seemed unafraid of it and wrapped around her legs instead. They squeezed her limbs until the audible cracks replaced her screams.

Blood textured the walls and floor as scientists were savagely ended. Silence conquered the room slowly as the scientists died almost unanimously. When the carnage ceased, the creature split into a dozen pieces and fled the room.

Walter leaned against a wall to regain his composure, but slipped on the blood splatter. He fell to the floor landing in the pool of viscera. A small tentacle remained in the sludge of human parts. The creature flung itself at him before he had a chance to scream, slithering its way into his mouth and down into his stomach.

Asylum for the Insane, somewhere on the east coast, 1918
"Did you get all that, Ms. Appleton?" the doctor asked.

"Yes, sir, I did."

"So, this is why you believe you are not actually Mrs. Weatherford, and are, in fact, Walter Cunningham trapped in Eleanor's body? Is this accurate?"

"Yes. I don't expect you to believe a word, of course. I am professionally aware of your obligation to keep me secured here for the rest of my life."

"This is not entirely true, Mrs. Wea—I mean, Dr. Cunningham. I have witnessed patients return to full health after even stranger delusions than this."

"Delusions?"

"Forgive me Doctor, I didn't mean to—"

"Listen to me, Doctor and Ms. Appleton, very carefully. There is something dark and ancient, destructive and savage, primal and chaotic, living inside of me, something that I never should have meddled with. And it's only one piece! There are hundreds more all over Brackish Harbor."

"Dr. Cunningham, if what you say is true, and these dangerous creatures are all over the island, then why haven't they been seen by any of the fishermen or locals? Why haven't they left the island?"

"I don't have those answers. I can only speculate. I believe they might be avoiding the salt water, or they are just lying dormant, like the one inside me. But I felt it awaken. This is the nature of my request. This is why I wanted to see you today. I need electrotherapy. Kill me if you have to. Or take me back to the island. But it is trying to get out. I don't know how or when, but eventually, I will lose control, and it will be free."

ACKNOWLEDGMENTS

As with all our publications, Tales from Brackish Harbor would not be possible without the help of some dedicated Crows. I would first like to thank our Assistant Editor, Damon Barret Roe. As with all our anthologies, this one would not have been possible without her. Assisted by our Acquisitions Editor, Stephen Black, we were able to sort through the mass quantity of submissions to pick out some amazing stories. I am grateful for them both. Damon also tirelessly led the Editing Team through this process, and I would like to extend my gratitude to the members of this team, including K.R. Wieland, JayLynn Watkins, and our Novel Editor, Eli Hayden Loft. I am always so honored to work alongside the Quill & Crow Editing Team, and this project was no exception.

Secondly, I'd like to deeply thank the inspiration for this project, William Bartlett. A longtime cosmic horror enthusiast, William inspired me to take a side-step from Gothic horror and dive into the otherworldly realm of eldritch horror. Not only did he provide a story for this anthology, but he designed the cover, which includes some of his own artwork. I am so grateful for his contribution, as well as the ideas from Luke Mann and Damon, to make this anthology a reality.

Lastly, I'd like to thank all the authors who contributed their stories. Having a pre-determined theme was a new adventure for us, and I was amazed by the way the authors capture the exact vibes I was hoping for. I thoroughly enjoyed every one of these tales.

Working on this anthology has been another enjoyable experience, and I hope you've enjoyed reading it as well. I appreciate everyone's efforts and look forward to seeing what more we can come up with as a publishing house.

Dreadfully Yours,

Cassandra L. Thompson

AUTHOR BIOGRAPHIES

WILLIAM BARTLETT is a regular guy with a full-time life. He is happily married with a son and a daughter who are as nerdy as he is. He is the Creative Designer for Quill & Crow Publishing House, and the author of *The House of Blood & Gold* and the dark poetry collection, *Nameless Here for Evermore*. His poetry is also featured in *Crow Calls Volumes II, III & IV*.

NICK BENNETT is a 31-year-old amateur author from the frozen wasteland of Michigan. He enjoys writing exclusively horror and humor. His biggest literary influences are H.P. Lovecraft, Michael Crichton, and Bill Watterson. Nick's other interests include but are not limited to: dinosaurs, robots, and robotic dinosaurs.

AMANDA M. BLAKE is a cat-loving daydreamer and mid-age goth who loves geekery of all sorts, from superheroes to horror movies, urban fantasy to unconventional romance. She's the author of horror titles such as *Nocturne* and *Deep Down,* and the fairy tale mash-up series *Thorns*.

AMANDA CASILE is a Speech Pathologist and writer who has just moved to New Jersey with her family and black cat, Lucky Nightmare. She writes mainly adult horror, but also dabbles in YA Science Fiction and Fantasy. Her story "The Thaw" will be in the upcoming *Step into The*

Light anthology from Bag of Bones Press. When not writing or teaching children to communicate, she can be found wandering the forest looking for ghosts. She's also active on Twitter.

FOX CLARET HILL is a transgender fiction writer who has been writing horror stories since he was old enough to spell. However, despite his adoration for the genre, writing was nothing more than a shadow-shrouded hobby until submitting his first story to DarkLit Press in 2021. That same story saw the light of day, and he has been confined to his office ever since. Born in Mothman's home state and raised in the hills of Malvern, Fox now resides by the beach in Australia with his husband and two dogs, Herbie and Gizmo.

LUCAS MANN lives in the beautiful Finger Lakes region of New York. In the abundant free time typical of being a parent of four children, physical therapist, and farmer, he enjoys writing in a mixture of genres. He has poetry featured in *Crow Calls Volumes II, III & IV*, has contributed to The Crow's Quill, and contributed to/edited *Grimm & Dread: A Crow's Twist on Classic Tales*.

MATTHEW SIADAK is based in the St. Louis area where he lives with his wife, daughter, two lizards, and three cats. He is currently working on his first novel, The Backwards Knight, the first of a planned fantasy trilogy with a touch of the dark and eldritch. His work has appeared in publications from Lost Boys Press and Herding Cats, and he has a selection of self-published shorts with his wife's art called *Arkadia*. When not writing, he loves to bake, tinker with tech, and make jam and soap. You can find him online at backwardsknight.com..

TEAGAN OLIVIA STURMER is a horror writer and Shakespearean actress and director hailing from the iron shores of Lake Superior where she spends most of her time in the woods making up scary stories and believing fairies exist. She is the author of *Floral Embroidery* and is represented by Amy Giuffrida of the Belcastro Agency.

MARY TAIT is an epic fantasy novelist and playwright living in northern Illinois. An archivist by trade, she is fascinated by the role information, history, and technology play in shaping our lives. While new to the horror genre, she suspects that her steady childhood diet of monster movies has something to do with her fondness for strange and terrifying creatures. She is currently writing *Ghost*, a fantasy web novel published weekly on her website, marytaitauthor.com.

R.B. THORNE writes slow-burn gothic horror, often with occult and supernatural elements. They can usually be found exploring forests, beaches, and cemeteries along the West Coast of the United States with their spouse. R.B.'s other passion is uplifting youth in their community. During the week, they lead an art program at a nonprofit for teens. You can visit Rose at rbthorne.com.

R. THURSDAY (they/them) is a writer, educator, historian, and all-around nerd. When not subverting Middle School Social Studies Curriculum, they can be found cooking spicy dishes, playing video games, reading, or writing about vampires, superheroes, queerness, space, wizards, and on a good day, all of the above. Their work has been published in Eye to the Telescope, The First Line, Poet's Haven, Drunk Monkeys, Sheepshead Review, Book of Matches, among many other fine journals, and placed 2nd for the 2021 Rhysling Short Poem Award. They live in the Pacific Northwest with the world's most copacetic cat.

WENDY VOGEL is a veterinarian, board game designer, and author of the horror novel *Trouble the Water* (JournalStone). As D.W. Vogel, she is the author of the Horizon Alpha science fiction series (Future House Publishing), and as Allison Rook she writes fantasy romance. Find her at wendyvogelbooks.com.

TRIGGER INDEX

- Child Death
  Low Tide

- Domestic Violence
  The Gift of Rakoska

- Emetophobia
  The Origins of Cora Deering
  A Bed of Eels

Discover more dark tales at Quill & Crow Publishing House
www.quillandcrowpublishinghouse.com

Made in the USA
Middletown, DE
26 August 2022